MURDER
OF A
TITANIC
SURVIVOR

MARGARET ILES

Murder of a Titanic Survivor

Margaret Iles

Print Edition ISBN: 978-1-77242-130-9

Cover design by Sara Carrick

Cover image used under license from Shutterstock.com

Carrick Publishing

For more information, contact Carrick Publishing: carrickpublishing@rogers.com.

Acknowledgements

There are many people who helped me write this novel. Brian Henry, first teacher and guide. Cheryl Freedman, editor, who offered great suggestions. Melodie Campbell, author and teacher, whose novels keep me falling off the couch. The staff at various libraries in Oakville and Burlington, Ontario. The Toronto Reference Library. The Toronto Archives, who assisted me in finding the information I needed. Donna Carrick, publisher, who gave a chance at publication. Sara Carrick, artist, for the breathtaking cover. Finally, my friend, Judy Glen, who gave freely of her time, going over the manuscript.

Each of you made my novel better.

Thank you, thank you.

Margaret Iles

CHAPTER 1

Burlington, Ontario—LaSalle Park, October 2000

Paulo leaned on his shovel to pull out a stubborn root. His breathing became laboured as he dug deeper. He could feel sweat in the centre of his back, causing his shirt to cling to him. The soft earth smelled sweet and woody as he lifted his shovel and pitched soil to one side. As he continued to dig, a fragment of black fabric appeared. Wiping his brow with his forearm, he stopped, cocked his head for a second, and then resumed. The handle bit into his hand, and he could feel the sting of a blister beginning. The shovel clanged against something hard. Paulo put his foot on top of the blade, pressed down, and pulled back. A skull appeared atop the dirt, dropped off and fell back into the hole.

A howl escaped Paulo's lips, as the shovel slid out of his hands. His mouth formed the word, "Jim," but nothing came out. He tried again and managed to call out the foreman's name. "Jiiiiim! Jim, over here. Come quick." A wild pounding had started in his chest, and he was having problems breathing.

The foreman looked up from the table where he had a landscape plan laid out for the park. Jim ambled toward the gardener, a quizzical look on his face. As he neared Paulo and saw his horrified expression, he began to sprint.

Paulo stood unmoving on the rim of the hole. He didn't look away from Jim until the foreman came up beside him. Then his shaking finger pointed down into the hole.

The vacant eye sockets of a skull, with a root protruding from its mouth stared back at the two men.

"Oh my God!" Grabbing the cell phone from his belt, Jim punched in 9-1-1. His breath quickened as he spoke. "My name's Jim Partridge. We're digging at LaSalle Park and we've just found a skeleton."

***

When the call came in, Roy Selby was sitting at his desk reviewing witness statements. He had a tranquil face and a stocky build with broad shoulders. But today, he looked all of his 59 years. Last night had been a bitch, with a violent domestic altercation and a shooting outside a bar. He'd slept only three hours.

"Detective Sergeant Roy Selby speaking."

"Road Constable Mulholland here, sir."

Selby listened for a minute. "Have you cordoned off the area, Constable?" He opened a drawer with his free hand and brushed the statements into it.

"Yes, sir."

"Don't let anyone leave. Block off the entrance, and instruct anyone inside the pavilion to stay put. I'll be there in fifteen minutes."

Selby grabbed his overcoat from the coat tree in the corner and strode out of the building. A black unmarked police vehicle stood near the side door of the police station. Selby hopped in. *LaSalle Park, eh?* He remembered how he and his wife Elaine had taken their daughter there for a picnic once when she was young.

When he reached the park, Selby pulled up near two cruisers and a small group of men standing clustered a few feet away from the yellow police tape warning, POLICE LINE, DO NOT CROSS.

P.C. Mulholland approached Selby's car.

Selby recognized the officer from one of their court appearances. "Who found the skeleton, Mulholland?"

The officer pointed to a man sitting on a nearby bench, puffing on a cigarette every few seconds. "His name's Paulo, sir. That's the foreman, Jim Partridge, beside him."

As Selby strolled over to the men he could smell freshly dug soil. He inhaled it and remembered the garden in his dad's backyard.

A low murmur came from the other workmen. Standing in front of Paulo, Selby introduced himself. "I'm Detective Selby, Paulo."

Paulo said nothing, just took another drag from his cigarette.

"I'm the one who called you," Jim Partridge said, as he reached over to the end of the bench, picked up a bottle of water and gave it to Paulo.

"Thanks, Jim." Selby turned to Paulo. "I'd like a few words with you, Paulo."

The man's face looked white as flour, and he trembled as he nodded. "OK. I tell you what I see." He made the sign of the cross and took a gulp of water.

Selby waited for the man to regain his composure. "What did you see, Paulo?"

Paulo crossed himself again and tilted his head toward the hole. In a quivering voice he told his story.

"Then we come here, sit down and wait for you," he finished.

"Thanks, Paulo. Don't leave yet. I need your boots, and Jim, I need yours too."

Paulo became agitated and jumped up from the bench, "Please sir, please. Don't take my boots. I need for work." Paulo spoke in a louder trembling voice.

"Don't worry Paulo, you'll get them back."

Turning to the foreman, Selby asked, "Jim, would you get another pair of boots for Paulo? You may have to send someone to his house. And get another pair for yourself. There may be some evidence stuck to the soles." Before he turned to walk away, Selby pulled out a package of gum and offered some to Paulo and the other men.

***

While Selby waited for the coroner and the rest of his team to arrive, he scanned the park. A white pavilion stood in the centre. The structure was in the shape of a barbell with an undersized two-story building on each end and a breezeway in the centre. The breezeway looked as though it could hold a band and several couples dancing. One of the compact buildings housed a high-end restaurant. Several employees of the restaurant had their faces pressed up against the windows, gawking at all the activity.

Behind the pavilion, a gentle hill sloped down to Lake Ontario. The detective strolled over to it and gazed at the lake. The sky had begun to darken and whitecaps lifted and dipped their frothy heads. Questions tumbled through his mind. Whose remains had Paulo dug up? How long had they been there? Was it possible they could be his missing daughter's?

He shivered at the thought, and a terrible sadness came over him. He turned away and began tapping his foot as he looked toward the entrance into the park. *Come on guys, come on. Where are you?*

At last, he observed several police cruisers and other unmarked cars snaking down the winding road toward the parking lot. "Finally," he muttered. "Now we can begin."

CHAPTER 2

The coroner, Dr. Phillip Maybrick, and the rest of Selby's team arrived in two cars. Dr. Maybrick was a small rotund man who looked more like Santa Claus than the chief coroner. Behind round glasses, his blue eyes sparkled. His white beard was neatly trimmed.

The doctor climbed out of his car and waddled over to the yellow tape. He stopped a few feet from Selby and pulled on plastic booties and gloves. Dr. Maybrick peered into the hole. "Looks like it's been here for a long time, Roy. The skull appears quite dry. You go in first, and then help me climb down."

Selby already had his plastic booties and gloves on. Watching his footing he climbed into the shallow hole and stretched out his arm to help Dr. Maybrick. The coroner removed a small brush from his pocket and delicately pushed the soil away from below the indentation of where the skull had been. The upper part of the skeleton appeared.

"Roy, I think the skeleton may be complete. The remains are wrapped in something. Help me out of here, and have your team pack up the bones and fabric and get them to Hamilton General Hospital. I'll be able to tell more when everything is assembled in the morgue."

Roy Selby climbed out and extended his arm. "Take a wing, Phil." The coroner grasped Selby's arm and climbed out.

Dr. Maybrick turned his white fringed head to Detective Kate Burton, who worked Forensics. The coroner smiled. "OK, Kate, you can take over now."

Detective Burton was the senior member of Selby's team. She managed trace evidence. Selby had watched her rise through the ranks over the last several years. Her mind was as sharp as a shark's tooth, and her tongue could be equally sharp at times, when she found incompetence in one of her colleagues. Her grey slacks clung to her lean frame, and a black turtleneck encased her swan-like neck. Her blonde hair was pulled back in a ponytail.

"I'll want photos and video before anything is disturbed," Kate said to Marie Dupuis, her assistant. Slowly and carefully, the two women climbed into the grave.

After the photos and videos were taken, Selby watched as Kate used tweezers to pick at some fabric entwined among the bones.

"Marie, photograph this bit, please, and then bag it," Kate said.

The women used trowels and small brushes skillfully and slowly to uncover the skeleton. It reminded Selby of a film he had seen on TV of archaeologists working at a dig. When the remains were totally exposed the women removed and carefully packed them. Marie climbed out of the hole and retrieved a large screen from the trunk of the Forensics van. She began piling the soil onto it, from where the skeleton had lain. Anything found in the dirt would be sent to the lab.

Selby and Maybrick turned and walked toward the parking lot. They stood beside Dr. Maybrick's car. It was one of the new models that looked like a hearse. "When will you do the autopsy, Phil?" Selby asked.

The coroner thumbed through a small notebook. "Looks like the day after tomorrow, Roy. See you then."

***

Hamilton Morgue

Selby gave a light rap on the lab door and pulled it open. "Hi, Phil."

Dr. Maybrick stood over the examining table where the skeleton lay neatly assembled. With a magnifying glass in his gloved hand, he looked up and nodded. "Roy."

The white tiles on the walls of the morgue glistened, reflecting light from a fixture that hung over the table.

"Have anything for me yet, Doc?" Selby asked with raised eyebrows.

"Well, I have bit of information, but it's still early and there's a lot more to come."

Picking up a pencil the doctor pointed to the neck region. "See that small U- shaped bone broken in two?"

Selby drew closer and bent over. "Uh-huh."

"As you may know, that's the hyoid bone. The break tells us the cause of death was asphyxia. Probably strangled with a ligature. A forensic anthropologist, Dr. Lisa Pallotta, is coming to examine the remains. She'll go over everything when she arrives," the doctor said.

Selby straightened. "Is Dr. Pallotta new? I haven't heard her name before."

"She is. She's just come from the East Coast. New Brunswick, I think. I met her last week."

"When do you think she'll be here, Phil?"

"Probably in a couple of days. I'll let you know."

Dr. Maybrick looked back at the remains on the table. "There are still a few more bones to come. I expect they'll find more from the sifted soil and maybe something from the gardeners' boots. There are only three or four missing from the hands. Also, some of the trace evidence that we sent over to the Centre of Forensic Science has been reported on. Your forensics team found shoes, some hair, clothing and fabric. It appears she wore a full set of clothes at the time of her death."

"Probably the best place to check out the shoes is the Bata Shoe Museum in Toronto. They'll be able to tell us the time period when women wore the type of shoe found in the grave," Selby added.

"Good," Dr. Maybrick said, and continued. "I believe your skeleton is female, judging from the brow, Roy. The male's brow has a bony ridge above the eyes. This one doesn't. And the subpubic angle is wider than that of a male. Dr. Pallotta will confirm when she arrives."

"Anything else you can tell me right now, Phil?"

"The preliminary report sent some photographs and an opinion on some fabric. They're still assembling more fragments of material." The doctor backed away from the examining table, put his face in his armpit and coughed. "More to come, though. But when I tell you what they found so far, it's going to blow you away."

Selby took a step closer, his curiosity aroused. "What, Phil?"

"One of the scraps of fabric is from a wool blanket. Some other pieces are from what looks like a shawl. They even said the shawl was homespun and from a sheep indigenous to Ireland. It's called a Roscommon Long Hair."

"Terrific. Those techs really know their stuff," Selby said.

"A label was still attached to one of the fabric remnants. Are you ready for this Roy? It said: RMS *TITANIC!*"

CHAPTER 3

Queenstown, Ireland, April 11, 1912

Mary Flynn stood on the small deck provided for third class passengers. Her family surrounded her. A stiff breeze grabbed her long auburn hair and held it behind her as the ship sailed out of the harbour. She clutched the railing with small hands and gazed back at Queenstown. A sigh escaped her lips as she soaked in the beauty of the island. Green, green hills and sheep. So many sheep. They covered the hillside like white polka dots on a green dress.

Her face puckered with mixed emotions. She was excited about going to America, but also sad leaving her friends behind. She also felt a tinge of fear. What would young people in America be like? Would they accept her? For seventeen years the only home she had known was in Cork.

The shore faded away. Mary's last glimpse of Ireland was of St. Colman's Cathedral spire standing out against a clear, blue sky.

Four days later, the only sounds in the Flynns' cabin were the muffled throb of the huge engines somewhere below and Mary's Da snoring. Her twin brother, Tom, was sprawled on one of the upper bunks, his clothes still on. A skein of black wool lay beside her mother as she sat at the end of the bottom bunk darning socks.

Mary shivered under the long woollen grey and white dress her mother had made for her, although it was warm in the cabin. "Oh, Ma, my stomach feels sick," she said, leaning over the side of the upper bunk.

"Shh, Mary, your father and brother are sleeping. We'll go out on one of the upper decks and get you some fresh air. Sure and you'll feel better," her mother said. Mary swung a black stocking leg over the side of the bed and slipped down.

"Here, take my shawl and wrap it 'round you tight, or it's your death you'll be catching."

Mary's mother began breathing hard as they both climbed several sets of stairs to stand on one of the small upper decks.

Mary shook. She grasped the black shawl closer. Goose bumps prickled her arms. The cold air felt sharp in her nostrils and it did quell her nausea. The water made a swishing sound as the ship sliced through it.

Two stewards strolled by. "Excuse me sir," Ma said, "I'd like to get m' bearings. Where are we now, and how soon before we reach New York?"

"Certainly ma'am," one of the stewards said. "We're approximately 390 miles off the coast of Newfoundland, Canada. We're scheduled to dock in New York in three days." He nodded his head and walked away.

Mary heard him say to his companion, "Button up, Peter, it's not summer yet. It's only 31 degrees."

The sea below Mary and her Ma appeared calm with only a smattering of ice pebbles on the surface. Stars twinkled in the black sky, and the air had a sharp bite to it.

"I'm still cold, Ma."

Her mother removed a wool scarf from her neck and tied it around Mary's neck. "Here love, take my shawl. Your teeth are clacking so hard, I fear they may fall out," Ma said.

Mary pulled the wool shawl up and covered her mouth. Looking down at the water now she noticed that the pebbles of ice had become large chunks, and an icy chill scurried down her spine. "Ma, look at the water."

Her mother gripped the railing and looked down. Her face darkened. "It must be freezing down there. Thank God we're up here."

Mary turned to her mother and touched her stomach. "I feel some better now, Ma. We can go back to the cabin." Mary took her mother's hand. It was warm, and she felt comforted. They'd just stepped away from the railing when they heard a loud crack like the sound of a large tree branch breaking, then a scraping and popping sound underneath where they stood. Mary lurched forward and stuck an arm out. Her hand gained purchase on the ice-cold railing.

She turned to her mother and screamed, "The saints preserve us! What's happening?"

They could hear the ship's engines still running as they passed by a mountain of ice. It glistened, and they had to tilt their heads back to see the top of it. "Most likely bumped that chunk of ice we did," Ma said through tight lips.

"But we'll be all right, won't we Ma? Won't we?"

Ma looked toward the stairs, then back at Mary. She clutched her daughter's shoulders and said in a steady voice, "Hold onto the railing, love, and wait here for me. I'd best be going back to our cabin to see after your Da and brother."

"No, Ma. I'll go with you."

Ma's eyes levelled on Mary. In a calm voice she said, "Mary, stay here and wait for us. One can go faster than two."

The expression on her mother's face surprised Mary. She had not seen it before. *Fear, I think she's afraid.* Mary never saw her mother afraid of anything. It scared her. The next instant Ma gave Mary a tight hug, turned, and made a frantic dash for the stairway.

Mary huddled deeper into her shawl and squeezed her arms against her sides to stop trembling. Thoughts tumbled through her mind. *Is the ship sinking? No, that's daft.* Her Da had told her the *Titanic* was the safest and finest ship in the world and built in Ireland. *Ma will be back in a few minutes, telling me to come down to the cabin, and that everything is fine.* She knew her mother would.

White knuckles showed as Mary clenched the railing. The ship gave a shudder. Then an eerie stillness descended. No sound from the engines. Only muted strains of music drifted down from the orchestra several decks above. She recognized a song she had heard a friend humming, "Autumn", and she could hear a few muffled voices speaking hastily. Mary felt a lump in her throat. Her body tensed as she peered at the stairway where her mother had disappeared. *Where is she, where is she?* Each minute seemed like an eternity. She could hear hurried footsteps on the stairs above. Mary looked to the stairs leading to the deck above her. Several crew members hurried down carrying grey life jackets, and she heard a whispered voice, "Good God, we've hit an iceberg."

***

"Here, Miss, put this on." One of the stewards stopped and held a grey life jacket out to her.

"No. Why would I need it? No trouble, is there?" she asked.

"No trouble, Miss. The captain's ordered us to tell the passengers to put the jackets on and go to the uppermost deck and wait there. Just a precaution, Miss, just a precaution. Nothing to be bothered about."

His face bore the same expression as her mother's— fear. She didn't believe him. More crew raced up and down the stairs carrying life jackets. *Maybe there really is trouble with the ship.* Her body tensed. *It can't be, it can't be.*

Another crewman stopped and rushed over to her. His voice was soft, but it had a ring of urgency. "Miss, Miss, leave off the railing. Put the jacket on, and come with me."

She didn't move. Mary's eyes remained riveted on the stairway where she had last seen her mother. She could hear the thumping of her heartbeat in her ears as she continued to cling to the ship's frigid railing.

Grabbing Mary by one wrist, the steward tugged. "Miss, Miss, we have to go. Please, leave off the railing."

"*No!*" she screamed. "I'm waiting on my family. Sure and they'll be here soon," she said, trying to pull away from the man's grasp.

The sailor looked into Mary eyes, hesitated, and relaxed his hold on her wrist. He smiled. "Don't worry, Miss. They'll be taken care of."

Something in his voice didn't sound right. He resumed a vice-like grip on her wrist, and it was stinging. She finally let go of the railing and let the steward guide her up the stairs to A deck. She continued to look back over her shoulder for her family. She was beginning to feel panicky. A knot formed in her stomach, and wild thoughts swirled and jumped around in her head.

Several passengers were already gathered on A deck. One spoke loudly enough for Mary to hear.

"What time of night is it, anyway?" a woman asked.

Another answered, "Almost midnight."

"And why do we have to leave our warm beds?" Mary heard someone ask. "I can see nothing wrong."

But there must be something terribly wrong, Mary feared. She looked around. Most of the men wore overcoats and caps. Some wore shiny top hats. Many ladies snuggled in furs.

The lifeboats hung just above them on the boat deck. Mary watched as two richly clad women climbed to the boat deck and got into a lifeboat. One was really just a girl and the other an older lady. They looked confused and frightened and they hugged each other. Mary felt the same way.

"Not to worry, Charlotte. We'll be well taken care of. Your father will see to that," the older woman said, patting the young girl's back.

Mary hadn't noticed the steward still held her arm. She jerked it back, and the steward let go.

"Just climb up the stairs to the deck above. You'll be fine, Miss. Just wait there with the rest of the passengers. Someone will help you into a lifeboat," he said.

Before Mary could protest, he let go of her wrist and disappeared somewhere down the deck.

Mary could feel panic welling up inside her again, but gulped it down and clamped her jaws. All the passengers appeared to be from first or second class, judging from their apparel. A few of them continued to climb the stairs, some with white handkerchiefs pressed against their mouths and noses.

Mary scanned the deck for her family. She saw no one familiar. Her face sagged, and then brightened. She remembered being told there were stairs on the other side of the ship. *Maybe they are coming up the other stairs.* She cheered herself with this thought.

Her eyes fell on an elderly couple standing nearby. The gentleman wore a black top hat. With a gloved hand under the woman's elbow, he gently guided her to one of the lifeboats on the deck.

"Just a step or two up, dear. Nothing to worry about. I'll steady you." The frail woman raised one foot tentatively to climb the step stool to get into the boat, and then stopped. She turned to her husband, reached up and held his face in her lined hands. Ropes of blue stood out on them. "My darling, I have been by your side since we were children," she said in a thin voice.

"It's alright, dear. I'll join you in a little while. Just get into the lifeboat."

"No. I love you with all my heart, and I cannot imagine a life without you. I will not leave you now."

The man looked down at his wife, and Mary could see the love and pleading in his eyes. Her heart ached, and her eyes became moist as she listened to the couple.

Holding both of the woman's hands, he said, "It's alright, dear. Just get into the lifeboat. I'll be in the next one just as soon as all the ladies and children have been taken care of."

The woman shook her head and put her arms around him. The gentleman's shoulders sagged, and he stepped away from the lifeboat, and tenderly held his wife.

***

"Women and children first, women and children first," second Officer Lightoller, who was in charge of loading the lifeboats, shouted out. A little boy of around six or seven stood beside him, tugging at his coat and biting on his lower lip.

"Do you know where my father and mother are, sir?" he asked, tears swimming in his eyes.

Mary saw him squint, trying hard to press the tears back. *Poor lamb*, she thought.

The officer took the child's hand, picked him up, and placed him in a boat. "They'll be right along, son. Don't worry. Your mother's probably in another boat."

Mary could see some of the children sitting in the lifeboat clinging to their mothers as they cried and shook with cold.

When all were seated in the craft, Officer Lightoller yelled to the crewmen, "Lower away." As the lifeboat lowered, one of the ropes would not extend with the others. The craft tipped at one end almost spilling the occupants out into the water.

Mary grasped the railing and looked down at the lopsided lifeboat. *Oh my God. If only I could help.*

"Help, help!" a woman screamed clutching the side of the craft with one hand and holding two children by the back of their coats with the other.

Officer Lightoller cupped his hands and hollered to the crewmen lowering the lifeboat.

"Get that blasted rope untangled before they're all dumped into the sea."

Wide-eyed, Mary covered her mouth. Amid screams from the lifeboat and gasps from the horrified spectators, the rope finally straightened out even with the others. The passengers flopped back to their places. The boat hit the water with a slap. Two crewmen sitting in the craft began to row away from the stricken ship. Mary stepped back from the railing and breathed a sigh of relief. *At least they're safe.*

Panic and desperation began to overtake her. "Where are they? Where are they?" she cried out as she scanned the faces coming up on deck.

Mary moved along with the other passengers as a steward herded them to the uppermost deck where the lifeboats were stored. Crewmen stripped off another canvas cover from a boat. Passengers were crowding onto the deck now. Two young women standing beside Mary sobbed into white hankies trimmed with lace. One was dressed in a maid's uniform, and the other wore stylish clothes. A man wearing a top hat stood near the women, looking sober and pale.

Another gentleman standing nearby gave a nervous laugh and said, "Nothing to worry about folks. Just a precaution. Right, Officer Lightoller?"

Mary studied the officer's face. It appeared tight and strained and then it brightened.

"Right, Sir. Just a precaution," the officer said.

Mary noted his clenched hands and she sensed a heightened alertness in his face. Her hands began to shake and fear for herself and her family engulfed her mind.

He took a few strides toward Mary and scooped her up in his arms. "Come Miss, you're next."

No longer able to control her panic, she screamed and struggled in his arms. "No, no, put me down. I can't leave now. Sure and my family will be coming soon."

Officer Lightoller paused for a moment. "Where's your family's cabin, Miss?" he asked as he put her down.

No reply. Mary's eyes focussed on the passengers coming up the stairs.

The officer took a step closer and put his hand on Mary's shoulder. "Which deck is your family on, Miss?"

Mary looked into the officer's eyes, uncomprehending. "Sorry, sir, what...what did you say?"

The man repeated his question.

"Oh, on F deck in third class, sir. But they won't be there now. They're on their way up."

Mary saw a flicker of fear cross his face, and then it was gone as quickly as a flame on a snuffed-out candle.

The officer's tone lightened. "Oh, don't worry Miss, they're probably on the other side of the ship boarding right now, or else they're already in a lifeboat."

A dark plaid blanket lay on one of the deck chairs nearby. Lightoller grabbed it and swaddled her in it. Mary's body stiffened as he deposited her in one of the boats.

The winches and davits creaked and groaned as the crewmen strained at the ropes that would lower the vessel. Mary could hear one of the officers trying to persuade passengers to get into a craft, but some wouldn't listen. She heard one passenger say, "Why should we? This ship can't possibly sink."

Before her boat began its descent, Mary heard one of the officers shout, "I want at least two crewmen and a couple of male passengers in each boat with the ladies and children. We need them to row."

Several crew men and a couple of male passengers stepped forward.

"Good lads, now listen. When you hit the water, I want you to row away from the ship, perhaps a couple hundred yards, and stay there." He added, "All of you can return to the ship when it's safe."

Mary heard the orchestra playing while she sat rigid in the boat. As it began its slow grinding descent, she craned her neck to look up at the passengers standing at the railing. She fingered the cross on its silver chain around her neck, desperately hoping to see a familiar face.

She didn't.

CHAPTER 4

The lifeboat hit the water with a smack. There were three sets of oars. Two of the crewmen took their place at the stern of the craft, each taking an oar, and rowed a short distance away from the ship. A steward shouted out, "We need more rowers."

Pointing a finger at a man in a fur coat, he asked, "You, sir, would you help?"

The gentleman sprung out of his seat almost before the crewman stopped speaking. "I'll take an oar," he volunteered.

Mary remembered an officer calling him Mr. Henry and assigning him to her lifeboat. She thought he had an alert look about him. She guessed he was in his mid-20s. Mary noticed another man in the lifeboat. He wore a black top hat. She recalled the man speaking to Mr. Henry before they got into the lifeboat. At the time, their conversation had appeared to be animated, and she guessed they knew each other. He'd stood beside Mr. Henry when the officer asked for rowers. After Mr. Henry volunteered, the man in the top hat grabbed the officer's arm and said, "I'll row," and jumped into her lifeboat. Now he sat beside Mr. Henry, an oar in his hand.

Mary looked up at the ship. Most of its lights still glowed. "Look everyone, the lights are still on! Everything is going to be alright," she said, trying to sound hopeful, although she suspected everything was not alright.

The glow from the lights threw a wide shaft of brightness across the water. The stars twinkled, shedding more light across the faces in the craft. Mary could see Mr. Henry was pale. His skin appeared translucent, his face set tight, jaw clenched. She sensed a determination about him as he grasped an oar with both hands. And somehow she felt less afraid.

Mr. Henry wore a fur coat. It looked like one made from raccoon she had viewed in a magazine.

One of the women with a Scottish accent guffawed when she saw him. "He's goin' to need that animal on his back tonight, I reckon."

The lifeboat could accommodate dozens more, with its spaciousness and high sides. Mary was puzzled. *It's less than half full,* she surmised. She remembered hearing an officer on deck, urging passengers to get into the lifeboats. They'd just laughed. One man in a tall hat said, "I don't see a problem, Officer. And if there is one, I can see another ship's lights winking in the distance. They can take care of the problem, I'm sure."

He and his companions laughed and strolled into the lounge, saying, "Let's have some champagne." The men wore evening clothes: black tails and shiny top hats. Some of the women wore elaborate evening gowns with fur stoles.

Mary remembered the frustrated officer throwing up his hands and giving the order, "Lower away!" to the crew manning one of the winches.

And the purser, Mr. McElroy, shouting at the people going into the lounge, "Don't go in there!" He strode over to where they were standing and placed his hand on one man's arm. "Stay out here, please! And wait for a lifeboat."

The man brushed the officer's hand away, smiled, and shook his head.

Mary shivered at the memory and wondered where those people were now. Her eyes stayed glued on the disabled ship as she began to list. Her lips parted in silent disbelief. *It can't be. This is the safest ship in the world.* As she continued to watch, more and more of the bow of the ship was gobbled by up the sea. It became clear to her the ship would sink. They would not be going back to the *Titanic*. *The Lord preserve us.*

Finally, she tore her eyes away and gazed at some of the survivors in the lifeboat. One weary looking woman with straggly hair only wore a flannel nightgown with a blanket over her shoulders. Mary could see a frantic look in her eyes as she stared back at the foundering ship.

Mary placed her hand on the woman's shoulder and said, "We'll be back on the ship soon, or another ship will come and help us."

A woman with blonde hair took her place beside Mary. In spite of everything, she seemed composed. She wore a green velvet coat, and socks—no shoes. Another older lady wore a home spun wool shawl, like Mary's. A small child sat beside the woman, a kerchief on her head, tied under her chin, and sucking her thumb.

A girl around four years old crossed her arms hugging herself and crying, "Mommy, Mommy where are you? My feet are cold."

Mary looked over at the child—no socks or shoes. She bent over and removed her own socks and held them out to the child. "Take these," she said.

The child looked at her with wide eyes, took the socks and said, "Thank you, ma'am."

A young mother sat huddled near the front of the lifeboat with a small child pressed close to her breast. She pulled her shawl around both of them and leaned forward trying to protect the child from the cold.

I hope we're not out here much longer. That mother and child may not survive, Mary thought, apprehension growing in her mind.

A set of oars in the centre of the craft remained to be manned. Mary nudged a young, sturdy-looking woman beside her, "come," and gestured with her hand. She followed Mary's lead, stayed low and crept with her to the centre where the oars remained idle. Mary lowered herself to the seat, and the woman sat beside her. Mary grasped one of the oars in her cold-stiffened hands. Silently, she thanked her Da for teaching her how to row.

"Help me row," she said, nudging the woman beside her. Mary pointed to the oar.

The woman looked toward where Mary pointed and grabbed the oar.

"My name's Mary. What's yours?"

The blonde woman pointed an index finger to her chest. "Anna, from Poland," she answered in a thick accent.

One of the crewmen gave the order to row. As the lifeboat moved further away from the sinking ship, Mary was surprised at the woman's strength and adeptness. They had put a distance of about one hundred yards or so between the great vessel and themselves, when one of the crewmen yelled, "Stop rowing!" The rhythmic splashing of the water stopped. Mary relaxed for a moment and let the warmth from rowing seep into her bones.

The lifeboat seemed to breathe a sigh as it came to rest in the water, with only small waves lapping against the side, and gently rocking its human cargo, like a mother soothing her child. Still and tense, Mary and the survivors looked back at the *Titanic*.

The two women sitting behind Mary began to scream, "It's sinking, it's sinking! It's going down!" Then they began to weep hysterically, crying out names. "John! Peter!"

Mary looked at one of the crewmen. His jaw clenched tight, and his lips formed a straight line. The bow of the great ship was completely submerged now.

"Please God," Mary prayed, "let my family be safe," although she knew in her heart that they were probably gone. She could feel it. She made the sign of the cross, leaned forward on her oar, and bowed her head. "Our Father who art in heaven..." Hot tears stung her cold face. At first, she was unaware that she'd prayed out loud and that her companions heard her. But as she raised her head to look back at the sinking ship one more time, she noticed several of the passengers had followed suit and were murmuring prayers.

Most of the lights on the ship still burned. The grand lady struggled to stay afloat as her bow slipped slowly and silently into the water below. The survivors watched in horror, as they heard an explosion...then another. One of the crewmen stood up and shouted, "The boilers are exploding!"

Mary watched as fire and debris shot up into the star-studded sky. It looked like pictures she had seen in a book of a volcano erupting and spewing its contents into the air. Sharp cracks which sounded like pistol shots reverberated in her ears. The sound reminded her of the time Mr. Peabody, a neighbour, had to shoot his dog. This time there were more—one, two, three, four. To Mary's amazement the next sound she heard was a dog barking in the distance!

Somewhere in the lifeboat a voice exclaimed in disbelief, "Was that a dog?"

A woman with brown curly hair, and wearing a shawl, sat a few seats in front of Mary. She turned and said, "I saw a toff smuggle a wee dog under her fur coat. She got into a lifeboat when we were waiting to get into one." Her mouth turned down and her forehead became creased. She spit into the ocean.

Several of the women covered their mouths with their hands as they stared transfixed at the dying ship.

One woman screamed, "My God, what's happening?"

Mary held her breath, hands glued to the oar. She watched the ship's bow slip slowly down into the water as the stern rose, the sea swallowing her bit by bit, like some hungry monster. She glanced around at the other survivors. Disbelief was etched onto each face. And silence, until...

"Holy Mary, Mother of God, they're jumping overboard. They'll freeze in that water!" a woman screamed. The starlit night illuminated the nightmarish scene, and still the lights twinkled from the portholes and decks like fireflies in the night.

The soft strains of the hymn "Closer my God to Thee" floated out across the water as the orchestra played on. Then the lights began to fade, and the music stopped.

CHAPTER 5

"The Lord saves us now. He best be bringing that other ship soon," one of the sailors muttered.

Mary gaped as the ship stood almost perpendicular, with only its stern still out of the water. A few seconds later the great ship split apart and began to slide into her watery grave. As the *Titanic* made her slow descent into the sea, screaming could be heard coming from the ship. And some passengers cried out, "Help!" and flailed in the frigid water. The last thing Mary saw was the white lettering stencilled on the black stern.

T I T A N I C

L I V E R P O O L

Mary sat silent and shivering, staring out into the night at the point where the ship had been. Now the only light came from the cold stars, which shone like diamonds in the sky. Then, the words she had just heard the sailor utter penetrated her numb mind. She remembered one of the crew telling some passengers that the wireless operator had telegraphed another ship. The memory ignited a spark of hope and lifted the heaviness in her chest.

A young mother clutching a small child began to shriek, "Oh, my God, we are all lost. I'll no see my Jim again," she wailed. "I'm going too." She clambered up the side of the craft and tried to jump overboard with her baby.

"Quick Jane, grab her!" shouted one of the ladies to another woman who'd been sitting near the distraught woman. They both leaped from their seats and grabbed the young mother by the back of her dress. The craft began to rock.

Their grip tightened on the woman's dress as they pulled her back. The baby began to wail.

"Shh, darling. We're trying to help mommy," one of the women said in a soothing voice. The woman gripped the baby tighter as they all fell backwards into the boat, arms and legs flailing. The women disentangled themselves and gently placed mother and baby in the bottom of the lifeboat. She remained there quietly weeping and limp, patting the whimpering baby's back.

Mary breathed a sigh of relief. Her heartbeat returned to normal as the terror she'd felt watching the scene began to subside. One of the rescuers sat by the young mother's side with her hand on the woman's back. Now Mary felt a new fear—fear of not seeing her family again. But she couldn't give up all hope, not yet. She rubbed her cross between an index finger and a thumb. The metal was cold.

Perhaps everyone in the lifeboat hadn't heard the sailor mention the emergency message the wireless operator had sent. The crewman had called it a CQD—the distress signal. She straightened her back, lifted her head, and spoke as loudly as she could in a shaky voice.

"Don't lose heart, there's a ship coming for us, there is."

"She's right. I heard it myself," a well-dressed lady sitting at the front of the boat said.

There were cries for help just a short distance behind them. The pleas tore at Mary's heart. She rose from her seat and spoke, turning her head to look at the rowers one by one.

"We have to go back and pick up survivors, or they will surely drown. Please! Our boat is only half full. And I for one don't want it on my head for the rest of my life that I did nothing to help them. We must do what we can."

A dowager with an ample bosom, clad in furs, a black wide-brimmed hat with a black plume on the side, hefted herself from her seat, rocking the lifeboat. "I am Lady Austen Prentice," she announced in an imperious tone, "and I forbid everyone rowing to go back. You will put all of us in jeopardy. Do not turn this boat around! I warn you do not turn this boat back, or you will pay dearly for it." She remained standing with a stiff, straight back, glaring at the rowers, her frame taking up a quarter of the width of the lifeboat. "I warn you again. All of us will be lost if you listen to this young lady."

The man Mary watched jump into the lifeboat just after Mr. Henry stood up beside Lady Austin Prentice. "Listen to reason, everyone. We'll be endangering ourselves, if we go back," he said, and sat with his hands in his pockets.

Mary shot to her feet and pointed a finger at the dowager. "And how will you answer, Lady Prentice, when asked why your lifeboat was only half full? And just a short distance away from people freezing and drowning? Why did you resist picking up any survivors? Maybe your husband or someone in your family is freezing to death in the water this minute," Mary blazed back at the dowager. Conviction rang in her voice. "We must go back. I have faith we will be rescued. Another ship will come." Mary suddenly felt older than her seventeen years. "Men, will you help me row back?" she pleaded. No one spoke or moved. Only the terrified pleas for help and splashing in the water could be heard.

She continued to stand and stare at the rowers for several seconds then sat down. With her tiny hands clenched on an oar, she nudged Anna and said, "Row."

Mr. Henry stared at Mary, then stood up. "The little lady is right, chaps. Let's do what we can." He elbowed the man beside him. "Row, sir," he said to the well-dressed man who had sided with the dowager.

Mr. Henry lowered himself to his seat, grabbed his oar, and began to row. His partner did the same. The crew dipped their oars and pulled.

Lady Austen Prentice spat out, "Fools!" and plunked down on her seat. The boat rocked.

The gut-wrenching cries for help grew louder. The lifeboat had only gone back a few yards when they saw a teenaged boy who had climbed up on an overturned lifeboat.

"Over here, over here," he yelled.

One of the crewmen shouted, "Grab my hand, lad."

The boy tried to grasp his outstretched hand, but he slipped on the wet boat and fell into the water. When he surfaced he was closer to the lifeboat. He stuck an arm out of the water.

The crewman grabbed it. "Got ya, hold tight."

Mary grabbed the belt on the back of the boy's coat. He was light, and they got him in without too much effort. His teeth were chattering, and he was pale as the snow on the chunks of ice around them. He appeared to be around the same age as Mary. Mr. Henry stripped off his raccoon coat and covered the freezing boy.

Mary scanned the water as they continued to row back. "Stop, stop rowing! I see more people over there, over there." She pointed a finger. "Let's try to get them."

Fifteen minutes later, they had pulled in 25 struggling, near frozen, people from the water. An older woman sitting in the stern removed a heavy-looking coat and gave it to a shivering young woman with just a night-dress on. The dress stuck to her thin frame like wet paper.

The lifeboat was full.

One of the crewmen pulled a compass from his jacket and pointed. "South, we row south, but not too far. The rescue ship was given the *Titanic*'s location just before she went down. If we move too far away they won't find us."

Glistening chunks of ice floated and bumped against the lifeboat. Mary could still hear a few faint cries coming from a distance. They ripped at her heart. The pleading gradually grew weak—then silence. It was a sound Mary would remember for the rest of her life, whether waking or sleeping—the weakening cries—then the utter silence.

The excitement of rescuing more passengers subsided, and a small finger of fear began to scratch deep inside Mary's chest. She dismissed it. *Da told me the Flynn's weren't quitters.* She could see the hopeless expression on the face of a woman who sat near her. It drooped and appeared vacant. She felt she must say something to encourage the woman, as her Da used to encourage her. The stillness of the night and the water seemed to amplify Mary's trembling voice as she spoke. "We must keep our spirits up until the rescue ship arrives. We've come this far for a reason. Don't give up hope now."

The woman's gaze turned toward Mary, and she gave a weak smile.

CHAPTER 6

A new day was dawning—April fifteenth. The horizon showed a tinge of pink above the darkness. The lifeboat rocked gently, lulling some to sleep. The atmosphere was hushed. A crewman slumped forward on his oar. His cap lay at his feet. Mary could hear soft snoring. She turned her head to look into the back of the lifeboat. Two ladies in fine clothes held hands and stared out into the pale light with gaunt faces. Most of the other passengers huddled together as close as possible with their heads lowered. The blankets covering them gave off little tremors.

Gradually, the ribbon of pink on the horizon increased, shedding more light across the sky. A faint flame of hope flickered in Mary's breast as she glanced toward the warming sunrise—then she *saw* it: a black speck on the horizon. She blinked twice and squinted. Her eyes grew wide. Her face beamed as she flew off her seat and pointed. "A ship! A ship is coming!" Her voice sounded like croaking in her ears. Only a few passengers appeared to have heard, and they raised their tousled heads. As the black speck grew larger, her voice strengthened.

"A ship is here!" she shouted. Mary crawled over to the woman who had tried to jump overboard. She lay curled in a foetal position in the bottom of the craft, her child pressed to her breast. Mary reached down and shook her by the shoulder. "Look, ma'am, a ship, a ship is here." The woman struggled to a sitting position and looked in the direction Mary pointed. She put both hands to her face. Tears of relief trickled between her fingers.

She bowed her head and clasped her hands. "Thank God, thank God."

Mary had given her plaid blanket to the woman. The woman held the blanket out to Mary, "I won't be needin' this anymore, Miss. Thank you, and God Bless."

Mary took the dark plaid blanket, threw it over her shawl and clutched it in front of her. Anna still dozed. Mary grabbed her sleeve. "Look, Anna, a ship is coming for us." She watched Anna as her face lost its dullness and brightened with a wide grin. It was only then that Mary noticed how attractive Anna was.

One of the women shouted, "Praise the Lord."

In spite of her heartache over her parents, not knowing whether they'd survived, Mary felt the knot in her stomach relax. Her teeth chattered and she hoped she wouldn't break a tooth. Her legs had stiffened from sitting in the cold. They felt like icicles, and she hoped she would be able to walk without too much difficulty. *If I can't, I'll crawl.*

***

The passengers in Mary's lifeboat were the first to board the *Carpathia.* She stood clenching the railing, watching the survivors come up the rope ladder which was hung over the side of the ship. Some small children had been placed in mail bags, and were being brought up by a crew member. The cold air pricked her skin like needles. Some of the passengers could barely climb, their legs weak and their fingers stiff. A crewman went down the ladder, picked up a woman sitting in the lifeboat, slung her over his shoulder and carried her up to the *Carpathia*'s deck.

Where could they be, Ma, Da and Tom? She prayed they were here, or on another ship. Mary could see sympathy in the eyes of the *Carpathia*'s passengers as each survivor came aboard. Some dashed forward offering a coat, or a blanket.

The crew poured cups of hot chocolate. One man pressed a cup into Mary's hands. The heat of the cup warmed her fingers.

"Come with me, Miss," one of the officers said. He put a hand under her elbow.

Mary shook it off. "No, I must stay here and watch out for my family."

In a gentle voice he said, "I understand Miss, but it's cold out here. You will be informed later."

"When, when will I know?"

"Captain Rostron will let you know later when everyone is aboard. Now come along. A lady has given up her cabin for you and for one of the other ladies from your lifeboat."

When Mary entered the cabin, Anna was sitting there taking off her boots. She felt relieved someone she was familiar with would share the cabin.

"Hello, Anna," she said and gave a tepid smile.

A steward entered the cabin behind Mary. "I need your names ladies, to put on the list of survivors to be posted in the lounge," he said and retrieved a small pad and pencil from his white uniform pocket. He wrote down Mary's name quickly and asked Anna, "How do you spell your last name?"

"Z-e-l-a-s-k-o," she said.

The steward wrote it down and deposited the pad and pencil in his pocket. "If there is anything you need, just call me. My name's Jenkins, Steward Jenkins at your service. I will be close by." He peered into the washroom and bustled around the room. "Fresh towels will be delivered shortly," he said with a smile. As he was about to leave, Mary asked, "Aye, there is one thing. Would you be having writing paper, or some kind of notebook and a pencil?" She was having difficulty remembering things. Her mind felt scattered with fuzzy gaps in her memory, like a fog closing in every now and again. It would help if she wrote things down.

"I'll see what I can do, Miss." And with that he left the cabin.

Mary lay on the soft bed with its satin spread and closed her eyes. Tired as she felt, sleep would not come. She tossed from one side to the other. Her eyes flew open when one of the gaps in her memory flooded with the terror of the night before. It was like a fast-running stream in Spring-time. Questions swirled in her head. *What's happened to my family? Have they been picked up by the* Carpathia, *or on another rescue ship?* Bone weary as she was, Mary jumped to her feet and ran outside, looking for Jenkins. He was standing a few feet away instructing some members of the crew. "Are all the survivors aboard sir? Are you still searching for more?" she asked.

He frowned. "Miss, you should be in bed. Yes, all the survivors are aboard. We're recording the names of all of them, and Captain Rostron wants everyone in the lounge in the morning. I'm afraid you will have to wait until then to see if your family's among the rescued."

Mary's voice screamed in her head, *Don't you know, I need to know now! I can't wait until morning.*

The steward's voice rang firm. She knew no pleading would change it. She let out a deep sigh, her shoulders slumped, and she turned away. Her footsteps seemed weighted as she trudged back to her cabin. Her whole body felt burdened with sandbags. This time when she put her head down, sleep came quickly from sheer physical and mental exhaustion.

***

"Mary, Mary, up, up. Breakfast."

Mary felt a gentle hand shaking her arm. Opening her eyes slowly, she stared into Anna's face and didn't recognize her for a moment. She sat up in bed and looked around the room. The enticing aroma of sausages and tea filled the air. Steam rose from the tea on a tray set to one side on a small mahogany table.

Awareness began to set in. Her head drooped, and she remained silent. After a while she looked up and stared disinterested at the food. As good as it smelled and looked, she didn't know if she could eat. The lump in her throat felt like a large plum. Pushing back the covers, she slid out of bed and tried to smooth the creases out of her dress. A pair of blue slippers rested on the floor beside the bed. Someone, perhaps Anna, had placed them there. Tears welled up again. *Ma used to put slippers beside my bed. She always feared I would catch cold or step on something sharp.* She swallowed and pushed the tears back.

Now fully awake, Mary took in her surroundings. She'd only seen such grand furnishings in the fine homes in Cork, where she occasionally worked. Beside the white wrought iron bed with the satin comforter, a small oak writing table with a chair stood under a porthole. A lamp with a multi-coloured glass shade provided light to the table. A dresser with a large oval mirror attached had small drawers on either side and was placed on the far end of the cabin. Wood panelling rose half way up the walls, and a persimmon and blue carpet covered the floor. *So this is what first and second class cabins look like.*

Her thoughts switched back to her family, and apprehension pressed down on Mary's shoulders. *What if their names are not on the list?* She needed to know now, one way or the other.

She dashed to the bathroom sink, splashed water on her face, and patted it dry with a fluffy towel. A silver comb, brush and mirror lay on the dressing table. Mary pulled the brush through her long chestnut red hair—quick strokes untangling the knots. Plucking up a piece of toast and nibbling on it, she gulped down tea. It burned her throat. Some tea spilt as the cup clattered onto the tray. Her mother's black shawl lay on the back of a chair. Mary drew it across her shoulders and looked at Anna.

She appeared to be dawdling, sitting at the table and pouring more tea.

"Come, Anna," Mary said, beckoning.

As they stepped out of the cabin, Anna drew back and said, "No. You go." Mary stopped and looked at Anna, a question mark in her eyes. Did Anna have family on the *Titanic*, or was she travelling alone? Mary wondered. Anna never mentioned any family, but then, she only knew a bit of English.

"Alright, I will go alone," Mary said.

Anna sauntered over to the railing and gazed at the sea.

A steward stood on the deck nearby. He approached Mary and asked, "Do you want to go to the lounge, Miss?"

Mary hesitated for a moment, and then she gave a nod. The steward led her to the lounge where the door stood open and survivors were queued to go in. She looked at the woman beside her and saw frightened eyes and grey-white skin. Mary guessed she looked the same.

A few officers and stewards positioned themselves at various places throughout the lounge. The names of all the survivors were recorded on lists pinned to boards at the far end. Mary prayed Ma, Da, and Tom's names would be on the list, or better still, they would be standing with open arms to greet her. She took a deep breath and entered the room.

CHAPTER 7

Mary felt a slight pressure on her shoulder. Turning, she looked into velvet brown eyes. Even when he wasn't smiling, his eyes seemed to be smiling. Mr. Henry, one of the survivors from the lifeboat, stood behind her. She remembered how he'd supported her plea to go back and pick up some of the drowning passengers. Her shoulders relaxed when she saw him. He spoke in a slow voice, which had a calming effect on her.

"Hello, Mary. When we boarded the *Carpathia*, I heard you tell the officer that you wanted to wait for your family. Are they here, or are their names on the list?" he asked.

"I've looked around, but I haven't seen them anywhere. The list is posted on a bulletin board, on the other side of the room. I'm almost afraid to look."

"Come, I'll walk over with you." He offered his crooked arm. Mary's breath slowed as she let herself be guided.

"My name's Andrew. Please call me that."

Mary nodded. They stood before the bulletin board. The black print stared back at Mary as she began to read the names. "Fairly...Flanagan...Flynn..," then the last name in the Fs--Francis. Only one Flynn listed, herself—Mary Flynn. Then the Gs began. "Perhaps I read the list too fast the first time," she said.

She read it again, her lips mouthing each name, willing their names to be there. They weren't. No mistake. She stood back from the list—bent over with her arms crossed in front of her. A muffled cry like that of a small, wounded animal passed through her clenched teeth. She began to rock and moan, saying, "They're gone...they're all gone—Ma, Da, and Tom...funny Tom."

An ear-piercing scream reverberated around the room. A woman stood near Mary, reading the list. She clapped her hand over her mouth and crumpled to the floor. Mary squeezed her eyes shut, but the dam broke, and hot tears scalded her face. Andrew turned her around and pulled her close. "It's alright, dear. Cry as much as you need to. I'm here for as long as you need me."

Every few minutes there were more agonized sobs until the air became thick with sorrow. There were a few elated exclamations when a name was found, but not many. Andrew led Mary out of the tortured room onto the deck.

A cold, dismal day with fog hovering above the water greeted them. They stood side by side, looking out to sea. Andrew kept his arm around Mary's slumped shoulders. She could taste salt on her tongue from her tears and the sea air. After a while she was able to speak. Mary shifted her gaze from the grey sea to the concerned eyes of Andrew Henry.

"I'm so afraid. What shall I do, Andrew? Go back to Ireland, or follow my parents' dream of a better life in America? I'm only seventeen and I'm scared. I don't know if I can do it without them."

Andrew stepped back, placed his hands on her shoulders and held her at arm's length. His tone was sombre and his gaze unwavering. "I think you would feel better if you continued on the path your parents planned. There are opportunities in Canada you wouldn't find in Ireland. All your parents' efforts will have come to naught if you go back."

Mary turned away from Andrew and didn't speak. When she turned back, she sighed. "Alright, I'll follow my parents' course, but scared, I am. I don't know where to start. My mind feels like it's frozen."

"Go and get some rest now," he said. "We will talk about it later. Will you meet me here at six o'clock? We can go to dinner together and discuss your fears."

Mary nodded.

She felt secure in his presence and wanted to linger. She took one last look at him, turned and stumbled a little as she went to her cabin.

***

At 5:30 that evening, after a fitful sleep, Mary began dressing. The purple colour of the dress which came up to her neck was enhanced by the cream lace ruffle circling her throat. The steward told her the garment had been left by a woman who gave up her room for a few female survivors. Although the dress was beautiful, Mary couldn't take any pleasure in it. Her sorrow was overwhelming. And she sobbed as she imagined her mother's proud and smiling face looking at her in this fine dress.

Anna also found a black wool dress. It did not reach the top of her black boots, and it creased across her hips. The hem of the dress whirled around her calves when she looked into the mirror. As she stood there admiring her reflection, she became aware of Mary's soft sobs. In a few seconds Anna bent over Mary. She threw sturdy arms around her. "No cry little one. Anna will help."

Mary grabbed a hank of her hair, and held it back off her face. She took the handkerchief Anna offered her and blotted her cheeks. "Thank you. I hope I do not look too wretched. I've promised to meet Andrew Henry outside the dining room at six o'clock for dinner. Come with me. I'm sure Andrew won't mind. I think he has a plan for us."

Anna cocked her head. "Andrew Henry?" she repeated in a long, drawn-out voice.

"Yes. You remember him, don't you? He wore a fur coat in the lifeboat, and he gave it to the lad we pulled from the water. Fur," Mary rubbed her arm as if ruffling fur, then gave it a smooth stroke. Anna nodded.

It was almost dark when Mary spotted Andrew standing near the ship's railing outside the dining room. He was talking to a *Carpathia* officer, who towered over him. Andrew's stance appeared casual, and there was a tranquil air about him in spite of the disaster he had just been through. It was not unlike men she'd observed in Cork, who had lived a privileged life. And his face had no deep creases between the eyes from frowning.

Mr. Henry turned his head and looked in the ladies' direction. His face brightened as he ambled toward them and offered an arm to each lady.

The ship's chef prepared a special meal: baked haddock with sauce, green peas, pureed turnip and boiled or roasted potatoes. And for dessert: plum pudding, ice cream, assorted nuts and fresh fruit. Almost no conversation could be heard from the nearby diners. Just some soft murmurs, and some sniffles. Mary watched as people toyed with their food, pushing it around their plates. Although the food looked delicious, she did not feel hungry. Several minutes passed as they ate in almost complete silence. Anna burped once or twice and said, "Excuse, please."

Much of Mary's food still lay on the plate when a waiter came to clear the table. Anna's plate looked as if it had already been washed.

Andrew patted his mouth and placed a white napkin on the table and turned to Mary. "I'd like to suggest a plan for you and Anna. I hope you do not think it impertinent of me."

"Oh no! Tell us your plan." Mary leaned forward and became intent on what he had to say. "What sort of plan?" she tilted her head sideways.

"I'm a barrister, living and working in Toronto, Canada. I live with my parents in a very large house. I'd like to extend an invitation to you and Anna to stay with us until you are able to get yourselves sorted out, and then you can find alternate accommodation."

She placed her hand over her mouth, and her eyes widened. A small voice in the back of her head whispered, *You don't really know him.* She brushed it aside like a cobweb and said, "Oh, Andrew, what a grand offer! But I don't know. I'm finding it hard to make decisions and my brain feels muddled, it does. What about your parents? They might not be keen to have us."

"I've already cabled them and they've replied. They are pleased to have you. They will be waiting for us when we dock in New York."

Mary glanced at her companion. Anna's eyebrows were arched and she looked from Andrew's face to Mary's and back and forth, like she was watching a tennis match.

"Andrew, Anna doesn't know what we are saying. I could not take you up on your invitation without hearing from her. I wouldn't want to go alone. Wouldn't look proper, see. Purser Jenkins is taking care of Anna and me. I will see if he knows anyone on the ship who speaks Polish and English. Then we'll see."

"Indeed. That sounds reasonable. She may have friends waiting for her in Canada or the United States," Andrew said.

In two or three days they would arrive at the port of New York.

CHAPTER 8

On the evening of April 18th, a curtain of darkness dropped on the day. "We will be docking in a short while, Miss," a steward informed Mary as she leaned against the railing, gazing out across the water.

She blinked as a knife of white light from a search light cut through the night. Hundreds of smaller lights moving like fireflies materialized a short distance away. She could hear another sound—*what was it, cheering?* And the sharp and sustained blaring of automobile horns amplified by the water could be heard.

The *Carpathia* went to the *Titanic*'s berth first, Pier 59, to drop off the lifeboats, and then over to Pier 54, the *Carpathia*'s berth. Mary and the other passengers stood at the railing, and could see thousands of people waiting and cheering. Some of the survivors near Mary gave weak smiles and waved white handkerchiefs.

Others looked frightened. Mary spoke to the woman beside her. "Do you have someone waiting for you?"

The woman's face appeared grey and dull as she answered without looking at Mary. "No, no, no one. And all my family... gone down with the ship, Joseph and my two babes," she said as she lifted her shawl to her face and began to weep.

Mary placed an arm around the woman, and said, "I'm sure there'll be help for you when we get off the ship. Don't worry."

The woman lifted her head. She didn't appear to have heard Mary's words of comfort. She just swept her tears away and said, "Only two and three my babes were. Now what'll I do?"

Mary felt her throat tighten and a heaviness in her chest as she continued to hold the woman. "There'll be help, I'm sure."

Some of the survivors had dead eyes—their faces still as corpses. "In shock," an officer from the *Carpathia* had told Mary. As the ship drew closer, she could see anxious faces on the dock, as they scanned the people at the railing. Their expectant eyes passed quickly from Mary's face.

Earlier, Andrew had said to her, "Only the relatives of the first and second class surviving passengers have been cabled from the *Carpathia*."

Mary knew no one in America, or Canada to inform—no relatives or friends. If it weren't for Andrew and Anna, she didn't know what she would do. Her small body shuddered at the thought. A whimper escaped her lips. *Why me—me alone? Why not Ma, and Da, or Tom?* Someday she may know the answer, but not now.

She wasn't aware Andrew had moved to stand beside her until she felt a light touch on her shoulder. "Mary?"

Startled, she turned toward him—then placed a hand on his arm. His raccoon coat had been returned to him, and the fur felt soft beneath her hand. "Thank you, Andrew. Thank you." They heard a familiar voice speaking a different language. They looked down the deck and saw Anna speaking to someone who spoke both English and Polish.

Anna's head bobbed up and down, and her face darkened. The interpreter said something to her, and she burst into tears. The gentleman put his arms around her and held her for several seconds. She looked up and swiped a fist across her face. Anna shook the hand of the interpreter and looked a little brighter.

They watched her for a few seconds until she looked down the deck and noticed them.

Anna rushed over, her dress flapping around her calves, like a flag in the wind. "I go now."

A swarm of reporters and cameramen stood on the dock, shoving and holding their cameras up above their heads. They craned their necks to snap a photograph, acting like bees droning around a hive.

"Look, Andrew," Mary said, pointing to some small boats which came out to the ship.

They were overflowing with cameramen and reporters with newspaper names stuck in the ribbon on their fedoras. They yelled up at the survivors at the railing. "What's your name? Where are you from?" Light bulbs flashed, illuminating the gaunt and desolate faces of some of the survivors. "Is your family with you? Where are you going when you land?" The passengers tried to shield their eyes from the flashing lights.

Mary's hands gripped the ship's railing and her lips formed a tight line. The reporters seemed oblivious to the suffering etched on the faces of the survivors. She glared down at them. "Go away, leave us alone," she yelled at the men.

The warehouse on the pier had been outfitted to receive the survivors. A long, one-storey building with a high ceiling and metal supports criss-crossing it. A "No Smoking" sign hung half way down from the ceiling. Lights fixtures suspended on long cords glared above them.

Mary squinted at the lights. "They look like upside down pie plates," she said to Andrew. The area along the side walls had large, square alphabetical letters hanging from a long metal pole that went from one end of the building to the other. A throng of people stood in the centre of the area. Her blanket from the *Titanic* lay folded on her arm. Her knees trembled.

Andrew's hand under her elbow steered her toward a sign with a large H on it. "Over here, Mary," he said.

Men in black uniforms with brass buttons and black caps with red stripes dashed about. The women working with them wore bonnets with red ribbons, and Salvation Army written on their jackets. They offered clothing and railroad tickets to whoever needed them.

Nurses with small white circular caps perched on their heads and large white, bibbed aprons stood beside tables, waiting for survivors. Each table had an alphabet overhead. Anxious expressions marked the faces of the doctors and nurses. Doctors with stethoscopes and white jackets sat questioning survivors and listening to their hearts. Everything seemed confusing to Mary. *This is all a dream and I'm going to wake up soon.* She didn't feel connected to anything, or anyone.

Mary and Anna stood with Andrew at the table with the large 'H'. A nurse positioned herself beside the table where a doctor sat. "Miss, were you in the water?" the doctor asked Mary.

She shook her head.

"Do you need anything, clothing, lodging, train ticket, medicine?"

"No, my friend here, Mr. Henry," Mary said turning in Andrew's direction, "is taking care of things for me and Anna."

Mary watched as the doctor looked at her and Anna from head to toe and then at Andrew. Two furrows appeared between the doctor's eyes. He exchanged glances with the nurse, whose eyebrows were raised.

Andrew stepped in front of Mary. "My parents have offered Miss Flynn and her companion, Anna Zelasko, temporary accommodation," he said.

The nurse and doctor seemed to relax. "Indeed. I see, very generous of them," the doctor said.

As she walked away, Mary overheard the nurse say, "Doctor McDermott, did you know that even the school children were darting about the city carrying collection boxes for donations to help the survivors?" A tear nestled in the corner of Mary's eye.

A woman shuffled beside her, holding the hand of a child about four years old. The child's face held the vacant expression of a sleepwalker. She looked straight ahead. Nothing seemed to be registering.

Members of the clergy attended a few people. Red Cross workers were sprinkled throughout the survivors, helping as well.

One of the workers approached Mary. "Do you need anything, Miss?" she asked.

Can you bring back my family? The impossible phrase rang in Mary's head. But she simply said, "I don't, but thank you anyway." When all the rescued were gathered in the cavernous room, they filled only a small area. It had been prepared for many more survivors. Doctors and nurses stood idly by their stations.

"Where are the rest of the passengers?" several people asked Mary, and each other. "More are coming, aren't they?"

Mary knew from the number of people she had seen in the lounge looking at the bulletin board that all the survivors were probably here. In a tremulous voice, she answered, "No, just us." There was a gasp from those closest to her, and handkerchiefs rose to the mouths of those who had asked. They blew their noses and dabbed at their eyes. People were speaking in hushed tones, and their murmuring seemed to echo in the dank, dreary place.

Mary began to lag behind Andrew and Anna. Then she came to a dead stop. Her shoulders were raised, her breathing quickened and her chin began to tremble. "No! I can't do it, Andrew. It's back to Ireland for me."

CHAPTER 9

Burlington, Ontario, November 2000

A week after the *Titanic* label was discovered, the telephone rang in the Selby home. Doug Selby picked it up, listened, and yelled out, "Roy, it's for you."

"Coming Dad," he said as he came from the kitchen, a coffee cup in his hand. He sipped from it before taking the receiver.

"It's Phil Maybrick, Roy. The forensic anthropologist arrived today. Meet you at the morgue in an hour."

"OK. See you then," Roy replied.

Selby strode into the lab at the Hamilton Morgue, and saw the new forensic anthropologist, Dr. Lisa Pallotta. She leaned over the assembled skeleton on the table. Dr. Maybrick stood by her side chatting.

They both turned and nodded in Selby's direction. "Hey, Roy," the medical examiner said.

Hmm, Maybrick forgot to mention how attractive the anthropologist is, Selby mused and sauntered over to the table.

The doctor turned his white fringed head toward Selby. "Roy, this is Dr. Lisa Pallotta, our new forensic anthropologist."

"Good to have you with us," Selby said, smiling and extending his hand. As he stepped closer, he caught a whiff of the fresh scent of Lily of the Valley. It reminded him of the delicate, white flowers his mother planted in her garden before she died. He savoured the fragrance. Dr. Pallotta's long black hair shone under the large light which hung over the table. It was the first time he'd felt an interest in a woman since his wife had died.

The snap of the doctor's surgical gloves echoed in the lab as she pulled them on and tied an apron around her waist. She reached up to adjust an overhead microphone. "Well, gentlemen, let's get started. I'll begin with the skull. Lots of info there." Dr. Pallotta pointed a pencil at the white orb on the examining table. "I believe this is part of the remains of a woman."

Selby opened a small book and began taking notes.

Dr. Pallotta continued. "The head is smaller than that of a male's, and the brow is not as pronounced," she said pointing to the brow bone.

"Ummm." Selby nodded and said, "Good head start, Doc."

She smiled. The forensic anthropologist pointed to several squiggly lines on the top of the skull. "We call these lines sutures. Calculating how close they come together, we can get a good idea of age. When you're born, the skull is in large separate pieces loosely joined together. As you age, the pieces grow closer and knit together. The squiggly lines demark the edges of the pieces."

Roy bent toward the skeleton, his eyes focussed on the skull. "I see what you mean, doctor."

Dr. Pallotta opened the jaw. "There's a fair amount of wear on the teeth, so that can also tell us something about age. I'll get back to you on that after I've studied them closely." She carefully placed the lower jaw back in its original position.

The detective noticed the care she took in handling the bones. She seemed to be giving the remains the respect she would give a living person.

"When I get a cross section of bone, I can confirm the age. There are tiny tunnels, called osteons. Depending on how many we find, they can be an indicator of age. I need to look at the bone under a microscope. As a person ages, the sternum hardens. As Dr. Maybrick informed you at the burial site, the deceased's death was a homicide, as determined by the fractured hyoid bone. She died of asphyxia."

"So you'll be able to tell us her age at the time of death?" Selby asked.

"Pretty close, after I finish my tests. I don't think she was very young, though. The sutures on the skull are too close together and judging from the amount of wear on the teeth, this isn't a teenager."

Selby's heart dropped for a moment, and then he felt hopeful. The skeleton wasn't his daughter's. Not Laura. A part of him wanted the mystery of his daughter's disappearance solved, even if it pained him to find her remains. Another part remained optimistic that she was still alive somewhere.

Stepping back from the table Dr. Pallotta said, "Excuse me gentlemen, but now I have to run some tests. I'll have a full report for you in a week. Good day. Nice meeting you, Detective Selby," she nodded to both men and turned back to the table.

***

Selby drove home, summarizing the doctor's info in his head, and reviewing what he had learned so far. The remains were that of a woman—not young, but not old. She may be from Ireland, judging by the shawl. Also, she may have had something to do with the *Titanic*. And she was murdered—strangled. Also, it appeared she'd been buried for a long time.

He pulled into the driveway of a red brick bungalow on Locust Street, where he lived with his father, Douglas Selby, a retired detective. Roy pulled open the front door and shouted, "Dad it's me," and hung his jacket in the hall closet.

"I'm in the living room, son. Just watching football," his father called out from his brown La-Z-Boy chair.

Selby went to the kitchen, opened the fridge and stared inside for a few seconds. "Any beer?"

"Uh-huh."

Selby dropped down on the sofa beside his father's chair. He poured beer into a glass and watched the white foam rise. "Remember the skeleton we found a week ago?"

His dad tapped the mute button with an arthritic forefinger and looked at his son. "What did the coroner and the forensic anthropologist have to say?" he asked, anticipation gleaming in his eyes.

A bit of foam clung to Selby's lip as he sipped his beer. He licked it away. "Quite a bit." He recounted the information he'd received from the two doctors. "Dr. Pallotta says she'll have a report within the week. I thought there might be a remote possibility that it could be Laura. But Dr. Pallotta said the remains are not that of a young person."

"Sometimes it's hard not to get your hopes up son, but our girl has been gone ten years and we don't know what's happened to her. Is she still alive or is she lost to us forever? Your team tried for years, working in their off-duty time to find some trace of her, but they came up empty."

Roy bowed his head. "I know, I know."

His father leaned forward in his chair. A bone in his spine gave a loud crack.

"Are you all right, Dad?"

"Fine, fine. Now tell me, they got any idea how old she was at time of death, and how long she's been buried?"

"I'll know soon. Both doctors think the remains are pretty old, judging from the degradation of the fabric found with the skeleton and the condition of the bones.

Remember I told you about the label attached to a fragment of a blanket with the name *Titanic* printed on it?"

"Uh-huh. That's a shocker." He lowered his head and rubbed the back of his neck. After a few seconds he said, "Back in the day, before you were born, Stan Burkowski— God rest his soul—and I worked on a case of a missing woman from our area. We ran out of leads. I wonder if there's any connection."

Roy touched his shirt pocket where he used to keep his cigarettes. Surprise registered on his face as he looked at the empty pocket. He had given up smoking about a month earlier. "What was her name?"

"Ryan… Mary Ryan. I've never forgotten it. Things from back in the day come to me easily. It's recent events I draw a blank on sometimes. Anyway, we could never crack the case. We had to put it in the cold case files."

Selby watched as his dad leaned back in his chair, seeming to drift away.

"Dad, would you like a cold one?" he asked.

"Huh? Yeah, that'd be good."

Roy set his bottle on the coffee table, meandered into the kitchen and opened the fridge door. "Last one!" he called out. The sweat from the bottle trickled onto his hand as he strolled back to the living room and passed the beer to his father. "Watch it. The bottle's wet." He took a few steps toward the sofa and plunked down.

His dad took a swig. "I was just thinking. Once in a while you get a case that buzzes around in your head like a mosquito. You swat it, but it just keeps coming back. The Ryan case stumped me, and I never forgot it. It's possible, I say just possible, that your skeleton is Mary Ryan."

"A-h-h, I think that's a stretch, Dad. She probably just ran off with some guy. Or she could've had an accident, bumped her head and lost her memory or something."

"No-o-o, not from what we learned about her. She had a child, a teenager when her mother vanished, and from all reports back then, the missing woman was devoted to her daughter."

"What do you remember about the daughter?" Roy asked.

"Sweet little thing. No bigger than a minute. Her mother called her Hope. I remember because Burkowski and I had a lot of contact with her after her mother went missing."

"Did the daughter live with her mother?"

"No. Hope lived in a convent before her mother disappeared, and went to her mother's home on the weekends. She'd call me every few weeks asking if we had any news of her mother. She gave me a picture of Mary. I made a photocopy of it for posters and brought one of them home. It's down in the basement somewhere."

Roy decided to humour his father. "OK, Dad. You find the photo and I'll take it to the forensic artist. I'm sure Dr. Pallotta will ask for a comparison between the image of the skull the artist puts on the computer and the photo you have of Mary Ryan."

"Another thing, we could never get a lead on where Mary Ryan originally came from." Doug's salt and pepper eyebrows came together. "It was as if she had just dropped out of the sky and landed in Burlington. It was called Aldershot, back then."

"How long did she reside in Aldershot?"

"Off the top of my head I can't remember, but I think I have some old notepads I forgot to turn in. There might something in them that'll jog my memory. They're in the basement with the rest of the 'memorabilia'."

"For once I'm happy you're a bit of a packrat, Dad."
Roy held the bottle to his lips, drained it, nodded and
pushed off the sofa. "Well goodnight. I'm bushed."

"Oh, one other thing I remember."

He stopped and turned to his dad. "What else?"

"During the course of our investigation we learned
that Mary Ryan visited a priest in Toronto, who referred
her to a convent in the Hamilton-Burlington area. But the
lead dead-ended because the priest died a few years before
Burkowski and I went to interview him."

A sigh escaped Roy's lips. "Sometimes we just run
out of luck. Too bad. Maybe he could have helped."

"And one more thing comes to mind. Mary Ryan's
friend gave us a box of clothing: old dresses and odds and
ends. It may still be in storage."

"Oh, no, Dad, the box would have been destroyed by
this time."

"Check anyway. You never know. Could have been
pushed to the back of the shelf and forgotten. Moth-eaten
by this time, I expect. Keep me in the loop on this one,
son." He leaned back in his La-Z-Boy and squeezed the
remote.

CHAPTER 10

The next day, Selby drove to Bronte Road Police Headquarters where the Property Evidence Room was located.

"Hello, Detective. What can I do for you today?" the attendant asked.

The officer was one of the new constables, young and anxious to please. Selby had met him a few times when he'd visited the Property Room. "Need to look at some old evidence boxes. May be something there related to a case I'm working on."

"Sure. Just sign in," the constable said, passing the entry register to Selby.

Once inside, Selby scanned the labeled boxes piled high on metal shelves. He looked on a bottom shelf where the older cases were stored. Rainer, Rennie, Robert, Ryan. His pulse jumped a few beats. As he reached down to dislodge it, a cloud of dust rose and he sneezed. Selby took out a Kleenex and gave a loud honk. He brushed the dust away. Now he could see the name clearly. 'Ryan, Peter.' His shoulders slumped in disappointment.

As he replaced the box, he noticed another box pushed far to the back. *Probably nothing. No harm in looking, anyway.* This box was old and tattered. Somehow over the years, it'd been overlooked. Selby leaned into the shelf and pulled the box forward. Dust partially covered the label. He drew his hand across the name. Ryan, Mary. *Finally a break.* He carried the box to a wooden table in the corner of the room, lifted the lid, and started browsing.

A pair of black shoes rested on top. They laced up the front, like Oxfords, and displayed a chunky heel. He thought they looked about the size his wife used to wear—size six. He placed them on the table. The clothes looked like something from the old movies his dad watched. A couple of outfits resembled ones he'd seen in photographs depicting the early 1900s. They were long—down to the ankle. And the colours were dark, except for a white long-sleeve blouse. He checked out the labels on what appeared to be the oldest garments. *The Robert Simpson Company* showed on them. One dress looked different from the rest—older. The purple colour made the cream lace at the top of a high neckline stand out. Ladies' fashions were not his forte, but the quality of the dress could not be mistaken. The clothes smelled of moth balls, and some items were badly creased.

Other clothing echoed a later vintage—shorter skirts and dresses, something like his mother wore. Selby started piling them back into the box. When he reached the last one, a calf length black skirt—he folded it and laid it on top. As he pressed the contents down he heard a slight crackle. He raised his hand and noticed the skirt had a small slit on the side for a pocket. Selby stuck his hand inside and felt paper. It had yellowed with age and was fragile. He opened it gingerly and read a clipping from *The Globe*, dated June, 1922.

It recounted a shooting in a downtown Toronto hotel, The Prince Edward. A Mr. Cyrus Henry shot and killed his wife's lover. Mrs. Madeleine Henry and Mr. Jeffery Adamson had taken a room there, and were just leaving when Mr. Henry approached them in the lobby of the hotel. He fired a small pistol, and killed Mr. Adamson, an accountant for one of Mrs. Henry's friends. A bullet hit Mrs. Henry's shoulder, but she recovered.

A Detective Kennedy had conducted the investigation. The article concluded with the fact that the Henrys' son, Andrew, had survived the *Titanic* disaster.

Selby stood back, rubbed his chin and felt stubble rough against his fingers. In the stillness of the room he could hear a clock ticking somewhere. *There's the* Titanic *connection again.* He'd need to go to the Toronto Reference Library where they had all the old newspapers on film. He took out his camera and snapped the shoes and clothing, then pocketed the newspaper clipping.

CHAPTER 11

New York, April 18, 1912

Mary stood trembling in the cold warehouse, which had been prepared for the survivors.

Andrew took her icy hand. "It's going to be all right, Mary. Everything is new to you. A new country, a new home, you don't know my parents, and it all scares you. That's natural."

Mary bit her lower lip and looked at Anna, who scowled back at her. *She seems braver than me,* Mary thought.

"Come," Anna said, twisting her head toward the exit and beckoning to Mary.

"Mary, give it a chance." Andrew said. "You have Anna and me for support, and if you still want to return to Ireland after you've been here for a while, I promise I will arrange passage home for you." He gave her arm a gentle tug.

Mary lowered her head and closed her eyes. *Ireland...Toronto....Ireland...Toronto,* bounced back and forth inside her head. *And what if I make the wrong choice?* She opened her eyes, pushed her shoulders back and looked in the direction of the door leading out of the building. Her chin stopped trembling. She took a slow step forward, and quicker steps followed.

Andrew's face relaxed into a smile as he walked beside her. Anna kept pace beside Mary, her boots clattering on the cement floor.

***

Madeleine and Cyrus Henry stood outside their Cadillac, shoulders pressed together. Their eyes were riveted on the exit from the Pier 54 warehouse. Their automobile sat purring and waiting. "I don't know if we made the right decision to have the young ladies come to our home," Mr. Henry said. "We have scant knowledge of their backgrounds."

Madeleine's brows shot up in surprised. She would do *anything* for her son, and Andrew wanted to help the young ladies. And if that's what he wanted, so be it. "There, there, Cyrus. I'm sure it will be fine. Andrew would not bring anyone to our home he thought objectionable. Trust his judgment," she said, patting his arm. Her gaze returned to the warehouse exit.

"Remember, Cyrus, when the black headlines slapped us in the face TITANIC SINKS. I went into shock and all I could mumble was 'Andrew, Andrew, Andrew.'"

Cyrus put his hand on his wife's arm. "It's all over now, dear. Thank God. When the telegraph came from the *Carpathia*, 'I am well, Mother and Father. Would it be possible for you and Father to take in two female survivors temporarily? They were in the lifeboat with me,' you almost fainted with joy. They'll be here any minute now."

***

Once outside the warehouse Mary could see a woman with outstretched arms rushing toward them, looking at Andrew. Tears of relief and happiness coursed down her cheeks. When they met, they held each other for several seconds.

Mary took tentative steps toward them and heard Andrew say, "Mother, I thought I might never see you and Father again."

She gazed past the mother and son, and her eyes fell on a gentleman standing a few feet away from Mrs. Henry. Mary assumed it was Andrew's father. He had relief etched on his face and she thought she could see tears glisten in his eyes. The gentleman stepped forward and put a firm hand on his son's shoulder. "Glad to have you home, son."

Andrew stood back from his parents. "Mother, Father, I would like to introduce my two companions from our lifeboat, Mary Flynn and Anna Zelasko, the young ladies I cabled you about. Thank you, Mother for extending a welcome and opening our home to them. They are very brave women."

Madeleine Henry extended a black-leathered hand. "You and Miss Zelasko are most welcome in our home."

Mary looked with admiration at Mrs. Henry. *She is quite beautiful and so well-groomed.* Madeleine Henry wore a grey hat with a large brim pushed back on one side. A purple and black feather made a curlicue on the side. Her dove-grey eyes were red and swollen. And she'd dropped one glove.

Mary retrieved it and held it out.

"Thank you, Mary," Mrs. Henry said with a warm smile. Some of the tension left Mary and she gave a little curtsy and smiled back.

"We will be taking the train out of New York to Toronto. The Grand Trunk Railway has put a special train on the line for passengers going to Toronto. We'll be more comfortable there," Mr. Henry said, looking at Andrew. "Stanfield will return the automobile home after he drops us off at Grand Central Station."

Madeleine Henry stood beside the rear door while the chauffeur opened it. "I can't imagine the ordeal you've been through, girls, but you must be tired, so just lie back and rest while we drive to the station," she said as she lifted her skirt and placed a fine-booted foot into the Cadillac.

Mary nodded, "Thank you, Mrs. Henry," and climbed into the back seat, followed by Anna.

Mrs. Henry's movements were slow and graceful. For some reason she had a calming effect on Mary. She didn't feel so anxious now.

Mr. Henry hardly spoke except to say, "Glad to have you home, son." He just kept slapping Andrew on the back.

As Mary and Anna settled in the auto, a man Mary had seen in the lifeboat came striding up to Andrew's father and clapped him on the back.

"Hello, Cyrus. You must be very relieved to see your son home. I was in the same lifeboat as Andrew. Glad we both made it," he said, and with that he hurried to a waiting automobile.

Mary recognized him. It was the man Andrew had been talking to on the *Titanic* deck and who leaped into the lifeboat. He was the one who supported Mrs. Austen Prentice's order not to go back to rescue survivors struggling in the water.

For some reason, not just the way he acted in the lifeboat, but for some other reason, he makes me feel uncomfortable. She couldn't quite put her finger on it. When everyone was in the Cadillac, Mary put her head back and tried to relax. The tension between her shoulder blades pained. She closed her eyes and, in spite of herself, dozed off.

"Grand Central Station coming up, sir," the chauffeur said.

Mary opened her eyes and looked out the window. Grand Central Station's lights twinkled, illuminating the enormous building. The entrance had three huge arches dozens of feet high, and above the middle arch was a massive clock surrounded by sculptured figures with wings.

When the small group gathered outside the car, a red capped porter approached them. "This way please," he said as he hustled around them, gathering the Henrys' small bags. "I'll take that blanket now, Miss."

The blanket rested, folded over Mary's arm. She'd been holding it ever since she left the *Carpathia*. She took a quick step back. "No, no, it's alright," she said, clutching it closer to her chest. The blanket held knitted memories, and she wanted to keep it.

They were shown to their compartment and their berths. Everything seemed to be moving so fast. Mary's head was spinning, and she felt exhausted. The grandness of the train barely registered. She climbed into her berth and fell asleep quickly.

CHAPTER 12

Although it was past midnight, not everyone on the train slept. Two men who'd followed the Henrys' black Cadillac were now on the same train. They sat in their Pullman coach. Lionel, the smaller man, leaned over to his partner and whispered, "We're on the right train, Sam. I sniffed them out at the dock. We've got the Henry family, alright. I spoke to their chauffeur while they were waiting for their son. We'll find out later who the gals are. Good-lookers, aren't they?"

Silence.

Lionel wished his partner talked a little more. He never knew what the guy was thinking.

Sam's face remained expressionless. He removed his bowler hat to reveal stringy black hair, a bit long for the day. He just looked straight ahead and nodded.

"Better get some shut-eye now. We'll take them by surprise in the morning. You shoot young Mr. Henry first," Lionel said.

***

The early morning sun knifed through the crack in the centre of the heavy green curtains. The light coaxed Mary's eyes open. She could see small dust particles in the stream of light. It reminded her of an old barn she had stumbled into one day. Some of the walls had disintegrated into weathered broken planks. The sun wiggling in through the cracks in the boards and specks of dust drifted in the light. She could almost smell the sweet scent of hay, and hear chickens clucking and scratching the wooden floor.

With a start Mary bounced out of her reverie. It took a few moments to collect her thoughts. Where was she?

Her eyes travelled around her berth, and she remembered: the car, the Henrys, the train. She slid the green curtain over to the side of the window and peered out. A dense, green pine forest rushed by. No sound came from Anna's bunk above.

Having no other clothes, Mary slept in her dress. She rolled out of her bunk and jerked her foot up when it touched the cold floor. Gingerly she put both feet down. She stroked her skirt and tried to brush the wrinkles out.

Reaching up, Mary shook Anna's arm. "Wake up, Anna. Breakfast."

A drowsy "hmmm" was Anna's only reply.

"Hurry, Anna. We have to meet the Henrys in the dining car."

Anna hung her legs over the edge of the bunk, rubbed her eyes and slid down.

Mary stepped into the compartment's washroom. She splashed water on her face and washed her hands. When she finished, Anna did the same.

When the girls thought they looked presentable, they left their compartment and headed for the dining car, where they found the Henrys.

***

"Don't be obvious," Lionel said to Sam. His sharp, dark eyes had a pinpoint of light in them when he spoke, and when he walked, he scurried. Lionel's nose twitched as he followed the heavy scent of coffee.

Sam reeked of tobacco. A yellowish brown colour stained his fingers, and his suit looked like a crumpled napkin. He carried his overcoat on his arm. When the men entered the dining car they saw the Henry group right away. Lionel pulled his cap down close to his eyes, and stepped into the aisle first, while Sam plodded behind.

Lionel passed Andrew Henry, then stopped and swung around.

"Get him, Sam."

Sam flung off his overcoat and aimed at Andrew Henry. There was a loud pop.

The group half rose out of their seats. Sam pivoted for a second shot and aimed at Mary.

She screamed and put her hands over her face. Another loud pop.

Cyrus Henry grabbed for the camera as Sam aimed it at Mrs. Henry. Sam whipped it behind his back.

Lionel pushed in front of Sam and said, "We'd just like a few pictures and a brief interview, Mr. Henry, something to give our editor about your son's rescue." Lionel yanked a small notebook from his pocket and held it in front of him, pencil poised.

"What is the name of your newspaper?" Mr. Henry demanded. Crimson covered his face. "Your editor will hear about this rude intrusion! Now get out of my sight, or I'll call the conductor and have you put off the train— before it stops," Mr. Henry added with a smirk.

Lionel looked horrified. He took a few steps back, out of Mr. Henry's reach, and regained his cockiness. "Thanks for the pictures, folks." He hurried down the aisle. "See you in *The New York Times*," he threw over his shoulder.

Mrs. Henry sat beside Mary and put her arm around her shoulder. "There, there, my dear. You're safe with us. Try to eat something," she said.

"I can't, I can't," Mary blurted out, still shaking. "Why won't they just leave us alone?"

"We will be home soon dear, and that will be the end of it." Madeleine Henry lifted a silver pot and poured a cup of hot tea and put milk and sugar in it. "Drink this. It will give you energy."

Mary took the cup and held it with both hands, taking one tentative sip and another. It did help steady her. She finished it and placed her cup on the saucer. "Ta, Mrs. Henry," she said.

"Come, Mary, let's sit in my compartment," Mrs. Henry said, rising and taking Mary's hand.

In Mrs. Henry's compartment, the women sat on the soft upholstered benches, across from one another. Mary recognized the faint scent of lilacs. Someone had given her mother a bottle of perfume at Christmas. The same scent emanated from Mrs. Henry. At the thought of her mother, tears welled up in Mary's eyes. Her head drooped and her eyes closed. She drifted into a twilight space, just on the rim of sleeping and waking. She could hear desperate cries and pleadings coming from the water...*Was one ma?* "Help, help, over here!" a desperate female voice cried out. A baby's wail, "Mama...mama ...mama," tore at her heart.

In her dreamlike state she tossed her head from side to side, but still the cries could be heard. Until one by one the voices ceased, and the water stopped churning. All became still. And the sound of silence was unbearable.

Mary shook off her trance-like state and heard Mrs. Henry's voice, seeming to come from far away. "Mary, Mary." She felt a hand on her shoulder.

"You fell asleep, Mary. I think you were having a nightmare. Are you all right?"

Mary sat erect and blinked at the faces across from her. Andrew must have come in while she was sleeping. He sat beside his mother. Anna sat erect beside her with a puzzled look on her face. It took a few seconds for Mary to fit the pieces together. It was like a jigsaw puzzle. Sometimes she would go off to another place where she wouldn't hear the voices around her, or feel the touch of her companions. She would forget where she was. *Was I sleeping and dreaming?* This never happened back in Ireland, but now it happened several times a day. Sadness swept through her like a chill autumn breeze.

"Mary, do you feel well enough to tell us a bit about yourself?" Mrs. Henry asked.

Mary paused, then nodded.

"Do you know anyone in America, or Canada?"

Mary shook her head. "When I feel better, I'll tell you about my family." She hoped there wouldn't be too many questions. It was painful to talk about Ma, Da, and Tom.

Mrs. Henry stood, walked over to the compartment door and opened it. She heard the conductor calling out, "Next stop Toronto." He stopped at their door and put his head in, "Tickets please."

Mary could feel the train slowing. When it stopped, they all rose, and walked to the exit.

Once inside Union Station, she was awe- struck. She turned slowly, gazing at her surroundings.

Mrs. Henry stood beside her and said, "Lovely, isn't it? Part of the station was destroyed by a massive downtown fire in 1904, but it's being rebuilt."

Mary thought the station appeared similar to Grand Central in New York. It displayed the same gargantuan space. The ceiling seemed to go all the way up to heaven. *Where have all these people come from? Throngs of people, rushing in and out the building.*

Although it was afternoon and the April sun was still weak, it drenched the building, pouring through long windows high up the walls. The foyer also had bright, warm lighting from a thousand bulbs. Outside the station, several taxis stood waiting for a fare. Mr. Henry hailed one. The men sat in the front seat and the women in the back.

The taxi turned off Roncesvalles Avenue on to High Park Boulevard, with its palatial homes and wide road. A new sidewalk had recently been installed. The houses were set back from the road about 50 feet, and the lawns were manicured to a precise height, with lush grass. Mary caught a whiff of thawing soil.

"There must be many families living in such grand houses, they're so large," Mary said as she pressed her forehead to the window, wondering what they looked like inside. It reminded her of Christmas morning, looking at the colourful wrap on the presents under the tree and trying to guess what was inside by the shape and size.

"Not really, my dear. In most cases there are just one family with four, five or six children, and various servants with quarters in the house," Mrs. Henry replied. Raising her hand and pointing a long slender finger ahead of her, she said, "Our house is near the end of the street, close to High Park."

"Stop right here!" Mr. Henry shouted. The taxi pulled over behind a Model T black Ford. Mary craned her neck and saw 'Police' written on the back of the parked car. Two men stood beside it talking in earnest. The one in plain clothes rested his foot on the running board. The other man wore a black uniform, with a tall hat that had a leather chin strap.

Mr. Henry sprung out of the car. "Good God, what's happened now?" His face flushed, and a frown creased his brow. He strode toward the men. "I'm Cyrus Henry and this is my house. What's going on?"

"I'm Detective Kennedy, sir." The plain clothes-man spoke in a quiet baritone. "I'm sorry to inform you, Mr. Henry, there's been a robbery. It took place during the night. One of your servants noticed the intrusion, an open window in the back of the house. The call came in this morning."

Mary sat still and listened, straining to hear. She looked from one man to the other, trying to read their lips. All she could catch were snatches of words: "robbery, window, called police."

Before the detective could say more, Cyrus spoke sharply to his wife. "Madeleine, take the girls upstairs."

Mary concealed her disappointment. She wanted to hear more, but stepped out of the auto as Mr. Henry had requested.

Mrs. Henry took Mary's hand and beckoned Anna. Mary looked back once over her shoulder. Andrew stayed outside with his father. Madeleine Henry shepherded the girls into the house and up to their room.

***

That night at dinner, Andrew's father referred only once to the incident. "Well, Madeleine, at least they weren't clever enough to take the Renoir. It's a small painting and they probably thought it wasn't worth much. Amateurs, I suspect. Just took some antique silver, and a few seascapes that weren't terribly valuable. And oh yes, a small amount of jewellery. Most of the valuable pieces are locked up in the safe."

Mary studied Mr. Henry's face. *He seems to be taking the robbery lightly. Are they that wealthy, and what's a Renoir?*

"That was a blessing." There was a sigh of relief in Mrs. Henry's voice. "There are some pieces in the safe that have great sentimental value to me, including my mother's emerald engagement ring."

A maid in a long black dress with a frilly white apron and cap entered the dining room, carrying a massive silver tray. She was a mite, and the weight of the tray seemed to pull her down. Mary hoped she wouldn't drop it. The novelty of being served made Mary feel shy.

Anna sat upright in her chair as she cautiously brought a spoonful of soup to her mouth and tasted it. She smiled at Mr. and Mrs. Henry and said, "Thank you, good." The diminutive maid continued to serve the meal, and cleared the table when everyone finished. She gave a little curtsy before leaving the room.

"Mary dear, do you feel well enough to tell us how it came about that you were on the *Titanic*?" Mrs. Henry asked.

Mary looked down at her hands in her lap. Her eyes began to mist. She didn't know if she could bear to speak about her family so soon after the disaster, but she swallowed hard to push down the plum in her throat. She raised her head, pulled her shoulders back, and looked at Mrs. Henry. "Times were hard in Ireland," she began, "and m' Da wanted a better life for us, he did. My parents, me and my twin brother Tom, boarded the *Titanic* at Queenstown, Ireland. It wasn't far from where we lived in Cork."

"It must have been costly for your whole family to purchase tickets. How did you manage?" Mrs. Henry asked.

"We all worked long and hard to save up the money and put it all in one pot. M'Da got the tickets. He paid around seven pounds for each of us," Mary said.

Andrew Henry turned to his father. "How much would that be in Canadian money?"

Mr. Henry placed his wine glass on the table. "About 30 dollars or so, for each person."

Mary continued. "Da fished the River Lee and my brother helped. They sold the fish in the market. And Da could fix anything, so he earned money repairing barns and houses."

Mrs. Henry nodded and smiled at Mary and took a sip of raspberry wine. "Go on."

"I worked after school in the Mayor's home, helping Cook and doing some cleaning. Sometimes I felt tired, but it was no bother. The rest of the family worked just as hard. Da didn't want me to work full-time and miss school. He was proud of my good marks. And the teachers said I could manage University—that's if we could pay the tuition." Mary offered this last piece of information with some pride.

"And your mother?" Mrs. Henry prompted.

Mary took a deep breath and squeezed her lips together. She could feel her throat tightening up. Could she bear to talk about her darling mother? They were so close. She would try.

"Ma sewed. She made gowns for the society ladies, and there were always bits and pieces of smooth satin, and silk light as air left over. The ladies said Ma could have them if she wanted. She would give them to me."

Mary paused and looked away from Mrs. Henry. She blinked away tears as she remembered pressing the fabrics to her cheek. The satin felt cool against her skin. And she would dream of a time when she might have a satin gown.

Mary came out of her reverie and continued. "Ma made most of the clothes for the family. When I was ten, she taught me how to sew dolls' clothes with the bits and pieces of fabric. And later I made some of my own clothes."

Mary grew silent again, as she envisioned her mother teaching her to sew and knit. They laughed when she cut the fabric on the wrong side, or when she dropped a stitch. Her mother never scolded her. She just said, "We learn by our mistakes," and "The dress could be worn inside-out and no one would notice. Besides it brought good luck." For an instant Mary could hear the click of the needles as hats, mitts, socks, and sweaters appeared in just a week or two. She held her bottom lip in with her teeth and her face tightened. She tried hard not to cry, but one salty tear escaped her eye and trickled down her cheek. Her face began to sag. And her head drooped. "I miss my mother very much." *I'll never hear her musical laugh again, or feel her warm hands,* she thought, but she couldn't tell Mrs. Henry all that she felt, or the dam would burst. She just said, "It will never be the same again."

Andrew and his father leaned forward as Mary spoke.

Mr. Henry coughed, and poured himself another glass of raspberry wine. There was a clink as he replaced the stopper on the decanter.

Mary lifted her head at the sound and looked at Mrs. Henry. Her eyes had welled with tears and she held her lips tight.

Then she brightened and said, "Well Mary, tomorrow I am going to take you and Anna downtown to the *Robert Simpson Company* and buy you some clothes. We'll leave early and have lunch in the Palm Room or the lunch room in the basement. How will you like that, girls?" she said looking at both of them.

Mary whispered, "Thank you," and tried to smile. She hadn't even thought about clothes. She needed someone to do her thinking for her just now, and Mrs. Henry seemed eager to help.

Andrew sat back in his chair and looked at his mother and father. "Mary hasn't told you anything about our time in the lifeboat. She is quite a heroine. Our lifeboat had room for many more people, and Mary insisted that we go back and pick up survivors."

"She did?" Mrs. Henry said with amazement.

"People were calling out and struggling in the water. Mary met with some resistance too, but she was adamant, thank God. She is responsible for saving at least another 25 lives," Andrew said as he turned and looked at Mary.

"Really? Well done young lady," Mr. Henry said. He appeared thoughtful for a moment and his face clouded. "I'm grateful it turned out well, but you could have put everyone in the lifeboat in danger, Mary. I'm sure there were some important people in your lifeboat. The boat could have been swamped by people trying to get out of the water."

Mary felt the hair on the back of her neck stir, and she could feel heat in her face. Her tiny hands tightened into fists. She tried to control her feelings. As angry as she was, she must respect her host. "Sure and everyone we pulled out of the water was an important person, too," she said in a tight voice.

Mr. Henry drained his glass and muttered, "Indeed, indeed."

Anna pushed her chair away from the table and excused herself, saying, "Tired, bed. Thank you."

Mrs. Henry placed her napkin on the table and rose. "Let's sit in the living room." She led the remainder of the group away from the dining room table.

***

The fireplace had been lit, and tall tongues of bright flames shot upward. It was still April, and a brisk wind blew off Lake Ontario. A draft could be felt inside the house. Andrew's father sat in a green, tufted, wingback chair on one side of the fireplace. His mother sat in a matching chair at the other side. Mary perched beside Andrew on a settee in the centre of the room. She could feel the smooth and rough texture of the brocade upholstery under her hand. A rectangular, carved mahogany coffee table stood in front of the settee.

Mary stared into the flames. *What will life be like in this new country?* she pondered. She felt protected by the Henrys just now, but what about later when she was on her own? Would she be able to manage?

Andrew switched on the stained glass lamp which rested on the table by the settee, and different colours sparkled like a kaleidoscope. It was the only light in the room, except for the burning fire which gave off a warm glow and a pleasant woody odour. Mary could feel the heat on her cheek.

The maid fluttered in carrying a small silver tray with four glasses of burgundy liquid. She moved noiselessly from person to person offering a glass. Mary said, "No thank you." She didn't know what the drinking laws were in Canada, so she better not touch the alcohol.

The corners of the room remained shrouded in a shadowy cloak. A potted palm rested languidly in one corner. Only its shape made it identifiable.

The shrill ring of the telephone in the foyer startled everyone, breaking the spell of relaxation. Mr. Henry rose and strolled out of the room. When he returned, he had a look of satisfaction on his face. "That was the police," he announced. "They've retrieved our possessions and have the thief in hand. They say it's one of our employees, Madeleine. They'll be over tomorrow to see us and return our property."

Mrs. Henry's eyebrows arched. "Oh no, Cyrus, which one?" Mr. Henry opened his mouth to speak when the telephone rang again.

"I'll get it Father," Andrew said. He spoke briefly and returned to the living room rubbing the side of his face. "That was one of the local newspapers. They want to interview Mary and me to find out how we got off the ship.

And they have heard about Mary persuading us to go back and rescue survivors."

Mary's body went rigid. She put her hand to her mouth. "Oh, no! I don't want to go back there. I only did what I thought was right. I couldn't leave all those drowning people in the water when we had room in our boat. I knew the boat couldn't be swamped. I was in a boat sometimes, with my Da. It was very much like the lifeboat. He told me if the sides of the boat were high no one in the water could tip it over." She felt sure the reporters would ask about her family, too. *Oh, Ma, Da, Tom*, she wailed in her head.

"Come over here Andrew, Mary. I have a suggestion." Mr. Henry said. He leaned forward in his chair. Andrew rose with Mary and the two of them moved across the dense carpet to stand beside Mr. Henry. His eyebrows knitted together and two tiny lines like railroad tracks became visible between them.

Mary was unsteady on her feet, and she began to feel a tingle of moisture on the back of her neck. *No more, no more talk about speaking to reporters!* she screamed in her head. Her face paled. Andrew put a hand under her elbow.

"The press is not going to let you alone until they have heard something from both of you," Mr. Henry said. "This disaster has reverberated around the world, and people want to know what happened and how the two of you survived. Grant *The Toronto Daily Star* or *The Globe* one interview. Let them know there will be only one interview to one newspaper, and no more."

Mary looked down at Mr. Henry, glanced quickly at Andrew. She dreaded the pain she knew she would experience by the retelling. Her heart was still an open wound, and the feeling of loss was overwhelming. She didn't know if she had the strength to talk to strangers about it. Her arms hung at her sides and her fists clenched. But she did not want to offend the Henrys and she didn't want to be any trouble. In a low, wavering voice she said, "Speak to the reporters, I will, but tell them I will speak but once."

Andrew put his hand on Mary's shoulder and said, "Don't worry Mary. I'll be standing right beside you."

Mr. Henry nodded and rose from his chair. "Good. And now, goodnight, ladies. Good night, Andrew."

Mary returned to the settee with Andrew. He patted her hand. His lips parted and he was about to say something when a white flash of light stabbed through the living room window. It lit up the room like a streak of lightening. Andrew rushed to the bay window. "Good God, it's those reporters and their cameras again," he said as he drew the velvet curtain shut.

CHAPTER 13

Mary did not sleep well that night. Visions of black water swirling around the helpless people filled her sleep, their wet clothes clinging to outstretched arms. She thought she saw her mother reaching out of the water toward her, a dark strand of hair stuck to her face, her eyes pleading. Mary shivered and twisted back and forth under the blankets. She heard a woman cry in the distance, "Take my baby! Someone, please, take my baby." The mother's desperate voice echoed in Mary's ears.

She woke with a start and her throat went dry. She threw back the blankets. A cold sweat trickled down the sides of her trembling body. She sat up and peered into the darkness. Where was she? She could feel the softness of the blankets and the smooth satin bedspread. She could hear peaceful breathing close by. She remembered—the Henrys' home, and it was Anna's breathing she could hear in the other bed. *Does she have dreams like I do?* She wondered.

Mary padded to the bathroom and retrieved a towel, her bed damp with perspiration. *There, that should do nicely,* she told herself, as she placed the towel on the damp sheet. She settled back into her bed, still afraid the dream would return. She could hear Anna's rhythmic breathing. It comforted her, and she closed her eyes.

***

After breakfast the next morning, Mrs. Henry spoke to the girls. "Get the coats I gave you, girls and wait for me in the front hall."

Anna dashed upstairs ahead of Mary to their room. Mary trudged behind her. She pulled the coat from the wardrobe and studied herself in a free-standing full-length mirror. Grey in colour, the coat had small lapels with three black buttons down the front. It fell to just below her hip, where each side cut away in a half circle to the back.

The coat was stylish, like the ones the first-class passengers wore aboard the *Titanic*. She wished she could feel some joy. Her body felt heavy, and she noticed a slouch in her posture as she gazed in the mirror. She pushed her shoulders back and looked at Anna.

Anna put on her coat, turned sideways and looked into the mirror. "Beautiful coat," she said, as she gave a broad smile.

Again, Mary wondered how Anna could appear so carefree after the tragedy. Perhaps she hadn't lost anyone in the disaster. Had she been travelling alone? Once Anna learned more English she could clear up some of the questions Mary would like to ask her.

Anna lifted her skirt and rushed down the stairs ahead of Mary.

Mary followed and stood beside Anna.

"We're driving downtown to the *Robert Simpson Company* for new clothes, Anna. Mrs. Henry told me we will be travelling through the city for several miles and we'll see Lake Ontario, electric streetcars, and a few automobiles, but mostly horse-drawn carriages like back home."

Anna tilted her head sideways, nodded and smiled.

"I know you can't understand everything I'm saying, but Mrs. Henry is going to get an English tutor for you and then you'll be able to enjoy yourself more," Mary said.

Anna's face lit up at the words "English tutor". She took Mary's hand in both of hers and said, "Yes, yes." It didn't seem to take much to raise Anna's spirits. Mary didn't know what it would take to lift hers, or if it was possible just now.

Boots scraped on the Henrys' concrete veranda. A narrow pane of glass framed either side of the door covered with lace curtains. Mary peeked through the lace and recognized the detective—the one who was in front of the house when they arrived from New York. A uniformed police officer stood beside him. She opened the door just as he was about to pick up the brass lion's head knocker.

"Good morning, Miss," he said raising his Homburg. "I'm Detective Kennedy and this is Constable Wickersham. We're here to see Mr. Cyrus Henry."

Mary's eyelids fluttered for an instant, like a butterfly's wings. Her eyes locked on his. She didn't move or speak for a few seconds. Although she'd only caught a glimpse of him a few days ago, something about him struck her. Then it came to her. The man bore a striking likeness to her father. His eyes were the same shade of grey blue and they held a similar expression in them—thoughtfulness.

She held the door open wide, and said, "Please come inside. I'll get Mr. Henry for you." Her voice sounded strange to her—it had dropped in pitch, and came out whispery. She could feel heat creeping up her neck and into her face. *For goodness sake, what's the matter with me?* she chided herself. She whirled around and disappeared into the back of the house looking for Mr. Henry.

When Mary returned, she found Detective Kennedy trying to make small talk with Anna, who just stood there smiling.

"She speaks very little English, sir."

"Thank you, Miss, I see that," he said, laughing. His laugh had a musical timbre and a softness to it. She felt awkward standing and waiting for Mrs. Henry. She wanted to speak intelligently to the detective, but felt unsure of herself. She could feel fluttering in her stomach.

Mary began to fidget. She glanced around the foyer, as if seeing it for the first time. She focussed on the oak panelling half way up the walls, then the oversized gilt mirror on one wall and the crystal chandelier above. The marble floor had a small Persian carpet in the centre. A round table with a vase of pink and white carnations decorated it. *Better not stand too close to it, I may knock it over,* she silently cautioned herself. She tapped her foot. Her green eyes finally came to rest on the detective's face. He was staring at her. A queer sensation crept into her body. It felt like excitement, but something else too. She didn't know what. The sharp click of Mrs. Henry's shoes on the marble floor caused Mary to look away from the detective. Mr. Henry appeared with Mrs. Henry, but broke into a stride when he saw Detective Kennedy.

He held out his hand and said, "By Jove, that was quick work. Good show. Thank you for coming Detective. I received your telephone message last night. Caught the scoundrel already, have you?"

"Yes, sir, we caught him down on Church Street trying to sell your property to a pawnbroker."

Mrs. Henry stepped forward and gathered up the girls. "Come girls, the auto is waiting. Goodbye Cyrus. We'll be home later this afternoon. And good day Detective."

They swept by the men, their long skirts dusting the floor. The girls hurried down the walkway to the waiting automobile, with Mrs. Henry close behind. She raised her navy blue skirt, stepped on the running board, ducked her head and stepped into the auto. The two girls climbed in beside her. Mary sniffed the fresh air. The frost had vanished and an earthy scent rose from the lawn. A slight smile crossed her face.

She turned her head to look at Mrs. Henry, and asked, "How long will it take us to drive to the store, Mrs. Henry?"

"Maybe about 40 minutes, dear. Just enjoy the scenery and get your bearings. You may want to go for a walk later," she answered.

As they passed one of the houses on High Park Boulevard, Mary could see the white and purple heads of crocuses peeking out from the soil. A vivid memory of her mother floated into her head. She had made herself a purple dress, with a white lace collar, the same colour as the crocuses. She wore it only on special occasions.

One Christmas Eve, her mother carried her upstairs to put her to bed. She held her close to her breast, and Mary felt the deep purple taffeta rub against her cheek. The memory flickered in her mind like a silent movie. She swallowed hard and bent forward.

A moment later she lifted her head and asked Mrs. Henry, "The houses are so large and beautiful on your street, Mrs. Henry. Are there many streets like this in Toronto?"

"Indeed, there are many beautiful streets in Toronto, but of course, not all. We live in the west end, in a fine area, Mary. The east end of the city is older than the west. So some streets in the east end are not nearly as nice as those in the west."

"A least 15 or 20 people could live in one house on this street," Mary said with amazement. All were two or three storeys high, with wide driveways and garages. Several houses stood with tall chalk-white pillars on spacious verandas. A boulevard flanked the road with maple and oak trees.

When they arrived at Roncesvalles Avenue and started toward Queen Street, Mary was surprised at the number of businesses on either side of the street. They all looked new, with bright rust-coloured bricks. An empty lot appeared every so often, between the new buildings like the gaps in someone's mouth from missing teeth.

There would have been work here for her Da and her brother Tom, something other than fishing. Her Ma could have easily found work sewing, as she noted the dressmakers' stores. She looked up above the shops and saw several lawyers' shingles. She wondered why they needed so many barristers. Pharmacies, millinery stores, dentists and physicians were open for business, as were butchers and barbers. It was like a small city right here. So much new to see. Some of her sadness was replaced with curiosity.

As they approached Queen Street, Mrs. Henry pointed ahead. "Lake Ontario is just in front of us, girls. Many ships come with goods and lumber to the port downtown. Passenger ships also bring in people from Europe and the United States."

Mary shivered as she remembered her father telling her cruel tales about the Irish Great Potato Famine in 1845. "When we had the Potato Famine in Ireland, a long time ago, did any Irish come here?" she asked.

A sad look crossed Mrs. Henry's features. "Indeed they did. Somewhere around 2,000 souls arrived in Toronto back in the mid-1840s. Many of them did not fare well and some even died of starvation, I'm sad to say."

Mary was horrified at the information. "Why were they starving?" she asked.

"No one would give them a job. They couldn't find work. It was a hard time for the Irish," she said sorrowfully.

The driver turned left on Queen Street and headed toward downtown Toronto. The buildings along Queen became more numerous, although there were some empty lots here as well. Mrs. Henry explained to the girls, "Toronto began its life in the early 1800s. It started in the downtown area, which was lower Yonge Street, and like rising bread it began to expand to the north away from the lake and east and west.

"The population is now over 300,000 and growing," Mrs. Henry said with pride.

The driver, Stanfield, brought the Cadillac to a smooth stop at the corner of Queen and Bay Streets. He walked around the automobile and opened the door for Mary, Anna, and Mrs. Henry.

"Please pick us up here at four p.m., Stanfield," Mrs. Henry said, and led the way across Bay Street and into the *Robert Simpson* store.

The elevator door opened at one of the upper floors. Standing in front of them was a tall, moustached gentleman with a surprised expression on his handsome face.

He took one step back and exclaimed, "Madeleine, how very pleasant to see you again so soon."

Mary watched Mrs. Henry as a pink tinge crept into her face. She began to stutter. "Jeffrey, y..yes, I suppose it's only been about a week or so since Sir Henry Pellatt's party. Let me introduce our two wards, Mary and Anna. They're survivors from the *Titanic* disaster. Girls, this is Mr. Adamson."

They both gave a little curtsy.

"Really, the *Titanic*! Welcome to Toronto, ladies. I'm sure your stay here with Mrs. Henry will be pleasant." He glanced over at Madeleine Henry and smiled. "Madeleine, may I have a private word?"

She nodded.

He led her several feet away from Mary and Anna. Mary glanced at the two of them and thought Mr. Adamson stood very close to Mrs. Henry, with his head turned away from them. She wished she could hear what they were saying. She watched as Mrs. Henry took a step back from Mr. Adamson. Mary heard her say a soft goodbye as she turned toward the girls. There was an expression on her face that Mary couldn't quite make out—a sort of not being here, a wistful look as if she was remembering something.

Mrs. Henry glided toward the girls and broke in with a cheerful, "Come girls, we have a great deal of shopping to do." Mary wondered why Mrs. Henry was speaking so quickly. And her hands were fluttering around. She grabbed Mary's hand and pulled her down the aisle.

Mrs. Henry turned her head to look back at Anna, but didn't break her stride. "Hurry, Anna. We have lots to do."

Puzzled, Mary could barely keep up with her.

The first items were long skirts in navy, black and grey. They were made of wool and serge, some with gore pleats all around. White blouses with lace trim, high necklines and long sleeves. Some of the sleeves were puffed at the shoulder and then tight-fitting down to the cuff.

Mary looked at the clothes and thought of all the times she and her mother had sat side by side and sewed. Some of the fashions were the same as she and her mother made.

So many things reminded her of her mother. She must hang on to the memories, or they might fade away when she was caught up in daily living. She would feel guilty if she didn't keep her family in her memory.

Mrs. Henry broke into her thoughts. "Now to the lingerie, girls. Next coats, and last, but not least, each of you must have three pairs of gloves. The hats will be purchased at the milliner's."

"I saw plenty of them on Roncesvalles Avenue," Mary volunteered.

At three p.m. they left for Simpson's lunchroom. A sign at the entrance stood on an easel announcing in large black letters the special for lunch, "a chicken pattie with bread and butter, and a pot of tea, 10 cents." The menu on the easel looked like one at the theatre announcing the feature act. Mary ordered the special.

Later, laden with shopping bags, the trio left the department store. Stanfield waited for them, just outside the car.

***

Mary spoke very little on the way home, other than to say, "Thank you, the clothes are beautiful, thank you." She was overwhelmed by Mrs. Henry's kindness. She guessed the Henrys were very wealthy. She heard the cashier present the bill to Mrs. Henry and say, "$110.56."

As they neared the Henry house, Mrs. Henry began to tell Mary about a school called Shaw's Business Correspondence School. "It's downtown close to the store we were just in. I would like to enrol you there, Mary, if you would like to attend."

"What do they teach, Mrs. Henry?"

"All the skills you will need to become a private secretary. There's typing, shorthand and bookkeeping. It's a respectable occupation for a young lady, Mary. And you would earn a decent wage. Would you like that?" she asked.

Mary looked away for a few moments. She would have to do something to pay back the Henrys. She felt indebted to them for their kindness. And if Mrs. Henry wanted her to go to business school, then that is what she would do.

Besides wanting to pay the Henrys back, she wanted to kick out on her own as soon as she could. Mary looked back at Mrs. Henry. "Yes, I would like that. I've already completed elementary school and almost all of secondary school, but one year."

"Good. You seem like a quick-witted girl. You should do well." Mrs. Henry turned to Anna, who had been listening intently, turning to look at each woman's face as she spoke. Mary believed Anna was picking up English faster than she expected.

"And Anna, as I told Mary earlier, I'm going to engage a tutor for you to learn English," she added.

Anna nodded her head, and said, "Yes, tutor. Thank you, Mrs. Henry."

CHAPTER 14

Burlington, Ontario, November 2000

Selby left the Police Property Department and drove home. He threw open the front door and strode in, hollering, "Dad, Dad, where are you?"

"For God's sake, what are you yelling about? I'm in the kitchen. Settle down, son."

Roy yanked out a kitchen chair so hard it almost tipped over. He straightened it and sat, watching his dad peel potatoes at the kitchen sink.

"I just made a fresh pot of coffee. Want some?"

Roy waved his hand. "No thanks."

His father put the potatoes in a pot of cold water and salt, and put it on the stove. He poured himself a cup of coffee and sauntered to the table. "What's got you so riled up?" he asked as he plopped down on a chair.

"You might have something," Roy said, "when you suggested the skeleton we found in LaSalle Park might be your missing Mary Ryan. How old was she at the time of her disappearance?"

Doug Selby's eyebrows rose. He left his cup untouched. "In her early 40s, I believe. But I've been rethinking my initial reaction to the discovery of your skeleton, Roy. It could belong to someone who didn't live around here. You'll have to do a lot of searching. And you'll need a lot of evidence to prove it's Mary Ryan."

Roy's excitement wasn't dampened. "I've just come from the Property Department. You said the evidence you collected from your investigation on Mary Ryan might be there, but probably not, because it was so long ago."

"Okey-doke. So?"

"The box was still there. And something else. An old newspaper clipping in the pocket of one of the skirts like the ones Mom used to wear."

His dad leaned closer, his eyes alive with curiosity. "How old, and what did it say?"

"Very old. 1922." He reached into his breast pocket and carefully withdrew the clipping and passed it over.

Doug's jaw dropped. "You took this from the Property Department?"

"Sorry, Dad." Selby looked sideways and gave an odd, crooked smile. "I wanted you to see it right away."

His dad's lips tightened. "You could be in a heap of trouble if someone finds out you have this, you know." The clipping shook slightly in Doug's hands. It was yellowed with age and small particles of paper dropped away as he began to read. The only sound in the room was the bubbling potatoes.

When he finished, he passed the article back to his son. "I see what you mean about the *Titanic* connection. I wonder why Mary Ryan had a clipping about the Henrys. It must have had some significance for her. Get this back to the evidence room ASAP," his dad said.

"I took photos of the clothes, and oh yeah, I forgot to tell you I found a pair of ladies' shoes in the box. I left film from my Canon at Eddie Black's, and told them to make prints. I'll have them in a few hours."

"Well, show me the pictures before you go downtown."

Roy nodded.

Doug rose from his chair and ambled over to the kitchen window.

Roy watched him and the silent snowflakes fluttering to the ground. "Dad...Dad?"

No answer. Roy figured that at 89, his dad's hearing was probably going.

Doug Selby made a slow turn to look at his son. "I was just remembering a time when you were around four years old and in the backyard building a snowman. You used cookies for his eyes, a prune for his nose and a banana for his mouth...and now you're building a person."

The room was still. Roy remembered, too. His mother had yelled at him for wasting food, but left him to his building, giving him a wry smile.

"What are you going to do now, son?"

Roy didn't answer for a moment. Coming out of his reverie, he stood. "I'm going downtown to the Toronto Reference Library. I want to look up the story in the clipping and look for any follow-up by the police. I'll take the photos with me. I want to compare the ladies' clothing styles back then. I'm sure there'll be some photos of dresses in the old newspapers."

His dad lifted his cup and took a sip. He grimaced. "Colder than Frosty the Snowman."

***

Selby was out the door and in his car in seconds. His Motorola cell phone rang at the precise moment he inserted his key into the ignition. He fumbled for the phone in his overcoat pocket and squeezed the talk button.

"Hi Roy, Phil Maybrick here. I just received some info from the tech people at the Centre of Forensic Science. They sifted the soil under the skeleton of the Jane Doe you're working on and found something."

"Great! What do they have?"

"It's a ladies' silver cross and chain. They say it's Celtic. You know the kind. It has a circle behind the upper part of the cross," Dr. Maybrick said.

"Yeah, they come from Wales or Ireland. My Grandmother had one. Umm, I wonder if our skeleton was from across the pond."

"That's a good guess, Roy. Thought you'd want to know."

"Thanks, Phil. Catch you later."

Selby got out of his Ford and went back into the house. As he strode into the kitchen, he could hear clunking and rustling coming up from the basement. Selby walked over to the cellar door and hollered, "Hey, Dad. Can you come upstairs?"

It took several minutes for Doug to climb the stairs. Roy guessed the arthritis in his father's knees was getting worse and slowing him down. He was out of breath when he reached the top. "Hold on Roy, until I get my wind back."

"OK Dad, take a chair. I have something to ask you."

The aging detective lowered himself into a chair at the kitchen table. "You sound excited. Why did you come back? You were going to Eddie Black's to pick up your prints, and then you were off to Toronto."

"I was, but I just received a call from Phil Maybrick. Can you remember if your missing girl, Mary Ryan, was of Irish descent? I thought Ryan was her married name. The techs found a Celtic silver cross in the dirt sifted from under the skeleton."

"Now you're putting my memory to the test, son. You know, the Property Department keeps all the used notebooks almost forever. Mine could be among them with the details from the Ryan case."

"OK, I'll go back and see if I can find them," Roy said.

"If Mary was Irish, it'll be in one of my notebooks. If you want to take them out, you'd better sign for them," his dad warned him with a frown on his face.

On Selby's way back to the Police Property Department he wondered, *Could it be... could the skeleton in LaSalle Park be his dad's missing lady?*

The traffic jammed on the Queen Elizabeth Way, so he decided to take Lakeshore Road. Hell, another jam, as he approached Bronte Road. He'd just drive downtown to the Toronto Reference Library. He could go to the Property Department tomorrow.

***

The traffic crawled north on Yonge Street until he finally reached Bloor, found a parking space, and entered the library. Selby approached the Information desk in the centre of the main floor.

"May I help you, sir?" the receptionist asked.

"I hope so. My first time here. I understand you have records of old Toronto newspapers on file?"

"We do. Just go downstairs to the newspaper room," she said, pointing to the stairs. "The person at the Help desk will assist you. Tell them what you're looking for, and they'll set you up. All the old stuff is on microfilm and some on *Proquest*, a new system we have."

"Thanks," Selby said and skipped downstairs. He approached the young man at the reference desk. The name 'Kurt' was on a sign on his desk.

"Hello, Kurt. I'm Detective Selby and I need to look at Toronto newspapers dating back to June, 1922. One would be *The Toronto Star*, another *The Telegram*, and the other *The Globe and Mail*."

At the word "detective", Kurt's ears perked up. Selby noted he seemed especially interested. Kurt rose quickly from his chair and came around his desk to stand beside the detective. "Certainly, Detective. We have all three newspapers. The names of the papers have changed slightly since 1922. *The Globe and Mail* was called *The Globe* back in the day, and *The Toronto Star* was *The Toronto Daily Star*, and *The Telegram* was called the *Evening Telegram*. So we'll look for those names. Follow me."

The far wall was lined with hundreds of small drawers. Each drawer had numerous small white boxes of microfilm which were year-dated. Kurt opened the drawers for *The Toronto Daily Star* and *The Globe newspapers for 1922*.

"Where do you want to start?" the librarian asked.

"Hmm, start at the beginning of June."

Kurt threaded the microfilm reader. "Watch me for a minute and I'll show you how to use this."

After Kurt left, the detective pulled out the clipping from his breast pocket. The complete date was not there. There was a hole in the paper where the day would have been, and he could only read June,—1922.

He settled in and began his search. When he reached June 25th, there it was: the identical article. He scrolled ahead looking for follow-up. A few days later, there was a small article stating Mr. Henry was out on bail, and there would be a trial at the end of the year. Selby sat staring at the screen, and then he had an idea.

Swinging around on the swivel chair, the detective pushed himself up and strolled over to Kurt's desk. Kurt was busy writing dates on the small, white boxes.

He looked up when he heard his name. "Yes, Detective may I help you?"

"You have a program here called *Proquest*, right?"

"We do." He nodded.

"Tell me about it."

Kurt stopped what he was doing and pushed the boxes aside. "You can enter a name and the program will scan the paper forward or backward to see if that name appears anywhere else in a particular paper. Let's go over to a reader and I'll show you how to do it."

The room felt stuffy, so Selby removed his coat, caught the back of the collar and slung it over his shoulder.

The two men stood at the bank of readers. "I want to see if the name Andrew Henry, of Toronto, appears anywhere before June 25th, 1922. I'm particularly interested in any interviews given by Toronto survivors of the *Titanic*. I know there was at least one," Selby said.

"Let me check for the dates first, when Toronto survivors returned here." Kurt got on a nearby computer and did a search. In just a couple of minutes the library technician returned with some dates. "OK, here they are," he said as he passed the paper to Selby.

There was an unmistakable glint of curiosity in Kurt's eyes. Selby guessed he was dying to ask him questions about his search.

"Had an old relative on the ship, Detective?"

Selby decided to give the librarian a tidbit since he had been particularly helpful. "No, no, not that. Might be a lead to a case I'm working on. But it's so long ago, probably won't lead anywhere."

"Oooh," Kurt said, looking like he wanted to know more.

Kurt went over to the bank of drawers with white boxes in them. He selected 1912 and returned. Selby sat in front of the machine, and Kurt leaned over his shoulder giving him instructions.

The detective scrolled, looking for anything about Toronto survivors. And there it was, on April 21, 1912, in *The Globe*. It read:

> *Mr. and Mrs. Cyrus Henry of Toronto welcomed their son, Andrew, home safe and sound after the* Titanic *disaster...*

Toward the end of the article, it continued:

> *...Miss Mary Flynn was in the lifeboat with young Mr. Henry and she was responsible for pulling several more survivors out of the water. Unfortunately, all her own family perished when the ship went down. Miss Flynn will be residing with the Henry family for an indefinite period of time.*

Mary Flynn and Mr. Andrew Henry were both survivors. It could be just a coincidence. Mary's a common name, but it was possible that Mary Flynn and Mary Ryan could be one and the same. A photograph of Mr. and Mrs. Henry, their son, Andrew, Mary Flynn, and another survivor, Anna Zelasko, appeared above the article. If Selby could find a link or a trail for Mary Flynn, it just might lead to Burlington, and the photograph was a bonus.

CHAPTER 15

Toronto, Ontario, May 1912

"You start at the school I was telling you about this coming Monday, Mary," Madeleine Henry announced at the dinner table that night.

Mary was sitting across from her. "Oh, so soon?" a slight quiver appeared on her bottom lip.

"Yes, Mary. You'll be studying Pitman Shorthand, typing and some bookkeeping. How does that sound?"

"I suppose it will help me to find a good job." She added with a little more enthusiasm. "I am very good at sums, so that should not be difficult, and I have seen people typing—it looks like fun. I met a girl back in Ireland who knew shorthand. She said there was a lot of memorizing, but I do have a good memory, so that should be all right."

She welcomed the distraction from her pain and grief. The studying would give her something to concentrate on and fill her mind.

The newspapers were still full of stories about the disaster. She read in *The Globe* that there were only 105 passengers from third class who survived. Whereas first and second class had approximately 600 survivors. Over 1500 passengers and crew had drowned. Many of the churches were holding large commemorative services for the dead. Mary and Anna had attended a service with the Henry family.

***

Two years passed. Mary was doing well in her studies. The shorthand gave the most difficulty, with words having three positions within two lines. And there were the vowels, with light dots and dark ones and light dashes and dark ones. Her brain must have grown twice the size for all the memory work it was holding. She would be finished her studies soon. It gave her pleasure knowing her parents would be proud. She could type 65 words a minute on her Underwood, but still needed more practice. Her baby finger had to be strengthened for the 'a' and the 'z'.

And Anna's English had improved. She spoke with confidence with few mistakes in grammar.

Mary returned to the Henrys' home at the end of the street, after a walk in High Park. She loved to feed the squirrels and watch the ducks flutter around on Grenadier Pond. She climbed the circular stairs to her bedroom. A beautiful, carved jade jar rested on her dresser. Mrs. Henry had given it to her last Christmas. She put her savings in it from money she earned typing for one of Mr. Henry's friends.

Mrs. Henry's birthday was coming up and she wanted to buy her a gift. As she walked toward her dresser, she thought about a pink and purple silk scarf she had seen. She removed the delicate lid and gasped, "Oh." It was bare. The money was gone. *Who could have taken it?* She ran out of the room, lifted her skirt, and took the stairs two at a time, calling, "Mrs. Henry, Mrs. Henry!" in a frantic voice.

Mrs. Henry's bedroom door flew open. She leaned over the railing. "I'm up here, Mary. What is it?" she said in a concerned voice.

Mary looked up with tears streaming down her face. "My savings have disappeared!"

When Anna did not return that evening, Mary looked in their closet. Anna's clothes were gone. Her heart fell. It became apparent her friend and fellow survivor had disappeared with the money. *But where could she have gone?*

CHAPTER 16

Toronto, August 1914

Mary sat at the breakfast table with Mr. and Mrs. Henry. She placed a Shredded Wheat biscuit in her bowl and said, "Just six more weeks and I will be finished my business course."

"That's wonderful news, Mary," Mrs. Henry said.

The exuberance in Mary's voice jolted Mr. Henry out of his concentration on the newspaper. "What's that you say, Mary?"

"My business course is almost complete," Mary repeated as she poured milk on her cereal. "I shall be looking for a position soon. I feel beholden to you and Mrs. Henry. I must begin to earn my keep."

Mr. Henry folded his paper and placed it on the table. "Now, now, my dear. There is no need to pay us back anything. We are indebted to you for the support you gave our son during the dreadful tragedy."

"Andrew also supported me in the lifeboat when some of the others did not want to go back and pull people out of the water. I would feel better if I could at least repay Mrs. Henry for the clothes she bought for me."

"Consider them a gift, Mary. I enjoyed doing it," Mrs. Henry said.

"When you have your business certificate, I may be able to help you with a placement," Mr. Henry said. "Let me speak to a few friends and see what I can come up with." He picked up his newspaper again.

The paper was full of news regarding Canada's entry into the battle with the Germans that was raging in Europe.

"Good morning, Mother, Mary, Father. What's for breakfast?" Andrew asked, as he entered the dining room. He looked at the sideboard, where there was orange juice, scrambled eggs, ham, toast, tea and fresh coffee. With a full plate, he sat across from Mary. His fork was in midair when he turned sideways to look at his father.

"I'm going downtown today, Father, to enlist in the Army."

Mrs. Henry gasped and placed her hand over her mouth. "Oh, no Andrew!"

Slowly, Mr. Henry lowered his paper. Some of the colour had drained from his face, and the paper shook ever so slightly. He folded his paper carefully and placed it beside him.

"It is only a short time ago we feared you had perished at sea, Andrew, and although it's honourable and courageous of you to volunteer, I am afraid your mother will be beside herself with worry, as will I."

"I would feel like a coward if I did not make a contribution to the conflict, Father and Mother. Many of my friends have already enlisted and are in training."

"I know, but…"

***

Mary went with the family to the C.N. Railroad station at the foot of Cherry Street to see Andrew off. She felt on the verge of tears, but held them back. "Good luck, friend," she said as she hugged him.

His mother's lips trembled as she clutched a white handkerchief. "Write as often as you can, son, and take care of yourself," Mrs. Henry said with her cheek pressed against her son's face, as she hugged him.

Mr. Henry took a step closer to his son, clasped his shoulder with one hand and shook Andrew's hand with the other. "Give them hell, son." Mr. Henry's hand shook almost imperceptibly as he grasped his son's shoulder, and his face was pulled tight.

Andrew's friend, Charles Simmons, was also there. He'd been rejected by the Army due to his poor eyesight, so Andrew had told his parents and Mary a few days earlier. "Come home safe, friend," he said, shaking Andrew's hand. Still holding Andrew's hand, he bent over and whispered something in Andrew's ear.

Mary could see Charles's eyes glisten as he stepped back from Andrew. Mary knew they were very close. She guessed Charles was having the same thought as she: *Would any of them see Andrew again?*

CHAPTER 17

Toronto Reference Library, November 2000

"Kurt, I want to try something else on *Proquest*."

"Sure. What is it?"

"I'd like to see if a name appears in *The Globe* in the years between 1912 and 1920."

Kurt put in the co-ordinates and the computer whizzed along and threw out a few Mary Flynns. Selby read the items and dismissed all but one dated May, 1919. His heart began to pump a little faster as he read:

> *More than two thousand lives have been claimed in Toronto by the Spanish Flu. The most recent death is that of a prominent executive of the Superior Railroad, Mr. Ulysses Howard. ... It's reported that Mr. Howard gave a* Titanic *survivor, Mary Flynn, her first job in Canada, and she was working for him at the time of his death.*

There's the Titanic *again.* And he knew now what she had been doing between 1912 and 1919. *But if Mary Flynn was Mary Ryan, why change her name?* Selby asked himself. *Marriage, maybe?*

He'd try the marriage announcements. After scanning the papers for some time, he could find no marriage announcement of Mary Flynn in any of the papers. Nada.

Selby pushed himself up and sauntered over to Kurt.

"Something else, Detective?" Kurt looked up at Selby with an eager expression.

Selby knew sometimes people were impressed by a police detective and were only too willing to help. That is, if they weren't of the criminal element. "Kurt, where could I find old marriage records dating back to say...1919 to 1930?"

Kurt answered immediately. "All the old marriage records for Ontario are at the Archives of Ontario. It used to be just down Bay St. on Grenville, but they've moved to the grounds of York University. I'm afraid it's quite a distance north to their new location. If there's a record, it'll be in the Ontario Archives."

"Kurt, I'd like a favour. Would you photocopy the pages I looked at today?"

"No problem, Detective. Just show me what you want," he said, rising.

While Selby waited for the photocopies, he thought about what it must have been like when the *Titanic* survivors were on dry land again. The relief, but also the sorrow over lost loved ones must have been immense. Then, surely, there must have been a multitude of members of the press and photographers. Where was it...New York? Yeah, he believed it was New York. He'd get Kurt to look up the newspapers in the city at the time the survivors arrived there.

Minutes later, Kurt returned with the photocopies. Selby thanked him and placed the copies in a brown briefcase.

"I just thought of something. Would you be able to look up a major newspaper in New York? I think *The New York Times* is the oldest. I'm looking for a photograph of the Henry family and two young ladies."

"No problem. And do you want a photocopy of the picture if I find it?" Kurt asked.

"It would be helpful. Thanks again."

Kurt returned about five minutes later with a wide grin on his face. "Got it, Detective." He handed the picture to Selby.

The quality of the photo appeared better than *The Globe*'s. He studied it for a few moments. The group of people appeared to be on a train. You could see the landscape through the train window. And the article accompanying the photo mentioned all the names of the people in the photograph—Mr. and Mrs. Cyrus Henry, and survivors from the *Titanic*, Andrew Henry, Mary Flynn, and Anna Zelasko. A smile slid across his face.

"Thanks again, Kurt, for your time. You've been very helpful."

Kurt beamed.

Selby slipped all the copies into his briefcase and left the library.

***

Four o'clock—rush-hour traffic. The detective decided to wait until the following day to go to the Archives and check the marriages.

Nearing his home in Burlington, he stopped for a red light at the corner of Caroline and Brant Street. His foot was on the brake when he heard a loud crunch in the rear of his Ford, and at the same instant his head jerked forward and backward. A searing pain pierced the back of his neck. The last thing he remembered was flying forward.

When he woke, he was in a bed in Joseph Brant Hospital. An antiseptic odour hung in the air. Alcohol and something else. A padded collar circled his neck. And he had the mother of all headaches. Nurses scurried in and out of the room. A fellow came in with a bucket of water and a grey mop, and began swishing the floor. A beige curtain hung open at the end of his bed.

"Glad to see you're awake at last, Mr. Selby," a pretty, doe-eyed nurse with black hair said. "I need to take your blood pressure and temperature."

The light in the room seemed to throb in his head, and he squinted as he asked, "Would you shut off the light please, Nurse?"

She went behind the bed and flicked a switch. "I'll have to turn it back on soon, though. Your doctor's coming in shortly to examine you."

Selby gave an abbreviated tilt of his head. In spite of the pain, drowsiness was enveloping him. *They must have injected me with something.* Slowly his eyes closed, and he felt like he was floating up and away. He could hear music and singing coming from the next cubicle. It was one of the old tunes his father liked. Rod Stewart had recorded some of the old favourites back from his dad's day. Stewart was singing "I'll Be Seeing You." After a few moments a black shade dropped in front of his eyes, and he no longer felt or heard.

CHAPTER 18

"Mr. Selby... Mr. Selby..." Someone was shaking his arm and calling his name. He opened his eyes, and a tall, bearded man came into focus with a nurse by his side.

"Mr. Selby, I'm Dr. Katz, and I'll be looking after you."

Selby whispered, "OK."

"You've had a bad whiplash and a slight concussion when you hit your head on the steering wheel. Do remember what happened?" Dr. Katz asked.

Everything was hazy for a few seconds and then Selby remembered. "I was stopped at a red light when I felt a sudden *wham* from behind, and an excruciating pain like an electric shock in the back of my neck. I'd forgotten my seat belt. I don't remember anything else after that, until I woke up here."

"Well, we're going to keep you for a few days. I want to run some blood tests, and a CT scan, OK? I'll see you tomorrow," the doctor said and strode out of the room.

"Um," Selby murmured, and drifted into dreamland again.

When Roy woke some time later, he could hear voices on the other side of the curtain. Soft and muffled, he couldn't make out the words. A male voice seemed to answer a female voice. Eyes still closed, but awake, Selby felt someone tapping his hand and calling, "Roy, Roy." He opened his eyes and blinked. His father stood beside his bed.

"How you feeling, son? You've got quite a shiner there and that horse collar looks like it could stretch your neck. Careful it doesn't choke you."

Roy tried to smile, but everything still ached, even the muscles in his face.

Just then a nurse bustled into the room, heading for the other patient's bed. "Mr. Essex, I have your medication. Do you have some water?" she asked.

"Essex… Essex… that name sounds familiar," his dad said. "Give me a minute. It'll come to me. What does your doctor say?"

"Give me a minute Dad, it'll come to me." They both laughed. And it hurt.

"You know, the usual." Selby recounted what the doctor had told him.

"It just came to me! Essex was the name of Mary Ryan's friend. An unusual name, isn't it? Like a place in England. I wonder if it's the same Essex. Burlington's a small city, you know, with lots of people who have lived here all their lives. Could be…" his dad said.

"Uh-huh." Selby muttered.

After a brief visit, his dad left, saying, "See you tonight, son."

***

Later that evening Selby sat up in bed, feeling much better. A tray of food was perched on a table at the foot of his bed. The room started to spin when he tried to get up and move the tray toward him. Selby flopped back into his bed and hit the buzzer for a nurse.

It was only a few minutes before she arrived.

"Would you move the tray up to me, please?" he asked.

The food wasn't as bad as some people made it out to be—a nice piece of sole, green beans and mashed potatoes. Applesauce for dessert, too. The meal gave him energy.

A large, black clock hung on the wall opposite the patients' beds and gazed down on them. Five minutes to seven p.m. A few minutes later, Roy heard several footsteps and conversation in the corridor. He turned sideways to look at the entrance, just as his dad strolled into the room. White shirt and tie, clean pressed navy suit as always when he went out. *That's my Dad,* Roy thought.

An elderly woman followed close behind. Smiling and a bit stiff-legged, she crossed the room to the other patient's bed.

All the curtains had been pushed back to the wall behind the beds. Roy and his dad could see the other patient sitting up, looking cheery. His visitor eased herself into a purple plastic chair beside the man's bed. She nodded and smiled at Roy and his dad. Her face and blue eyes seemed to come to life and shine as she looked at the patient. *His mother,* Selby assumed.

Doug Selby sat close to his son's bed. "Do you feel well enough to tell me what you found at the Reference Library?" he asked.

"I found one small follow-up to the shooting of Mrs. Henry's lover. It stated a trial would be held at the end of the year, and Mr. Henry had been released from jail and out on bail. I used the library's new electronic program to search for Mary Flynn's name. I'll tell you about it later. I'm too tired now. I just want to get out of here as soon as I can. Have you found anything in the basement yet?"

"Still looking."

They chatted for a short while longer.

"OK, I'll be back tomorrow." His dad stood and pushed his chair away from the bed. The visitor at the next bed also prepared to leave. She bent down and kissed Mr. Essex on the cheek. She glanced at Roy and his dad and nodded as she passed by.

Doug took a quick step toward the lady. "Excuse me, but I heard the nurse call the patient you were visiting Mr. Essex. By any chance are you his mother?"

The woman stood still for a moment, a curious expression in her eyes. "Why yes, I am. And who might you be?"

"My name's Douglas Selby. I'm a retired detective."

She cocked her head sideway. "Yes?"

"I investigated the disappearance of a young woman way back in the day. I interviewed a Mrs. Essex at the time, a friend of the missing person. I just wondered if there's a connection. It's not a common name around here."

Roy stretched out an arm. "Dad—No, Dad," he pleaded, his forehead covered in furrows. His dad just couldn't stop being a detective.

"Why yes, I'm Daphne Essex," her eyelids fluttered, then settled on Douglas Selby's face. She tilted her head and continued to stare at him. Her voice softened and sadness crept into it. "I had a friend who disappeared a long time ago."

The men's eyes widened as they focussed on the woman. They glanced at each other before they looked back at Mrs. Essex.

"Yes, it was a long time ago, but I remember the name Selby. You must be that nice young detective, who came to my house asking about my friend, Mary Ryan. Nothing ever turned up, or did it?" she asked with a hopeful note in her voice.

Doug took a few steps closer to Mrs. Essex and leaned forward. "Sorry, not back then, but there might be something now. My son Roy, here, is a detective working on a case that might be related."

"Dad, I don't think you should be talking about this right now." The frown on Roy's face deepened and a tinge of pink appeared on his cheeks.

His dad ignored him and went right on talking as if he hadn't heard his son. "If you don't mind Mrs. Essex, would you leave your telephone number with me? Between the two of us, we may be able to help my son."

Roy watched as the patient in the next bed rose, put on a bathrobe, and strolled over to where Mrs. Essex and his dad were standing.

Tying the belt on his bathrobe, he said, "I remember my Mom telling me about her missing friend when I was a youngster."

"And I remember you when you were in diapers," Doug Selby said with a chuckle. He fished a notebook from inside his jacket, and unclipped a gold-tipped fountain pen from his breast pocket. "What's your number, Mrs. Essex?"

After Mrs. Essex left and her son climbed back into bed, Roy spoke quietly. "Please, Dad, don't go to Mrs. Essex's house until I'm out of here, and then the two of us can go if you want."

"OK, OK. I guess I'll have enough to keep me busy rooting about in the basement for any old items that might help."

CHAPTER 19

Two days later Roy was home, a collar holding his head upright.

His dad called Mrs. Essex to get her address. "I can hardly believe it. Mrs. Essex is still living in the same house."

"You old fogeys stay in the same place forever. You put down roots and stay planted. Nowadays, young people move around a lot more, every five years, so the stats say."

"Well, look at us. You're back living in the same place where you were born. Guess you're becoming an old fogey, too."

"Got me there, Dad."

It was lunchtime and the two men strolled into the kitchen. There was a delicious scent of maple syrup lingering in the room. "I roasted a ham last night. We can have ham sandwiches with Dijon mustard," Doug Selby said.

"Sounds good. Have any pea soup?"

When the men finished their lunch, Roy pushed away from the table and stood. "Very tasty, Dad. Thanks."

"Now let me see what you got from the Reference Library, before we visit Mrs. Essex," Doug said.

Roy went to his bedroom and returned with his briefcase. A sharp click sounded as he pressed the brass button and withdrew the contents.

Doug took the papers in his outstretched hand and began to read. After a few beats, he said, "You've got some real interesting stuff here. And the photos are pretty good. I can't wait to compare them with the photo I made for the poster of the missing woman."

"Neither can I," Roy said.

A stiff wind blew up from Lake Ontario and rattled the kitchen window. "Phone Mrs. Essex and ask if we can go over now. You seemed to have made an impression on her."

Doug rose with a smile and an expectant look on his face and hurried into the living room to make the call. A couple of minutes later he was back. "It's OK. Mrs. Essex says she'll see us now. Better bundle up, though. I looked at the outside thermometer. It says 20 degrees Fahrenheit. That is... I think its Fahrenheit. This Celsius thing has me all confused when I hear them give the temperature on the news. Shoulda just left the temperature alone," he said.

"If it was Celsius, you'd be taking off your sweater, Dad."

They took Roy's Ford. Doug recited the address, then kept giving his son instructions all the way.

Roy glanced at his dad and smiled. "It's all right, Dad, I know the street. I wonder if Mrs. Essex will remember anything new about her missing friend. What do you think?"

CHAPTER 20

Toronto, Spring 1914

True to his word, Mr. Henry gave Mary a letter of reference addressed to a Mr. Howard, one of his friends. She hurried down the street clasping the envelope. Mrs. Henry told her Mr. Ulysses Howard was an executive at the Canadian Superior Railroad.

The envelope was unsealed, and Mary's curiosity got the better of her. She knew she shouldn't open it. It was not addressed to her, but she could see no harm, she rationalized. Feeling a little guilty, her fingers fumbled as she withdrew the letter. After reading the first few lines, the dimples started to show in her cheeks. Her steps slowed and shortened as she read:

> *She is an intelligent young woman*
> *and a hard worker, and I am sure you will*
> *find her quite satisfactory. She has her*
> *diploma from business school and is*
> *therefore fully qualified to fulfil your needs.*

She folded the letter and was replacing it in the envelope when she felt her shoulder bump against someone.

"Really, young woman! You should look where you're going." A stout, red faced woman pushed by her and did a half turn to stare back with a scowl.

Mary stopped and looked at the disgruntled woman. "Oh, I'm very sorry ma'am."

"You should be!" And with that the woman huffed off down the street.

The Howards' house stood on the same street as the Henrys', High Park Boulevard. Like most houses in the area, it climbed three storeys high, with red brick and white trim. Tall pillars stood on either side of a wide veranda, supporting a narrow balcony above it. It looked larger and grander than the Henrys' house. She guessed some Canadians must have a great deal of money to live in such houses. She remembered the Mayor's house back in Cork, where she worked after school. Even his house was not so grand. Mary rang the bell and heard chimes. She clutched the letter in her gloved hand as she waited.

"Yes, Miss?" A thin, middle-aged woman with black hair pulled back in a tight bun stood in the doorway. A long black dress with a white collar fell to the floor, making her look even thinner. The door stood half way open. Looking into the woman's pinched face Mary wondered if she was the housekeeper. She had a condescending air about her, just like the housekeeper at the Mayor's home in Ireland.

Mary took a step forward, handed her the letter and said, "I'll be thankin' you to give this to Mr. Howard. I am delivering it for Mr. Henry."

At the mention of Mr. Henry's name, the woman's face thawed a little, and she almost smiled—almost. Long bony fingers plucked the letter from Mary's hand. As she began to close the door, the woman offered a begrudged courtesy. "Thank you. Good day."

***

Two days later Mary was standing beside Madeleine Henry when the telephone rang.

Mrs. Henry picked up the receiver and listened. "Hello Ulysses. I trust you are well?" She stood in the foyer with the cone-shaped receiver pressed to her ear. She listened for a few seconds. "Yes, Ulysses, I'll tell Mary. She's right here. Give my regards to Mrs. Howard."

Mary had been about to go out for a walk. Her ears perked up and she stood still at the front door when she heard her name mentioned. *Could it be Mr. Howard calling so soon?* Her heart began to pound at the prospect of starting her first secretarial job. In the next minute, irrational apprehension began to creep in. Would she be able to do the job? Of course she would. Why she received the highest marks in the class at secretarial school!

Mrs. Henry replaced the receiver on its hook. She turned to face Mary, a trace of a smile on her serene face. "Mary, that was Mr. Howard calling, the gentleman my husband referred you to. He says your credentials are in order, and he would like you to start working for him on Monday. He is a very pleasant man Mary, and I am sure you will get along well."

"Monday?" Mary gasped, putting a hand over her mouth. "So soon? Does he not want to interview me first?" Her voice trembled. She tried to hide it by speaking louder.

"Mr. Henry spoke with Mr. Howard about you yesterday, and Mr. Howard was pleased with my husband's comments."

***

Mary showed up promptly on the following Monday morning at 9:00. The same gaunt woman to whom she had given the letter answered the door. "Come in Miss, you are expected. Wait here." Mary stepped into the foyer clutching her purse. She was glad she was wearing gloves—she was sure her knuckles were white. The housekeeper disappeared like a wraith, floating to somewhere at the back of the house. Mary waited, trying to keep calm. She felt prickly beads of moisture on the back of her neck. *Stand up straight, keep your hands still and only speak when you are spoken to.*

Mr. Howard entered the foyer with a woman trotting close behind, her ample bosom thrust out. "How do you do, Miss Flynn?" the gentleman said. "I am Ulysses

Howard and this is my wife, Mrs. Howard." He stepped aside.

Mary felt the blood drain from her face. She couldn't stop her eyes from growing wide. She tried to compose herself and hoped she hadn't betrayed her feelings. Her embarrassment began to subside. She said simply, she hoped without emotion, "How do you do Mrs. Howard." Here, in front of her, was the woman Mary had bumped into on the street.

In an icy voice, Mrs. Howard replied, "Yes, I remember you. You're the young lady who does not watch where she is walking." Mrs. Howard's eyes and lips narrowed as she scanned Mary head to toe.

Mary looked directly at Mrs. Howard, pushed her shoulders back and said, "I'm sure it will not happen again." *Oh, sweet Jesus help me,* Mary prayed under her breath. Was she going to be dismissed before she started? She felt sure Mrs. Howard had told her husband about the incident and that the clumsy young woman was reading a letter when the collision occurred. And Mrs. Howard probably suggested the letter she was reading was the letter of introduction addressed to him. But if she told her husband, he never mentioned it, only their collision.

"It was just a small accident, was it not, Victoria? Nothing to make a fuss about, I'm sure," Mr. Howard said quickly. His brow furrowed as he looked at his wife.

Turning to Mary he said, "In a few moments Mrs. Sylvester, our housekeeper, can show you to your room and to where you will take your meals. I would like to discuss your duties in my office now."

"Thank you, sir." And under her breath, *Thank you, God.* Mary exhaled and let her shoulders relax.

Mr. Howard beckoned Mary. "In here Miss Flynn," he said, holding the mahogany door open for her. The room was off the foyer several feet from the front door. Just before she entered Mr. Howard's office, she looked over her shoulder, back to where Mrs. Howard stood. Her new boss's wife was rooted to the spot, watching them. With eyes narrowed, she looked down her nose, and her mouth became a thin pale line. If Mrs. Howard thought she could bully Mary, the lady had another think coming.

Just before Mr. Howard closed the door, he said, "Excuse me for a moment, Mary," and a few seconds later Mary heard him tramping upstairs.

Still smarting from Mrs. Howard's cruel remarks, she decided she would be co-operative, but would not be bullied. She remembered a time when she and her Da were at the post office. A fine lady had stepped in front of Mary in the queue. Her Ma and Da had taught her she was as good as the next person. Her Da said, "Don't let her get away with that. Tell her you were here before her." And she did.

She had stepped in front of the lady with the frilly umbrella and said, "Excuse me, Ma'am. This is my place." A frown rippled across the woman's face, and she sniffed and backed away. The next instant she swung around and was out the door, leaving a cloying perfume in her wake.

Mr. Howard returned, closed the door, and sat behind his desk. "All right Miss Flynn let's get to work."

CHAPTER 21

Toronto, 1918

Today marked four years since Mary had started working for Mr. Howard. For the most part things had gone well, except for the occasional unpleasantness from Mrs. Howard. Mary sat in her office reading from her shorthand notes. The clicking of the typewriter keys produced a pleasant sound, although it was loud, so she didn't hear Mr. Howard enter the room.

"Ah, good morning, Mary. Are the letters I dictated yesterday ready?" He towered over her, even with his stooped posture. His brown wavy hair was just beginning to show a strand of grey, and his hairline had started to recede. There seemed to be a kind of urgency about him, in his quick movements and in his voice, which was breathless at times.

Mary stopped typing on her new Underwood and swivelled around on her chair. Perspiration glimmered on Mr. Howard's face. And his hand shook when he reached out to take the letters. She was puzzled, because it wasn't warm in the house.

"All ready for your signature, sir." Mary took a closer look at him. "Are you feeling unwell Mr. Howard?"

He began to rifle through the file marked "correspondence". "Thank you, for your concern Mary, but just a bit of a cold, I expect. Oh yes, good, here they are," he said picking up the letters. "Would you mind taking them up to the post office as soon as I have signed them?" He began to cough violently, and pulled a handkerchief from his pocket to cover his mouth.

Mary rose, startled. She became frightened when he couldn't regain his breath. The only thing she could think of was to get him some water. "Sit down Mr. Howard, I'll be right back."

She dashed to the kitchen and shouted, "Mrs. Sylvester!" No reply. She looked around the kitchen puzzled. "Mrs. Howard! Mrs. Howard!" No reply either. A second or two passed, and then she remembered seeing the housekeeper and Mrs. Howard leave the house that morning. Gone shopping, she suspected. She went to the sink and let the cold water run for a few seconds. She had no idea where the glasses were, but luckily one stood on the counter. She filled it and hurried back to Mr. Howard.

He was slumped in the chair, mopping his forehead. He'd stopped coughing, but he looked limp and pale as if he had lost all his energy. "Drink this sir," she said as she held out the glass. After several long swallows he handed back the empty glass. He took a couple of deep breaths and put his hand in his pocket. When he withdrew it, several coins lay nestled in his palm. He selected a penny, and placed it in her outstretched hand.

"Take this for the newspaper, Mary. Please pick up *The Globe* for me. The delivery boy missed me this morning."

Irritation sounded in his voice, and a frown appeared on his face. It wasn't like him. Usually he treated people with patience. Mary concluded the impatience came from his illness, whatever it might be. She did up the buttons on her belted sweater coat, pulled her cloche down over her ears and headed out.

The fresh spring breeze brushed against her face. She enjoyed its clean scent, inhaled it, and pulled up the collar on her sweater. She reached Roncesvalles Avenue, deposited the letters in the red mailbox, purchased *The Globe*, and started home.

As Mary walked back to the Howard home, she passed the Henry's house. She felt blessed and grateful to the Henry family for taking her in and giving her opportunities outside her class. Mrs. Henry and Andrew were not as rigid regarding class as some were. But even so, if they had not been brought together by the *Titanic* disaster, they probably never would have met. And perhaps her parents, if they'd survived, would not have been able to provide the secretarial training she needed to better herself. But her Da would probably find a way.

Mr. Howard paid Mary well. Out of her fifteen dollars per week, she had saved several hundred dollars. She made most of her clothes when she still had her sewing machine, and seldom had to buy anything new. The few clothes she did buy were of a classic design: white blouses, with high necklines, a sprig of lace at the throat, and long sleeves. But the styles were changing. Skirts were getting shorter. She had purchased a black one.

Mary's mother gave her a sterling silver cross and chain at the time of her Confirmation into the Catholic Church at the age of twelve. She seldom took it off.

She did not want to live in the Howard home much longer. She wanted her own place with her own things. She had seen advertisements in the *Daily Star* under *Rooms to Let*. There were several in the High Park area for young working ladies.

As Mary neared the Howard home, she saw an ambulance in front. Her pulse quickened. It must be Mr. Howard. She *knew* something was wrong—not the Spanish Flu, which raged in the city, she hoped. The newspaper under her arm stated thousands of people were dying from it in Toronto and millions throughout the world.

She rushed up the walkway, and the door opened just as she reached it. Ambulance attendants came out carrying Mr. Howard on a stretcher.

Mrs. Howard followed close behind, dabbing at her eyes. She saw Mary. "Mary, Mr. Howard collapsed a few minutes after Mrs. Sylvester and I returned from shopping. He was bleeding from the nose and mouth. Dr. Fraser says it's the Spanish Flu. Thank the Lord, the doctor lives next door. We summoned him straight away."

"Is there anything I can do, Mrs. Howard?" Mary asked.

"Take care of the children when they return home from school." She stared at Mary for a few moments, panic and sadness written on her face. "Thank you, Mary. He is very low," she said as she followed the stretcher into the ambulance.

Two days later, Mr. Howard was dead, and Mary felt shock and sadness. He had been a kind gentleman, and she would miss him. She was out of a job and a home.

Where to now?

CHAPTER 22

Burlington, December 2000

Roy Selby parked in front of the Essex house. His dad didn't remove his seat belt and just sat there, staring at the property. "It looks better than the last time I saw it." Yellow grass peaked through a sprinkling of snow. Evergreens hugged the front of the house. "Nice paint job, too, charcoal grey and white," Doug said.

"Well, Dad, you haven't been here for decades, so I suppose the house has been painted several times since then. OK, let's go," he said as he slipped out of the car. He walked to the passenger side and opened the door. His dad clutched the door frame and struggled to get out.

Doug stood on the sidewalk, gazing at the house and holding his son's briefcase.

"It's all coming back to me now. I came here twice. The first time my partner, Burkowski, came with me. I remember Mrs. Essex as a pleasant young woman, rather attractive. Although, she looked like she'd been beaten down—older than her years, I suspect. Poor, but neat and clean. The house looked spotless, and she'd made cookies and tea for us."

The morning snow lay in small borders up either side of the stairs. Doug clung to the black wrought iron railing as he climbed to a postage stamp-sized porch.

Roy pushed the buzzer. He heard background music and some dialogue. Sounded like a soap-opera playing on the TV. The door opened. Mrs. Essex's blue eyes sparkled. "Come in gentlemen."

She led them to the kitchen. "Have a seat," she said, as she busied herself at the kitchen counter.

Roy watched as his dad's eyes roved around the room. Doug said, "I see you've updated your kitchen, Mrs. Essex. The old Aga stove's gone, eh? And nice white ceramic tile. More durable than the old linoleum."

Mrs. Essex turned her head. "Oh, heavens, yes. Gotta keep up with the times you know," she said, smiling. A teapot with a yellow knitted cozy sat on the kitchen counter beside an electric coffee maker. "Tea or coffee, gentlemen?" she asked.

When they settled down with their refreshments, Mrs. Essex asked, "Is your neck feeling better, Detective?"

"Getting there, bit better each day. Thanks for asking," Roy replied.

"I'm very glad you came today. I've never stopped thinking about Mary. She was such a good friend to me. There's something I have to tell you that I didn't mention when Mary went missing."

Both men leaned forward.

"I didn't want to shine a bad light on her at the time. I mean, some folks might not think too kindly of her," she said, looking at Roy's dad, then at him. "But I can't see that it matters too much nowadays."

Doug opened his mouth to say something, but his son shot him a look that said, "Sit on it."

"It's OK, go on, Mrs. Essex," Roy said.

She nodded and a lump appeared and disappeared in her throat.

"Anyway, one night in September, a long time ago, September the nineteenth, to be exact—it was my birthday—Mary came over with a bottle of wine and a cake to celebrate. After a few glasses she became very relaxed and started talking about her past. I thought it unusual, as she tended to keep most things to herself."

"How long ago was that, Mrs. Essex?" Roy asked.

"Oh, just about a month before she went missing. 1939, I believe it was. Well, she started telling me about Hope's father. She'd told her employer, Mr. Martin, that her husband had died—it wasn't true. She'd never been married." She paused and took a sip of her tea and bit on a chocolate chip cookie.

The eyes of both men were riveted on the woman. Roy put his hand in his breast pocket and pulled out a small pad and pen. "Did she mention his name or where he lived?"

"Only that his name suited his character. And he lived in Toronto somewhere. And here's the sad part, he'd forced himself on her! That's how she got in the family way. He'd been one of her part-time employers." The elderly lady leaned back in her chair, looked at her hands folded on the table and sighed.

The detective made notes.

"Does your son live with you, Mrs. Essex? Sorry, I've forgotten his name," Doug asked.

"His name is Richard. His marriage broke up a while back, so he's temporarily living here, that is, he will be after he's discharged from the hospital."

Roy stopped writing and looked at Mrs. Essex. She was leaning back in her chair, and the tenseness had disappeared from her shoulders. "Do you think she ever told her daughter any of this? I mean, the daughter must have asked questions about her father."

"Hope did ask, but Mary told her he'd died a long time ago. When Hope pressed her for more information, she said her father was not a good person and she didn't want to talk about him. That's what Mary told me," Mrs. Essex answered.

"Could I have a glass of water, please, Mrs. Essex?" Doug asked.

"'Course. Would you like some bottled water instead? I have some in the fridge."

"Sure."

Mrs. Essex put both hands on the table, pushed herself up, and moved to the Frigidaire.

Doug nudged his son. When Roy looked at him, his dad smiled and held a thumb up.

Mrs. Essex returned with the water and handed the bottle and a glass to him.

"And Mary's parents, what did she tell you about them? Were they from Ireland, by any chance?" Roy asked when the lady was seated.

"I believe they were. Mary spoke with a slight Irish accent. The only thing she said is that they all drowned in a boating accident, her mother, father and brother. She refused to say anything more about it. 'Too painful,' Mary had said. And another thing—Mary's brother had been her twin. That's why I felt sorry for the kid when her mother went missing, no father around, no brother—an orphan," she said.

"A real nice kid, too," Doug chimed in.

"Would you know where the daughter is now, Mrs. Essex? And if you have any photographs of Mary and her daughter, could I borrow them?" Roy asked.

"I'm not sure about photos, but there might be something in the basement, and I may have an old address. We've lost touch over the years, but there may be something. Oh, there's one other thing I remember. Hope married and I attended the wedding. I believe I kept the wedding invitation and a few letters. I remember you were there too, Detective," she said looking at Doug.

"That's right. I received an invitation too. I believe I kept it," Doug Selby said.

Mrs. Essex turned to Roy, "I'll see what I have in the basement. It'll take me a few days, maybe even weeks. Lotta junk down there."

"I have some old pictures I want you to look at Mrs. Essex," Roy said, reaching down for his briefcase. The clasp gave a sharp click as he pressed it and withdrew the photos. "They're photos of some survivors from the *Titanic* and a short story attached to each of them. Please look at them closely and tell me if you see any resemblance to your friend."

"Whew! The *Titanic*?" Mrs. Essex's eyes widened.

"Read the article first, and then take a good look at the photographs." Something warm pressed against Roy's leg. He looked down at a sleek, grey cat who'd strolled into the room. Its white nose, white bib, and four white paws were clean as fresh fallen snow. An attractive feline. He leaned over and stroked its smooth coat. It began a soft purr. Very friendly, too. Roy loved cats and dogs.

The elderly lady rose and walked over to the kitchen counter where her eyeglasses lay. She picked them up returned to the table and lowered herself to a chair, adjusted her glasses and held out her hand. A small tremor became visible as she took the photocopies.

Both men leaned forward as Mrs. Essex studied the photo from *The New York Times*. The ticking clock over the stove seemed to grow louder.

Drawing the photo closer to her eyes she said, "I don't know…it's not very clear and of course it's in black and white."

"Take your time, Mrs. Essex."

"The shape of the face is similar, and the long hair. Mary had long hair when I first met her, but later she styled it short and it was auburn. Oh, I wish I could see this picture in colour." She continued. "Same wide set eyes, full lips, but I can't be sure. This girl is very young," she trailed off.

Roy felt sure his dad could see the disappointment on his face. He guessed Mrs. Essex could see it, too.

She placed *The New York Times* photo underneath the one from *The Globe* in Toronto. She squinted for a few seconds. "This resembles Mary, too. Again, the woman in these pictures is much younger than Mary was when I last saw her. When were these taken?"

"In 1912," he answered.

"Whew! Look at how long the dresses are. And the hats! Look at how large and ornate they are." She became silent for a few seconds as she read the story below the picture. "It says here her name is Mary Flynn, and she survived the *Titanic* disaster. You think this young woman could be Mary Ryan, Detective?"

"There's a possibility. Still a lot more investigation to do, though."

Mrs. Essex studied the photographs again. "Just a minute," she said, rising. She went into the living room and came back with a large magnifying glass. She placed it over the upper part of the picture. "The young woman has something around her neck, but I can't make it out—a necklace of some kind. But the bottom half is tucked in under the top of her dress."

"I'm going to have the photos enlarged, Mrs. Essex, and I'll return when I have them. I'd like you to take another look later," Roy said.

"That may help," Mary's friend answered.

A few seconds later Mrs. Essex brightened and said, "I just remembered something. One Sunday I brought a small Kodak camera with me to take pictures of the choir. And I got one of the girls to take a picture of Mary and me. I wouldn't have thrown it away. It has to be downstairs in the rubble somewhere. I'll start searching right away and call you when I find something."

The chairs scraped against the tiles as the men stood. "Thank you, Mrs. Essex, you've been very helpful," Roy said.

She gave the men a pleased smile and walked them to the front door.

"Call when you find that wedding invitation and any pictures. If you think of anything else, let me know," Roy said.

Mrs. Essex waved her hand in front of her face like a windshield wiper and nodded.

***

Roy felt a pain in his neck as he stabbed the key into the ignition. He wished to hell he could rub it, but the padded horse collar prevented it. "Got any Tylenol on you, Dad?"

"Think so. I usually carry some." Reaching into his coat pocket, he withdrew a vial and passed it to his son.

"We got a lot of new information from Mrs. Essex tonight. Too bad we didn't get it back in the day when the investigation began. I always told Burkowski someone from Mary Ryan's past was responsible for her disappearance," Doug said.

"Umm. We may never know, but sometimes a path in the forest leads to a destination we didn't expect. I think now that Mrs. Essex's memories of the past have surfaced, she's going to remember more. We'll speak to her again soon."

CHAPTER 23

Toronto, 1919

The first thing Mary had to do, now that Mr. Howard had died and her lodging was gone with him, was to look for a new home. She checked *The Toronto Daily Star* advertisements, found one in the High Park area and approached the address. The house stood tall on Indian Road, red brick, three storeys high, with a pointed roof which reached toward the sky like a church steeple.

Mary pressed the buzzer. A lady opened the door, brushing a bit of flour off a rosy cheek.

"I'm here about the advertisement in the newspaper for a room to rent. May I see it please?" she asked. Mary felt timid, as this would be the first place she had ever rented.

"It's on the third floor, dearie. Bathroom's down on the second. You'll be sharing it with two other tenants if you want it. I'm Mrs. Thorndike, the landlady."

They trudged up two steep flights of stairs that were covered with a tatty scarlet runner. Mary could see the hardwood underneath. When they reached the top, Mrs. Thorndike hung on the railing for a bit, puffing and catching her breath. After several seconds she removed a large ring from a belt around her waist. Several keys hung from the ring. She used one to unlock the first door, and Mary pushed it open. Her eyes roamed around the room. A slight odour of mould floated on the air. *Oh well, can't have everything.* "It will do nicely, Mrs. Thorndike. I'll take it." A more pleasant scent replaced the other as they left the room. Mouth-watering aromas of cinnamon, apples and bread floated up from the kitchen. Mrs. Thorndike apparently liked to bake.

Mary found another secretarial job working for a doctor on Queen Street near Triller Avenue. She could walk up to Roncesvalles and take a streetcar down to Queen, then walk the rest of the way.

The early morning sun cast a wedge of light on the wooden floor. Mary stretched and yawned as she lay on her bed. It was Saturday morning, just a few hours to work this morning, then she would be off until Monday. Her eyes roved around her room. Her brass bed faced the window wall.

She swung her legs off the bed and sauntered to the window. One of the branches of an ancient elm tree brushed against her screen. A mother robin had built a nest there, and she perched on the edge of it, a pinkish worm hanging from her beak. The baby robins chirped, demanding their breakfast. The scene touched Mary's heart. It reminded her of a time when her mother would put out bread crumbs for the birds. The image grew in her mind, and she felt a painful tightness in her throat. *Poor Mother, gone, gone. Will my heart ever stop aching for her?* Should she take the 'tonic' now to ease the pain?

One day a while back when Mary still worked for Mr. Howard, she sat at the kitchen table finishing her dinner of cabbage and sausages. Maude MacDonald, the Howard's cook, stood beside her peeling apples for the next pie. Flour smeared her apron and hands. A pumpkin pie had been placed in the oven already. The flavour seeped out and Mary began to salivate. She slumped in her chair, put her head down and started to massage the back of her neck.

"Feeling poorly, are you love?" Maude patted her hands on her apron and plunked herself down on a chair beside Mary.

"Aye, I haven't been sleeping well, and I have a throbbin' noggin," she said as she glanced up with droopy eyelids.

"Indeed, I know that one. Mr. MacDonald used to suffer something terrible with headaches after he had a pint or two. He went to see Dr. Longridge, and the doctor wrote him an order to take to the chemist. A few hours after taking it, he was right as rain. I'll give you the doctor's address. Tell him your problem and ask for an order for the 'tonic'.

"And he'll give it to me you think, that tonic?" Mary asked.

"Oh, yeah. He gives it to lotsa ailing ones, just like handing out sweets to the bairns. And if ye run out, Mr. MacDonald found out how to make his own tonic. You're a dear lass and I'll get you some if you need it."

"Ta, Mrs. MacDonald," she said and gave the cook a grateful smile.

***

Ever since then, Mary kept in touch with the MacDonalds and Dr. Longridge. Mostly she would take the tonic at night-time, but sometimes on her days off, too. It worked like a magic potion at bedtime, and she slept soundly. The nightmares only came once in a while now. Queer enough though, it smelled like her Da's Irish whiskey. Oh well, she wouldn't bother her head about it. It did its job. *Careful though*, she cautioned herself, *not today*. Mary stood in front of the wooden washstand, lifted the white floral pitcher and poured some water into the washbowl. She splashed water on her face and patted it dry. She brushed her teeth and dressed. The office would be busy this morning, and time would pass quickly.

Three hours later, Mary finished working at Dr. Tricklebank's office. She walked along Roncesvalles

Avenue on her way home, enjoying the early summer warmth on her face. The gentle sun produced a feeling of well-being in her. Buds were bursting on the trees, and freshness filled the air. The tulips lifted their bright faces of red, yellow and pink to drink in the golden nectar.

She would go home and change into something cooler. She still wore a winter coat. Confessions were being heard at St. Vincent de Paul Church this afternoon, and Mary thought of going. She wondered if drinking the 'tonic' was a sin. Oh well, she'd think of something to confess.

Mrs. Thorndike possessed a Singer sewing machine, and she told Mary she could use it once in a while. Last week she'd made a pale green dress. It was lighter than the one she had on, and she was anxious to wear it. As she changed, she munched on some bread and cheese saved in wax paper. She hurried up Fern Avenue to Roncesvalles Avenue to St. Vincent's.

After Confession, Mary strolled along Roncesvalles. She felt calm and peaceful, and the pain in her chest had lessened. Above the chatter of people on the street, she heard someone behind call her name. Surprised, she whirled around. Her dress swished around her legs and clung for a moment.

"Mary!" The voice was insistent.

She turned and scanned the throng walking behind her. Her eyes stopped on a man hurrying in her direction. As he got closer her vision settled on a pair of cornflower blue eyes—eyes she'd seen before that reminded her of her father's. An expectant light shone in them.

Mary had not forgotten Detective Sergeant Paul Kennedy and the giddy feeling she'd experienced when he'd visited the Henry residence several years ago. While the Henrys were in New York picking up their son Andrew, Mary and Anna, a theft had occurred at the Henrys' home.

Paul Kennedy waited for them in front of the house when they arrived. His image had appeared in her mind's eye a few times since then. Although her grief was overwhelming at the time, he was one of the few bright spots in her life.

In the beginning, she had hoped she would see him when she was out shopping or at the lending library or when she went to church, but she never did. Occasionally, she would read his name in the newspaper reporting a case he was investigating. She read the newspaper daily—a habit she'd inherited from her Ma and Da.

She stood still facing the detective, and a tiny shiver ran up her spine. With a wide smile on his face, Detective Kennedy rushed forward.

"Detective Kennedy, is it?" Mary's voice shook a bit, as that weird feeling she felt when she first met him swept through her again. Her face was hot, and she hoped she wasn't blushing.

The detective took a step closer. "You remembered me. I didn't think I would be so fortunate," he said. "Please call me Paul."

Trying to sound casual Mary said, "Been to church have you, Mr.Ken…I mean Paul?"

"No, I just stepped out for a moment to pick up a packet of tobacco for my pipe. There's a smoke shop a few blocks up the street. I was on my way there when I recognized you in the crowd. Have you been well? I know you're no longer at the Henrys' home. Where are you living now?"

"Not far from here, just a few blocks away. I have a cozy room, at Mrs. Thorndike's rooming house for working young ladies." *Is he asking just from his detective habit, or for something else?* she wondered.

"Let's not stand out here on the street, Mary. There's a small tea shop up the street. Would you accompany me there? We could have a hot cup of tea and a chat."

Mary's mouth turned up at the corners and she nodded. "If you have a mind to." *I don't need anything to make me warmer.*

She wondered if he was feeling any of the same excitement. She blinked and put a brake on her thoughts. *Jesus, Mary, and Joseph, what am I thinking? A romance is not in my plans just now, and that's a fact.*

The detective extended his crooked arm and led her to the tea shop. Inside, the waitresses were bustling about. Several of the people from the church had stopped in. The enticing aroma of fresh baked bread and scones moved toward them like a welcoming host. Somewhere in the back of the tea room, a radio was playing "A Pretty Girl is Like a Melody."

Paul shepherded Mary to the back of the room. "Let's sit here," he said pulling out a bentwood chair for her. As she was about to sit, she noticed his hands had left a damp impression on the back of the chair.

A waitress approached their table, pencil and pad in hand. "Tea and scones with strawberry jam and whipped cream, please Miss," Mary said and swiped her tongue across her lips. She glanced around, taking in her surroundings. The shop was spacious and airy with a white tin ceiling that was marked off in squares.

Paul's forehead crinkled, and he tilted his head slightly to one side. "I see you've cut your hair. It's very becoming." Mary's hair was in the latest fashion, with deep waves close to her head and bobbed at the back.

Mary reddened and lowered her head, hoping he wouldn't see the blush. "Ta," she murmured and quickly slanted the subject away from herself. "Your name was mentioned in *The Globe* as one of the policemen investigating the shooting by Mr. Henry at the King Edward Hotel," Mary said.

"Yes. It's big news, with Mr. Henry being a prominent person. A constable has been assigned to me and we're working together. Terrible tragedy though," the detective said.

"I cried when I heard the news," Mary's eyes began to water.

"From what I remember regarding the theft from his house, I thought Mr. and Mrs. Henry were fine people."

"It's hard for me to grasp that Mr. Henry would do such a cruel thing," Mary said.

"Hmmm. As you may know, their son, Andrew, is back from the war. I interviewed Andrew concerning the shooting. He's taking this family calamity very hard."

"I know. As soon as I read about it, I rang him up straight away. Andrew's been a very good friend to me ever since we met. I couldn't do much for him though. Right now he's beyond any comfort."

"Too bad about his leg," Detective Kennedy said.

Mary nodded. "His mother treated me like a daughter. And Mr. Henry paid my tuition for secretarial school and helped me find a position. I owe the family a great debt."

She paused and thought about the poor uneducated young women who were working in factories sewing and earning two dollars a week. Or else they were in service, some of them worked half to death. At least she had been spared that, thanks to the Henrys.

Her mind returned to their conversation. "The write-ups in the papers did not give many details." She leaned forward in her chair and asked, "Would you be getting into trouble if you told me something more? I was shocked and puzzled when I heard what Mr. Henry did."

Paul was silent for a moment. His face took on a sombre appearance. He picked up his teacup and took a sip and carefully placed it back on the saucer. He appeared to be contemplating how much to tell her. "The case is still under investigation, so I really can't say much more than the papers reported. It's a scandal for certain."

"*The Globe* didn't give any motive as to why Mr. Henry did it. Do you know why?" Mary asked.

A deep sigh escaped his lips. "Well, the newspapers will have the whole thing soon enough, so.... Mrs. Henry was having an affair with Mr. Adamson, who did accounting for one of the Henrys' friends."

Mary's jaw dropped and she spilt some tea in her saucer as she put her teacup down. "What?" Her voice had risen. The people at the next table turned around.

"I met Mr. Adamson once while I was shopping with Mrs. Henry. A gentleman, or so it seemed at the time. Though I did think they appeared keen on each another. But I put it out of my mind, not wanting to think ill of Mrs. Henry."

"First impressions are not always true, Mary. However, Mr. Henry suspected something was amiss when one day his wife didn't arrive home when she told him she would."

"Perhaps she was ill," Mary offered.

"No, that wasn't the case," the detective said. "Daisy, the maid, told Mr. Henry his wife mentioned going to Mrs. Phipps' home and she was fine when she left."

"Well, maybe she became ill later," Mary said in defence of Mrs. Henry.

Detective Kennedy raised one eyebrow. "Mr. Henry telephoned Lavinia Phipps, the friend his wife was supposed to be visiting, and Mrs. Phipps informed him that Mrs. Henry had left around three o'clock, stating she wasn't feeling well," the detective said.

"Well, maybe she really did feel ill and took a stroll in the fresh air thinking it might help."

Detective Kennedy didn't speak for a moment and just stared at Mary. "It must have been a long walk, because she didn't arrive home until just after six o'clock. Mr. Henry told us that when he asked his wife at dinner that evening how she was she feeling, she said 'Fine.' When he mentioned speaking to Lavinia Phipps, he said she appeared nervous."

"That must have surprised Mrs. Henry. I mean that her husband was checking up on her," Mary said.

"Perhaps. Mr. Henry reported that she'd brushed the incident off quickly and said, 'Just a spot of queasiness, Cyrus. Nothing to fuss about.' I don't think he believed her, because after that Mr. Henry engaged a private detective. The private investigator followed Mrs. Henry for several weeks with nothing unusual to report until that fatal day."

"It must have put Mrs. Henry on her toes, after she learned her husband was checking up on her. It's hard to believe Mrs. Henry being involved in something like this. Such a lady, but what did the detective say?" Mary asked.

"Well, on the day Cyrus Henry shot and killed Mr. Adamson and wounded Mrs. Henry, Mr. Henry's investigator had reported that Mrs. Henry and Mr. Adamson had checked into the King Edward Hotel around three-thirty."

Again, Mary looked stunned. "Good Lord, what could Mrs. Henry be thinking? Her husband must have felt humiliated." She pulled her chair closer to the table and leaned forward. "Can you tell me anything else the detective said?" Mary asked, looking directly at Detective Kennedy without blinking. She wondered if she were pushing it too far.

Paul lowered his eyes and took a sip of tea. "At the time we interviewed the private detective, he reported that Mr. Henry seemed calm in a cold sort of way. 'Thank you. I'll take care of it,' were the only words he uttered."

"Mr. Henry must have been seething inside," Mary said, shaking her head.

"Probably," Paul shrugged. "The investigator said he did notice Mr. Henry's jaw tightening and he looked pale."

"It's hard to believe Mrs. Henry could be involved in a deceit like this." Mary slumped back in her chair.

"I know you held the greatest respect for Mrs. Henry, but remember, Mary, idols have clay feet. She made a mistake, a fatal one, and she's paid dearly for it."

"But to shoot her and Mr. Adamson? I can barely believe it," Mary's voice cracked as she spoke.

The detective leaned back in his chair, took out his pipe, and struck a wooden match on the side of a tiny matchbox. "Mr. Henry arrived at the hotel in a taxi, entered the hotel, and took a seat in the lobby.

"A newspaper was lying on a small table beside a wingback chair. Mr. Henry picked it up, and opened it. One of the desk clerks told us he noticed Mr. Henry peering over the top of the newspaper. His eyes were riveted on the elevator doors. When he saw his wife and Mr. Adamson emerge from the elevator laughing, arm in arm, I suppose he took leave of his senses."

"I can imagine the shock Mrs. Henry must have felt when she saw her husband. She must have been frightened out of her wits," Mary said.

"Indeed. The witnesses in the lobby said Mr. Henry seemed composed as he approached the couple. They further reported that Mrs. Henry took a step backward and covered her mouth. Mr. Henry reached into his overcoat pocket and took out a small revolver. Two loud cracks, which sounded like firecrackers going off, pierced the air, so some of the guest told us."

"They must have feared for their lives," Mary said.

"Indeed. It became chaotic after the shots. Women screamed. In the guests' haste to take cover, vases of flowers, tables and chairs were knocked over. Some guests crouched behind the furniture. One of the men pushed a woman to the floor."

"And the desk clerk who recounted the scene, what was he doing?" Mary asked.

"He crouched behind the counter and peered over it, watching the whole frightening scene. He said poor Mr. Adamson lay on the floor on his back, bleeding from a hole in the middle of his forehead."

"And Mrs. Henry?"

"She collapsed in a heap beside him. The desk clerk could see blood staining the shoulder of her powder-blue jacket. He could see a red puddle growing beside her as she lay on the floor."

Mary's hand closed into a fist and covered her mouth. And her eyes filled with shock and fear for Mrs. Henry. In a tight voice, she managed to squeak out, "Oh, no."

"It's alright, Mary. She lost a lot of blood, but she's going to be alright, at least physically."

Mary leaned back in her chair, retrieved a small handkerchief from her pocket and blew her nose. "I know, but it's just the image of her lying there bleeding and in pain that bothers me."

Paul touched her arm. "The desk clerk told us he crouched all the way down to the floor and managed to pull a telephone off the desk and call us."

"Did Mr. Henry leave then?"

"No. When we arrived, Mr. Henry was seated in the lobby, looking frozen in the moment. A Smith and Wesson 38 revolver was lying on the floor beside him, and the pungent odour of cordite still hung heavy in the air when we arrived." Paul leaned back and took a pull on his pipe. "Now you know almost as much as I do," he said with a mirthless smile.

Mary lowered her head, nibbled on her scone, and became pensive. Hearing it out loud made it all the more real. She felt a vacant spot in her chest and a deep sadness. There would be a publicized court case and Mrs. Henry would most likely be dragged through the mud, her reputation in tatters.

She felt anger toward Mr. Henry. *He had choices. For one, they could have agreed to live separately.* Her mind drifted back to her survival from the *Titanic*, and she contemplated how precious life is. *Mr. Adamson didn't have to die, and Mrs. Henry being wounded and all.*

Mary was startled out of her reverie. "A penny for your thoughts, Mary," Paul said.

She told him, and finished with, "He didn't have to shoot them."

"Mary, perhaps you don't understand a man's pride. Mr. Henry felt wronged and humiliated by his wife's illicit affair and betrayed by Mr. Adamson. In his mind, he felt justified in his actions. He stated to the press, 'They got what they deserved.' I believe a separation and even a divorce would not have given him the closure he could live with. And it doesn't appear taking her back was an option in his mind. I don't believe his pride would have tolerated it," Detective Kennedy said.

"Nor would she want it." Mary's voice rose and tightened. Her lips and eyes narrowed. "Are you defending his action, Detective Kennedy? I certainly hope not all men would be so puffed up with pride that they would go along with Mr. Henry's solution."

Paul's chair scraped the floor as he shifted and pulled it closer to the table. He placed his hand near Mary's. "No, no I'm not defending him. I'm just explaining what I think was in his mind. I'm sorry if I offended you. That was not my intention." His voice became soft and his face took on a sincere expression.

Mary looked askance at his explanation.

"In my experience of a crime like this, by men of Mr. Henry's stature, I have learned something of their reactions to things of this nature, that's all. Please forgive me," he said.

Not totally convinced of Detective Kennedy's explanation, Mary picked up her gloves and prepared to leave. *If I stay any longer, I may say something I will regret. I do like him.*

She looked at her small Bulova wristwatch and turned in her chair. "I have to leave now. I promised to meet one of the choir members this afternoon. We've planned on taking a stroll down the street."

"Could we meet another time?" he said rising. "There's a very good vaudeville act at the Brighton Theatre, I'm told, and it's close by."

"Yes, another time. But today I want to see what's happening down Roncesvalles Avenue. My friend tells me they're building an enormous entertainment park near the lake. It's to be called Sunnyside, just like the train station at the corner of Roncesvalles and Queen Street. There's to be a bathing pavilion and a beach where people can swim in the lake. There're going to build a wooden staircase leading down to the park. It sounds exciting." Mary headed for the door. "Thank you for the tea," she said over her shoulder.

Paul called out to her. "I'll get in touch with you at work. Where did you say you worked?"

"I didn't. But it's Dr. Tricklebank's office. You may call me if you have a mind to, but not for a while. Good day, Detective."

CHAPTER 24

Burlington, November 2000

Roy and Doug Selby arrived back at their home on Locust Street after their visit to Mrs. Essex. Roy hung his shearling jacket in the hall closet. The rich aroma of roast beef and sweet onions greeted him. "How'd you do it, Dad? It smells delicious. My favourite," he said as he walked into the kitchen.

"Slow cooker."

After Roy's mother died a few years ago, his dad had learned to cook. Doug watched all the cooking shows on TV and made some of the dishes. Nothing complicated at first, just cheese omelettes with diced tomatoes and roasted squash with brown sugar.

Steam floated out of the pot and clouded his glasses as he lifted the lid of the cooker. "Not bad for an old bachelor, eh?"

Both men had lost their wives to cancer several years back. After Roy's wife died, he and his daughter Laura had moved into his dad's home.

"Did you pick up the photos of the contents of the evidence box yet?" his father asked.

"Not yet. I'll get them in the morning. I went straight down to the Toronto Reference Library, and you know what happened on the way home."

"You're getting close, son. Remember I told you earlier there might be a connection? But then I changed my mind. The skeleton could have come from anywhere. Now I'm back to square one. Look, how many people have gone missing in Burlington over the years?" He answered his own question. "Not many. Most of them have been found living someplace else. Some women fled from abusive relationships—moved away from the area. And how many have been called Mary?"

Roy rubbed his chin. "Just one that I can think of. We still need a lot more info from the forensic anthropologist and the Forensics Centre in Toronto."

A hissing sound came from the stove. The slow cooker had been turned on high when they arrived home, and now it bubbled out. Doug kicked back his chair and hurried over to the stove.

Roy busied himself setting the table. "After I speak to Dr. Pallotta—"

His father interjected, "Who?"

"The forensic anthropologist, Dad."

"Oh, yeah."

"After I see what she has to say, I want you to look for your old notebooks. There might be pieces of information there that'll fit into this puzzle."

As Doug spooned their dinner onto plates, he said, "It won't be easy. I'll have a lot to plough through. I hope the dust doesn't choke me."

As they sat down to eat their dinner, Doug said, "Some of the boxes haven't been opened in decades. I'll see if I can find anything related to the Mary Ryan case. Mrs. Essex reminded me about Mary Ryan's daughter's wedding. I think the invitation is down there with the 'memorabilia,'" he said as he cut a slice of beef.

"It'll probably take you weeks, Dad. In the meantime, I'll have to go back to Dr. Pallotta's lab."

"Umm. There is one thing I remember about Mary Ryan's daughter Hope. A few years after you were born, she left Burlington for Toronto. Said she wanted to be an actress."

"How old was she then?" Roy asked.

"Around 18 or 19. We kept in contact for a while, but gradually the letters and phone calls trickled off. Until one day a wedding invitation came in the mail. It was addressed to Burkowski—God rest his soul—and me. Poor Burkowski's weight had skyrocketed. The tobacco, hamburgers, chips and Coke finally got to him. A massive heart attack took him while he was sitting right at his desk. Or did I tell you that already?" his dad chuckled.

**

The next day Selby called Dr. Maybrick. "Phil, I'd like to meet with you and Dr. Pallotta today at the morgue. When can I see both of you?"

"I'll call back and let you know after I speak to Dr. Pallotta," Dr. Maybrick said.

At three o'clock two people in white coats stood at the morgue's reception desk. Selby strode toward them. Everyone smiled.

"Follow me, Detective. I have a further report for you," Dr. Pallotta said.

Selby followed her back to the examining-room.

She walked over to the assembled skeleton which had been found in LaSalle Park. Picking up a pencil, Dr. Pallotta pointed to the head. "Skulls from different races have particular differences. I have some photos I want you to look at." She turned toward a small side table at the end of the examining bed. "These are photos of three distinct types—Caucasian, Negroid and Mongoloid. If you compare the first one, the Caucasian, you can see the bone structure of the face is narrower than the other two. Also, the Caucasian has high bridged nasal bones just like our lady."

Selby murmured, "Another piece of puzzle—she was Caucasian."

The anthropologist pointed her pencil to the lower section of the skeleton, the pelvis and the subpubic area.

The two men drew closer. "As I told you before, our victim was female. Look at the subpubic area," she said pointing down. "When a woman delivers a child, the bones in this area widen. I can tell you this woman had delivered a child. When more than one child has been delivered, a small notch appears on the pelvic bone."

Selby kept his eyes on the area. "Is there a notch? I can't see one," he asked.

"No, there isn't. So our victim had delivered a child, but only one."

Did Dad ever mention more than one child in the Mary Ryan case? He didn't think so. *Looks like another piece of the puzzle,* he thought. "Have you been able to estimate her height, Dr. Pallotta?"

"Please call me Lisa, Detective Selby," she said, smiling.

Did he imagine some personal interest in her tone?

"I measured the femur," she said pointing to the thigh bone. "I calculated that she was five feet and three inches give or take a fraction of an inch. Age—somewhere in her early forties."

"Very good, doctor...Lisa," he said stepping away from the table. "You've given me another piece of the puzzle. Thank you."

It was the first time Selby had been present at an anthropologic examination. Dr. Pallotta impressed him with her knowledge. The remains he'd seen examined in the past all had some soft tissue remaining which gave off clues. Most of the time they knew the identity of the victim, or found out soon after the discovery of the body.

Dr. Pallotta put her pencil down and walked to the other side of the table. "I still have more work to do, but the people over at the Forensics Centre have something for you. I think it's about the hair that was found at the burial site. Excuse me gentlemen, but I have to get back to work now."

She walked Selby and Dr. Maybrick toward the entrance and added, "I thought it would be a good idea if I asked the forensic artist to make a cast of the skull and do a facial reconstruction."

"I have some photographs for you, Lisa, of a woman that went missing in Burlington several decades ago. They may be useful in the facial reconstruction," Selby said.

Lisa Pallotta's eyebrows arched. "Really? Bring them in as soon as you can. That'll help."

***

Outside, Dr. Maybrick and Selby walked toward the parking lot. "Is Dr. Pallotta new in the Hamilton area, Phil? I haven't heard her name before."

Dr. Maybrick took a few extra steps to keep up with Selby. "She is. I heard she left St. Mary's University in Halifax, where she was a professor, and came here. She wanted to work in the field."

"Is she living in the Hamilton area now?"

Maybrick turned sideways to look at Selby and smiled. "Why the interest, Roy? Caught your eye, did she?"

"Well, she is very attractive and knows her stuff. I just wondered."

"Uh-huh. If you want her number, the morgue has it," he said as he approached his blue Mazda.

Selby walked toward his car and then came to a sudden stop. He remembered what Dr. Pallotta said about Forensics having something to report on the skeleton's hair. He'd drive to the Toronto Centre for Forensic Science now. He retrieved his map book from the glove compartment. The Centre was on Morton Shulman Drive.

Selby showed his credentials to the information attendant and was directed to the lab. He saw several people working, dressed in lab coats, gloves, some with masks, and some with goggles. An array of high-tech microscopes stood on the tables. He approached the first tech he saw, a latte-skinned young woman. "Detective Sergeant Roy Selby," he said, showing his badge.

"Kitty Malone," she replied, holding out her hand.

"Dr. Pallotta, the Forensic Anthropologist in Hamilton, said you have something for me from the skeleton we unearthed at LaSalle Park."

She lowered her mask and revealed teeth as white as Chiclets. "Follow me."

They walked to the other side of the lab where a tech was preparing a tray with eight or ten troughs in it, getting gelatine ready for a DNA test. "We thought it might help if we got some DNA from the hair found in the grave. No roots left, degraded a long time ago, but we're going to try to get mitochondrial DNA from outside the nucleus. Do you have anything to compare it with?"

"Not yet. But it may be possible to get something later. When you finish your tests, call me, will you?" he said and handed her his card.

"Oh, there is one more thing," Kitty said. "We found a few short, dark hairs on the clothing you sent us, along with the red ones. We'll test them also."

He was quiet for a moment. *This could be my lucky day.*

***

As Selby drove home, he sifted through the facts. The remains are that of a woman about five feet three inches tall, red hair, Caucasian, and she'd delivered one child. Age, early forties, and Dr. Pallotta believes she's been buried a long time.

The beeping of his cell phone broke into his thoughts. He pulled off the road and answered the call.

"Roy, is that you?"

"Yes, Dad, it's me, your son Roy," he smiled.

"My hearing's not too good these days, son. Guess I'm going to have to get a hearing aid. Been putting it off, it's so damn expensive."

Roy could hear irritation in his dad's voice. *Just doesn't want to admit he's getting old,* Roy thought.

Doug's voice became animated as he began to speak. "Thought you'd like to know I've got some good news and some bad news."

"Give me the good news first."

"I've been rooting about in the cellar and I found a copy of the flyer I made of Mary Ryan at the time of her disappearance. I used a photograph her daughter gave me when we started the investigation."

"Great," Roy said.

"I'm still looking for the wedding invitation. Now here's the bad news." His dad's voice lowered. "We've had some water leakage in the basement. The flyer's partially damaged by the water."

Roy was disappointed. "Mmm. I just thought of something. When Mary Ryan went missing, did a photo of her appear in the local newspaper?"

His dad brightened. "I believe it did. Not right away, but a while later. The Burlington Central Library has all the old *Burlington Gazette* newspapers on film."

"OK. I'll drop by the library on the way home. Meanwhile, put the flyer in a file folder. If I can't get a photo from the library, we'll have to use the one you found. I'll give it to Dr. Pallotta and the forensic artist."

CHAPTER 25

Toronto, May 1922

Sunday was Mary's day off. *Should I have a drink before church? A small jigger, that's all it'll be,* she rationalized. She reached into the battered night-table beside her bed and withdrew the medicine bottle. A small glass rested on the table which she filled half way. Two swallows, and she emptied the glass. It burned her throat going down and the heat seemed to continue, as it travelled all the way to her toes. Warmth filled her body and the small nagging anxiety, which always seemed to be there, dissolved.

There, that's better. Mary replaced the cap and put the bottle back in the drawer. She filled the glass with water and took a long swallow. She smiled. She wouldn't want Father Brennan to smell alcohol on her breath when she went to Communion. Although, it was gossiped in the parish that Father Brennan himself sometimes got carried away with the sacramental wine after Communion and at Baptismal celebrations.

It'd been several weeks since she last saw Detective Kennedy. He'd tracked her down at Dr. Tricklebank's office and asked her out. *Him being a detective and all, it would have been easy,* she guessed.

Massey Hall was their first outing together to hear the new Toronto Symphony. Paul said the director, Luigi von Kunits, was one of the best.

Afterwards, as they walked out onto Victoria Street, Paul offered his arm and asked, "Did you enjoy the concert, Mary?"

"Oh, thank you so much, Paul. The music is still ringing in my ears, and," she opened the program she grasped in her gloved hand, "Mr. DeBussy's "Clair de Lune" sounded so sweet, it made me weep. This has been the grandest night of my life," she said with a shy smile.

He gave her hand a pat, and smiled back. "Have you ever roller skated, Mary?"

"No, but I've seen it, kids rolling down the sidewalk. It looks like fun, but I never tried it. Too afraid of falling and looking ridiculous."

"Don't worry, I'll hold you up. The *Trillium Ferry* boat takes people over to the Toronto Island to an outdoor rink, and they rent skates. I'd like to take you next week."

"Oh, a shame it is, I can't go next week," she said frowning. "I'm moving to a larger room on the first floor of my rooming house, and I'm taking in typing to do in my spare time. My father told me to save my money if I wanted to get ahead."

"My, my, Mary, you certainly are industrious. Well, another time."

Mary noticed Paul was taking a longer route to her house and driving slowly.

Without warning, Mary grabbed his coat sleeve. "Paul, stop the car! I think I just saw my friend, Anna from the *Titanic*." Mary looked back at the woman wearing high-heeled laced boots, which came up to her knee. Her skirt rose several inches above the top of the boots. She leaned against a lamp-post and the light illuminated her brassy blonde hair.

As Paul backed the car up, he said, "Didn't you tell me she had stolen some money from you when you were living at the Henrys' home?"

"I did, and I haven't seen her since."

Mary craned her neck. Paul had stopped the car under a lamp-post, and Mary could see Anna clearly as she approached, with a smile on her bright red lips. Anna bent down and leaned inside the car. Her expression froze. She recoiled. "Mary! Sorry, sorry." She straightened, turned on her heel and ran down the street, ducked into a doorway, and began pounding on a door.

"Want me to go after her?" Paul asked.

"No, poor soul. It appears she needs the money more than I do."

***

Two weeks later Paul called at Mary's duplex. It was Saturday afternoon and she was home doing some dicta-typing. Papers were scattered on the floor, and an empty cereal bowl and a glass of water stood on the desk beside her. The doorbell startled her. She peered through the lace curtain covering the oval glass on the front door. Mary's heart fluttered as she recognized Paul Kennedy. She jerked the door open.

"Are you ready to go roller-skating on Toronto Island?" he said with a wide grin.

"If you'll hold me up," she laughed. "Wait here until I put on a shorter skirt. Wouldn't want my dress getting caught in the skates. I'm handicapped enough. I'll be back out in a minute." She closed the door and her heels clicked a staccato beat down the hallway to her room.

Mary returned and jumped into Paul's auto as he held the door open for her. They headed to the Toronto docks.

They sat outside, on the upper deck of the Trillium Island ferry. The island was only about a mile from the Front Street dock. Mary breathed in the invigorating air as they chugged across Lake Ontario. She snuggled into her sweater coat, and was knotting the belt when Paul reached for her hand. Their hands collided, just as she pulled the band tight and let go. Mary giggled, and said, "Wait a moment sir!"

He reddened, and gave a self-conscious laugh.

"Sorry," he said, as he gently placed his hand on top of hers.

His hand felt steady and strong and she felt safe and protected with him. She shifted in her seat and faced him. "Look Paul, I brought some lunch for us. Ham sandwiches, and pickles, and a few hot biscuits with jam. I baked the biscuits myself," she said with pride, glancing down at the wicker basket. "There's a thermos of hot tea, too."

"You think of everything, don't you? When did you get all this ready?"

She hesitated, and looked out at the Centre Island dock they were approaching. A tinge of pink coloured her cheeks. "Last night I was in a baking mood, and Mrs. Thorndike has provided a mutual kitchen for the roomers. I had the use of it for an hour or two last night."

In fact, Mary had been planning the picnic for days. She hoped she sounded convincing. She knew she was a terrible liar. When she was a child, she occasionally tried to lie to her parents. She stuttered, looked down, her eyes shifting back and forth, and they knew.

"Well, it sounds delicious. Thank you, but really you didn't have to. We can buy some refreshments on the island. And I forgot to mention that they rent canoes and rowboats. Perhaps later we can take one out."

Mary remembered another time on another boat, and her voice quivered. "I think this ferry boat ride is enough for one day. At least I can see the shoreline. I don't care much for boats. I think you can understand."

Paul pressed her hand a little more tightly. "Please forgive me. I wasn't thinking."

***

The *Trillium* arrived at the dock. It was a brilliant fall day and the sunlight glittered on the water. The *Trillium* had been filled near capacity, and everyone appeared happy and excited, as they disembarked. Paul brought an auto rug, and had it folded over his arm. He steered Mary in the direction of the roller-rink. After a short walk Paul said, "Here it is. What do you think?"

The rink was an enormous, white gazebo with an unobstructed view of Toronto. Mary pulled on her skates and wobbled onto the rink. Music was playing. Mary recognized "St. Louis Blues". Paul placed Mary's arm across her waist in front of her, and took her hand. He put his other arm behind her waist, and put his hand on her left side. As they skimmed around the perimeter of the rink, Paul took his hand off Mary's side, and pointed toward the city.

"In 1904, a great fire raged in this part of the city," he said waving his hand across the view in front of them. It reduced several acres to rubble and caused some damage to Union Station."

Mary felt a pang of pain as she looked at the station and remembered how she felt when she arrived there with the Henrys. Desolate.

After half an hour of skating, Mary slowed down. "I think I'd better be having a rest now." Her calves and ankles had started to ache, but she felt more confident on her skates now. She broke away from Paul and skated toward a bench. Her movements were choppy and staggered as she turned and lowered herself to the seat.

Paul glided toward her. He picked up the blanket he had brought. "I have a suggestion, Mary. If you could bring yourself to get into a rowboat, there is a small island in the centre of the river that's quiet and private. The water is shallow, and you can see the bottom quite clearly. We could eat our lunch there."

Mary nodded. "I'm ready for lunch, but I'm still not sure about the boat. I'll have to see it first." They took off their skates and returned them to the rental booth. Strolling beside the river, Mary looked toward the water. She could see a cluster of small crafts in the centre, some white rowboats and red canoes. Dirty seagulls screeched and circled overhead. Someone had thrown a piece of bread into the water. Their hungry mouths opened wide in anticipation, as they dived toward an enticing meal.

Men in rowboats dipped their oars into the water and pulled on them as the women reclined in the back of the crafts. Large floppy hats shielding their eyes from the glare of the afternoon sun. Mary edged tentatively to the shoreline. She could see the sandy bottom of the river and it reassured her... a little.

"Will it be alright?" Paul asked, placing a hand on her arm.

"Will there be life jackets in the boat?"

"If there isn't one, I'll get one for you," he said drawing her closer to the rowboat.

Mary gave a slow nod.

Paul paid the attendant for the boat and approached Mary with a wide grin. He carried a bulky-looking life jacket and his car blanket. He knelt and held the boat close to the dock. She placed the lunch basket in the bottom of the craft and stepped in. It rocked gently and she crouched down and grabbed the sides. "It's a soggy lunch we'll be having if I tip this boat."

She looked back at him with a nervous grin and adjusted the lunch basket, which had tilted on its side.

After a leisurely row around the petite island in the centre of the river, Paul steered the boat toward its bank. "Let's stop and have our lunch here." He pulled the boat all the way out of the water and left it behind a bush. There were shrubs and immature trees running all along the perimeter of the island. He led Mary toward the centre, where the greenery was denser. Mary couldn't see the river from where she stood. But, she could hear light laughter coming from someone in a boat, and soft splashes as paddles and oars dipped and lifted in the green water. Paul spread the blanket on the ground in a tiny clearing. Mary unpacked the lunch basket.

When they had finished eating, she leaned over to brush a crumb from the side of his mouth. He caught her hand and kissed her palm.

Paul lifted his head, and she could feel his breath on her face, and a pleasant scent of pipe tobacco, just before he kissed her. She was stunned for an instant, and then savoured the warmth of his lips. With his mouth still on hers, Paul placed his hand on Mary's back, leaned forward, and slowly lowered her down to the plaid blanket. He stretched out beside her, pressing his body close to hers. Mary's eyes were closed and her lips partly open. It was her first kiss. She felt a feathery touch tracing a path down her side and moving forward. Her whole body tingled. She felt like she was floating on air.

The next moment she plummeted to earth and sat erect, as if coming out of a dream. "Paul, we can't do this! I'm afraid. I've never done anything like this before. And besides, we're out in public. People will see us and report us. And we might be arrested! And you a policeman." There was panic in her voice.

He touched the side of her face. "Forgive me Mary. I've wanted to kiss and hold you for what seems like forever. Today, with the sunlight on your hair, you seemed to be glowing. Being really close to you for the first time, I couldn't resist any longer." His voice was very quiet. "We'll leave now, if you like. Don't be angry with me," he said.

"No, no, I won't. It's all too much for me just now, it is." The sun disappeared behind an ominous-looking dark cloud as Paul rowed back to the boathouse. They were both silent. Mary's face was drawn tight, and she looked straight ahead. His face was closed and distant.

The wind came up and Mary gave a small shiver as they waited on the dock for the ferry. "Here, take my jacket dear. It'll take the chill off." Paul leaned forward and placed it around Mary's shaking shoulders. She smiled up at him, relieved the awkward silence had been broken.

Paul spread the auto blanket across both their legs as they sat on the inside deck of the *Trillium*. He surreptitiously put an arm around the back of the bench where Mary sat. "I hope I didn't upset you too much when we were on the island? I'd hate myself if I did anything to interfere with our friendship." She thought he looked nervous as he spoke and she began to pity him. She put her hand on top of his and gave it a little squeeze.

CHAPTER 26

One week later, Mary curled up in the corner of her settee holding a new mystery novel, *The Mysterious Affair at Styles*, by Agatha Christie. She was devouring the book when the doorbell jolted her concentration. *It must be Paul.* He mentioned last week that he would be coming today to take her to the new amusement park, Sunnyside. But he was early. Mary did not expect him for another hour. In any case, she felt delighted that he was here. Her feelings for him grew stronger each week.

She put a marker in her book, placed it on the side table and sprang off the settee. A smile curled on her lips, she glanced through the curtain on the front door. Her demeanour changed in a flash. It wasn't Paul. It was *him*, one of her typing clients, clutching a brown paper package tied with string.

The caller removed his black bowler. "I was in the area and thought I would drop this typing off for you. Being the weekend, I thought you could work on it and have it ready on Monday. May I come in? I have some things that need explaining," he said, as he took a step forward.

"Mrs. Thorndike, my landlady, is very strict about her lady tenants having visitors. She lives right next door," she said glancing to the far side of the duplex. She hoped he would get her drift. The money she earned working for Dr. Tricklebank wasn't enough for what she wanted to do. Mary wanted a better place to live, and the rent would be higher than what she was paying Mrs. Thorndike, so she decided to take in typing assignments on the weekend. Mr. Henry had referred this client to her.

When Mary went to pick up her first assignment from this man, she remembered him from the lifeboat. He had supported the dowager's command not to go back for survivors. She also recalled Mr. Henry Senior speaking to him when they were off the ship and on the dock in New York. As he was a friend of the Henrys, she supposed it would be alright for a few minutes, even though she didn't like him. She needed the money. She'd get rid of him as quickly as possible.

"Just for a few minutes, then," Mary said.

The visitor pushed the door open wide and sprang in. She led him the few steps down the hallway to her room. Looking behind her once, she saw only his back as he looked behind him. She felt a cold finger on her spine. Her door was ajar. He slid by her soundlessly and shoved the door shut.

"Open the door," Mary shouted.

"I'll only be here for a few minutes and then I'll be gone," he said in a cajoling voice. A small table stood on the other side of the room. He strode over to it and placed the package on it and stood aside. "Come and look at it, and I'll explain what I want."

Mary's apprehension was growing by the second. His refusal to open the door put her teeth on edge. *He's in now, so just get rid of him as soon as possible.* She walked over to the table and began to untie the package. He stood behind her. Her fingers trembled and were white as she wrestled with the tightly tied package. The small hairs on the back of her neck had begun to rise like antennae. The next second a cold hand clamped down on her mouth. One of her arms was being twisted behind her back. Her wrist burned in his grasp as she was being steered toward her bed. "Don't cry out," he hissed, "or it will be the last sound you ever make."

In spite of his threat, she spit out a strangled, "No!" His fist crashed into her face. All went black and she felt like she was spinning into an abyss. When she regained consciousness, her dress was under her chin. Her body ached in every corner, especially where he violated her. Humiliation scorched her body. She forced herself to look in his direction. He stood at the table straightening his clothes and picking up the package he had used to gain entrance and her trust.

Mary's shoulders slumped and her head hung down. Long red hair covered her face and she did not brush it away. She welcomed the shield. Sitting on the edge of the bed, she tried to put her clothes in place. Her underwear lay in tatters on the floor beside the bed. All Mary could think about at this moment was a very hot bath. She could feel her eye puffing up like a balloon. Her vision was blurred as she looked up and saw the rapist hurrying toward the door. He paused and snarled over his shoulder.

"If you speak of this ever, the words will be your last."

***

The steam from the hot water in the bathtub rose up and clouded the mirror on the medicine cabinet. Mary was glad of it. She didn't want to see her face. She tested the water with her toe—too hot, but she got in anyway and settled down up to her chin. A facecloth and soap rested on the back of the tub. She grabbed both of them and began scrubbing her body with such intensity that her skin, which was already pink from the hot water, became pinker. At this moment she loathed her body. The next moment a horrible thought struck her—what if she were pregnant?

Some water splashed over the side of the tub as she sank deeper into it. After soaking for a few moments longer, she rose from the tub and stepped out onto a cold floor. Shivering, she put on a bathrobe and skittered to her room.

Dressed in fresh clothes, Mary went to a small cupboard in the corner and pulled out a bottle of alcohol marked 'tonic'. Her hand trembled as she splashed whiskey into a glass and drank all of it in one swallow. She poured another. Slowly, numbness seeped into her body and mind. She held a cold wet cloth to her left eye and picked up the bottle to pour another drink when the doorbell rang. She knew it must be Paul this time and wondered if the heat of shame would show on her face. Her mind raced. *Oh, sweet Jesus, what can I say?* She'd get rid of him as fast as she could. Mary opened front door a crack and stood behind it.

"Mary, it's me, Paul. I've come to take you to Sunnyside." He blinked when he saw the white cloth she was holding to her eye. "Good Lord, what's happened to your eye?"

The disgrace she felt kept her from telling the truth. "I stumbled on the back porch, fell and hit my eye. I can't… go out today Paul. I'm a bit shaken, and I want to rest." She hoped her voice sounded convincing.

"No! Let me help you. Let me see your eye," he said as he peeked through the crack.

"It's alright, Paul. I'll see you next week when I feel better. Stand back." And with that she put her full weight against the door and closed it. Quivering like a wounded bird, she returned to her room and emptied the small bottle of alcohol.

***

A week later, the purple discolouration and swelling of Mary's left eye grew faint but did not disappear. Now it was yellowish. The day after the assault she'd tried applying the small black leech she purchased from the pharmacy. It was said the leech would draw out the blood under the skin, but for all her loathing, putting the ugly thing to her face, it did little good.

Mary seldom wore makeup, but she purchased a small box of Woodbury's face powder. She dabbed a pinprick of cold-cream under her eye first, and then patted on the powder.

Mary telephoned her employer, Dr. Tricklebank, on the Monday after the attack and said she wouldn't be in for the week. The excuse she used was that she had been clumsy, fell and hit her face, and needed to rest. Now, a week later, she appeared at Dr. Tricklebank's office.

When the doctor greeted her, his eyebrows arched, but the only thing he said was, "Happy to have you back, Mary. Hope you're feeling better."

As each patient approached her desk, she wondered if they could see the yellow dappling under the makeup. Shame stunted her self-confidence, and she lowered her head when she spoke to the patients. She needed to confide in someone, *but who? No one, except…perhaps Madeleine Henry.*

CHAPTER 27

Toronto, 1922

Lise Marois, Madeleine Henry's mother, sat on an ornate cream settee sipping tea in her home on Kingsmill Park in the Kingsway. Her daughter sat opposite. Mme. Marois, a widow, sat straight as a ruler in her chair. Her silver hair was meticulously coiffed in deep waves close to her head in the latest style.

"Are you feeling better today, dear? I know your shoulder has healed well. The doctor told me the bullet just nicked your collar bone. He said you were fortunate it wasn't broken. I know you have a great deal to think about, but I was wondering if you had made any plans for your future."

Madeleine put her teacup back in its saucer and nibbled on a small cookie with white icing and a cherry on top. "I feel much better when I'm here with you, *Maman*, but my mind is still numb with grief. I cared a great deal for Jeffery. It's hard for me to believe he's really gone."

"It will take time to lessen the pain of your loss. And after that, he will come into your mind at odd times, and you will think for an instant that he is still alive."

"I know. That happens now." Madeleine squeezed her eyes shut at the memory.

Mme. Marois leaned back in her chair and sighed. "With the law being what it is today—and given who he is, your husband will probably be let off. He's out on bail right now, isn't he?"

Madeleine nodded. "I received papers yesterday. He's filing for divorce on the grounds of adultery. I won't give him any trouble on that point, and besides he has proof.

The hotel register had Jeffery's name on it with "guest" beside it. I expect it will be granted quickly. Just as well. We should have divorced long ago."

"Je suis tres désolé, Cherie." Her mother leaned forward and put her hand on her daughter's.

"I feel so guilty. If it weren't for me, Jeffery would still be alive. I know it wasn't right that we were together, but I was just so lonely, and Jeffery appeared attracted to me. I was flattered, and attracted to him. We did resist each other for a while, but then we just let go and let our feelings take over."

Mme. Marois' face showed compassion as she nodded.

Madeleine's brow furrowed and her eyes were barely opened as she stared at her teacup. Her cheeks flushed when she thought about the scandalous situation.

"Madeleine, there were two of you in the relationship, and it's wrong for you to assume all the responsibility for what happened. You did not trick or lure him. He took it upon himself to pursue you, and he booked the room, remember that."

Madeleine did not comment on her mother's remarks. She slumped in her chair. "I would like to stay here for a while *Maman*," she whispered.

Mme. Marois' face shone. "I'd be delighted to have you, dear. Since the Spanish Flu took your father, and your brother left to live independently, I've been at loose ends, rambling about this old castle of a house. Now tell me, how is Andrew, and what's he doing? It's a shame about his leg. My grandson is very dear to me."

Madeleine rose and went to the tea trolley and poured herself another cup of tea. "He's moved out of our home and has taken rooms with his friend, Charles. He's able to get about on crutches quite nicely and he's gone back to work at his old law firm. I believe he still loves his father, but he can't forgive him for trying to kill me. He's confused about the whole affair. I suggested we rent a house together, but he said, 'No, not just now.'"

Mme. Marois placed her teacup on the table beside her and rose. She was tall and elegant and stood very straight. "I'm going to take a nap now, dear. We will discuss this later, if you wish." She began to walk out of the room, but stopped and turned.

"Oh, I forgot to tell you that your young Irish guest, Mary, stopped by when you were at the bank the other day. She enquired about your health and said she would be getting in touch with you when you're fully recovered."

A pensive expression appeared on Mme. Marois' face, and she added, "Just a feeling, but I thought there was some urgency in her visit. I could be wrong."

Madeleine's eyebrows puckered, "Oh? I do hope everything is all right. I haven't heard from her for some time. I'll send her a note."

CHAPTER 28

Toronto, 1922

Mary had been in Paul's head for the last week. His mind drifted while working, and she would appear in his mind's eye. He could almost smell her—Lilacs and Ivory soap.

He'd felt concern when he last saw her. She was injured and in pain. And something else: she seemed frightened. *Of what?* Surely not of him. He would see her today. The idea excited him. He knew this couldn't last forever, but he felt compelled to continue seeing her.

The amusement park, Sunnyside, opened last week, and Paul wanted to take her there. He hoped she felt better as he rapped on the door and removed his Homburg.

***

Mary pushed the lace curtain to the side of the oval glass in the door. Her face was pale and her manner subdued when she greeted him. He spoke gently. "I thought I could take you to Sunnyside today. It would be fun, and the fresh air from the lake will do you good." He nodded his head a few times. "Yes?"

Paul leaned forward placing his face in the slender opening. She felt grateful that he seemed genuinely concerned. His brown eyes reminded her of velvet. Mary believed she had nothing to fear from Paul, but the dreadful memory of letting in the wrong person came back. "I've work to do, and I'm tired." She spoke quickly, and there was an edge to her voice.

"Come out just for a short while. I promise not to keep you longer than you wish."

Mary sighed and pushed her shoulders back. "All right, all right, but just for a couple of hours." During the last week she had barely spoken to anyone except Dr. Tricklebank's patients. She startled easily when someone spoke to her while she was typing or writing. Maybe a bit of fresh air and some company would do her good. Paul had never given her any reason to fear him, but now she harboured a suspicion of all men. A few moments later she sat beside him in his automobile. He parked his black Ford on the Lakeshore and they strolled into the throng of people.

Sunnyside amusement park buzzed with laughter and excitement which seemed to zing in the air. It smelled of chips and vinegar. The park encompassed several rides: a Merry-Go-Round, The Whip, and when Mary looked up, she could see The Flyer, a white roller coaster. She could hear the cars creaking to the top, and the riders' screams as the cars plummeted down a long dip. The sweet aroma of candy floss floated on the air.

Mary didn't eat many sweets, but the scent of the sugar was enticing. "Paul would you buy some of that pink confection?" she said, pointing to the candy floss.

"Certainly." He returned a few moments later holding two brown paper cones filled with pink floss. As they began to peck at their cones, Mary heard someone call out Paul's name. Paul turned to look at a gentleman striding toward them.

"Hello, Paul. See you're enjoying the park. It's really something isn't it," he said, smiling at Paul and looking at Mary.

"Well, I'll be on my way. Don't let that candy floss stick on your face." He turned to leave, but stopped half way and said, "Give my regards to May and the kiddies."

Paul looked stunned, and his face turned a deep crimson. He began to speak, but stuttered. "He's…he's one of my co-workers, Detective Jim Butler."

A puzzled expression appeared on Mary's face as if she were trying to solve a mathematical problem. A moment later her face hardened as the penny dropped.

"I want to go home, Paul. Now." Her lips narrowed, and ice water seemed to drip from her words.

He looked down and fumbled in his pocket for the Ford's keys. "Certainly, certainly, but I can explain."

"No need. I get the drift," she said, glaring at him. She turned on her heel and struggled through the crowd in the direction of his auto.

Although it was a warm July day, the atmosphere in the Ford was frigid. *Thank the Lord, it's not a long drive home,* Mary thought.

Half way there, Paul tried to mutter some feeble excuse. "I was going to tell you. I…I was just waiting for the right…and I do care for you."

Mary breathed a sigh of relief when the auto stopped in front of her house. Paul rushed to the other side of the car to open her door. It flew open and she hopped out with the speed of a rabbit. "Don't bother with the door, we both know you're no gentleman, and I'll thank you not to call on me again. You've spun a grand tale and deceived me." Mary flung the door shut with a loud crack and bolted up the walkway to her front door.

Once inside her room, she dropped down on a side chair. Agatha Christie's novel lay on the table beside the chair. She picked it up and smashed it down. Hot tears coursed down her face. She doubled forward and put her face in her hands.

Over the next few weeks, Mary focussed on her work, trying to keep the horrendous memories of the rape squashed down. But they would bubble up in the evenings at home. She tried to anaesthetize herself with alcohol. Finally, she decided she had to take some kind of action. It felt like her spirit was being crushed, and she could not—or would not—tolerate the feeling of being a victim. *But what of his threat of violent retaliation?* And it was too soon to know if she was pregnant, but she had to take some kind of action. Mary gave her notice to Dr. Tricklebank and decided to move to another part of the city, the east end of Toronto, near Sherbourne Street. It would be a step in the right direction. She'd find another job.

There was a girl in her church choir who she liked and admired. Her name was Phidela Betts. She was quiet and self-assured. Mary never heard her gossip as some of the other girls did. She decided she would ask Phidela to go to the police station with her, telling her only that she needed some moral support to report a crime.

"What is it, Mary? What happened?" Phidela asked.

"I'm sorry, Phidela, I just can't tell you now except that a man hurt me. I'm so ashamed."

Mary and her friend took their time walking up to the desk sergeant at number Six Police Station at the corner of Queen and Cowan Avenue.

Trying hard not to stammer, Mary said in a clear voice, "I would like to speak to a police officer, sir."

And what is the nature of your complaint, Miss?" He placed his folded arms on the high counter and leaned forward.

"It's of a personal nature, sir. I just need to speak in private to an officer."

The sergeant studied her for a few seconds, then turned and picked up a telephone from the far end of the desk. He spoke quietly, then hung up. He returned to where

Mary waited. "Take a seat on the bench over there," he said, pointing across the room.

Mary sat down and began looking at her fingernails and pushing the cuticle back. She squared her tense shoulders. A gnawing pain had started between them. Sooner than she wanted, a police officer approached. Looking at her with keen eyes, he said, "Follow me, Miss."

"Wait here for me, Phidela," Mary said. "I'll be back as soon as I can."

***

It took Mary only two or three steps to reach the chair that stood in front of a battered oak desk. The policeman walked behind it and sank down on his swivel chair. "My name is Constable Brixton," he announced, taking out a small notepad. "And who might you be, Miss?"

Mary pushed her shoulders back and sat as straight as she could. Perspiration made her hands clammy. She closed them into two small fists and held them in her lap. "Mary Flynn, Sir."

"That's F-l-y-n-n, correct?"

She nodded.

He dropped his pencil beside his notepad and leaned forward. "Why are you here, Miss Flynn?"

Mary hoped she wouldn't sound incoherent as she fumbled to find the right words. "I was interfered with and beaten by one of my secretarial clients, sir. He also threatened to do me harm if I spoke of the attack to anyone." There, it was out. Some of the tension and queasiness left her body. She had finally told someone.

"When did this alleged attack occur?" the officer asked.

"Two weeks ago, at the beginning of July."

The constable's eyebrows rose. "Why is it you're just coming forward now? Why have you waited?"

The room became stifling hot. Mary could hear the disbelief in the policeman's voice. "He threatened to do me harm if I told anyone, as I told you before. I was afraid to come sooner. It's been dragging me down over the last while. So speak out, my brain's been telling me." Mary slumped back in her chair.

The constable stared at her for several seconds without speaking. She could feel the heat creeping up her face and hung her head. She felt like he was judging her.

"Tell me where the attack took place and precisely how it came about."

Mary related the entire incident, trying not to blush. But how do you cut a blush? Giving the details was excruciatingly painful. The policeman listened, nodding his head occasionally, and saying, "Go on," when she hesitated.

"What's this client's name?" he asked.

When she answered, he lifted his pen, his eyebrows arched, and his eyes widened.

"Would you repeat that, please?"

She did.

The officer paused and stared at Mary for a few seconds before continuing. "You mentioned you were rendered unconscious and your eye was badly swollen and discoloured. Pity you didn't come sooner, and show us the evidence," he said. "Why would a single woman let a man, whom she knows only professionally, into her room?"

"I told you, it was not my idea, but his. I did try to dissuade him, but he insisted. Him being a client and all, I thought I would be safe."

"Doesn't your landlady have rules about male visitors in her female tenants' rooms?"

"Yes, she does, but—"

"And what about the torn undergarment? Where is that? It would be evidence."

Mary could feel her heart sinking. From the constable's attitude she could see he didn't believe her.

The constable stood up, shrugged his shoulders and closed his pad. "The police can't go to a respected member of the community with a flimsy accusation like this. You have no proof, and it's just your word against his. If you had followed your landlady's rules, nothing would have happened. That is...if it did."

Her shoulders slumped as she realized it was no use. The police would do nothing. She rose slowly as if a large stone pressed on her shoulders, pushing her down. Then anger gave her a surge of energy. She looked directly at the officer and said in a firm voice. "I want my complaint recorded. There may be more victims who have suffered at this man's hands. Then you might take my attack seriously when another woman comes forward."

"I'll mention it to my captain," he said with little enthusiasm. The officer stood and came from behind his desk and nodded. "Good day, Miss Flynn."

Once out the office door, she raced toward Phidela, her eyes blazing. "We're finished here, Phidela. I have to go home and get my things together right away. I'll be moving, dear, so I won't see you for a while, but I'll write."

Phidela looked stunned. "Aren't the police going to help you with your problem?"

"I don't think so, but if they do make enquiries, someone will come looking for me and not with good intentions."

CHAPTER 29

Mary sat in her new room on Bleeker Street in the east end of Toronto. It wasn't as clean or comfortable as her old room. Well, she could do something about that. The floor was covered with worn and faded linoleum. The pattern had all but disappeared. She'd scrub it and cover a portion of it with a small carpet she'd purchased from a second-hand furniture store on Queen Street. She measured the windows. Some bright fabric would cover the paint-chipped window frames. Her Singer sewing machine would do up some curtains nicely.

The position she'd found at the Toronto General Hospital would be too public, she thought. Instead, she purchased *The Toronto Daily Star* and turned to the Help Wanted ads. She spread the newspaper on a table, scanned the ads, moving a pencil down the column. *The Toronto Daily Star* wanted women to take classified ads in their advertising department. Mary thought she was qualified for that one. The applicant needed accurate spelling and good English. *Maybe.* Another position was for a secretary at a doctor's office. This one was close by. And working for Dr. Tricklebank had given her the experience needed.

Since the attack, Mary feared being out in public. When she was out, she would frequently look over her shoulder. A job close by suited her. She kept the door to her room locked at all times and only opened it for the landlady.

She jotted down the doctor's number. A tenants' mutual telephone hung on a wallpapered wall in the hall. Telephone numbers had been pencilled on the paper. She dialed the telephone number taken from the ad and made an appointment for an interview. It was for that day at two o'clock. Mary selected a navy blue dress with a white collar from the few clothes she owned. Just right for an interview, she thought. Her hair bobbed in the fashion of the day fit just right under a navy blue cloche. White gloves finished the outfit.

***

Mary perched on the edge of a chair in front of Dr. Ludwick's paper-laden desk. She handed him the letter of recommendation from Dr. Tricklebank. As he read the letter, Mary studied him. Dr. Ludwick appeared to be middle-aged, between 45 and 50. He wore circular steel rimmed glasses. His face looked thin and lined, possibly from too little sleep. His black hair laid slicked back. The dark suit he wore looked like it could use a good pressing, and small white flakes salted his shoulders.

He held a black fountain pen poised over a sheet of white paper like a hypodermic needle ready to inject someone. Occasionally he would lower it and jot something down.

Dr. Ludwick finished reading the letter of recommendation and placed it on the desk in front of him. Still holding his pen, he began to ask Mary questions and make note of her answers on the letter of recommendation. It struck her that he was writing very slowly and carefully. *Odd.* An occasional "Yes, yes," accompanied his languid pen strokes.

When the interview finished, he leaned back in his chair, and the corners of his mouth curved upwards. "Everything seems in order, and Dr. Tricklebank recommends you highly. How soon could you start?"

Mary was taken aback by his sudden decision. She had an odd feeling about him, something she couldn't quite put her finger on. "I'd like to think about it for a few days, Dr. Ludwick."

Two deep creases appeared between his eyes and his lips became a thin line. He snapped, "If you're not sure about the position, why did you come?"

"I just need a little time, personal things I have to attend to. I'll let you know tomorrow."

Dr. Ludwick nodded and stood up. "Good day then, Miss Flynn."

The uncertainty about the doctor persisted all evening. *But I have to work, don't I?* Her savings were running low after buying the carpet and curtains and a few other odds and ends. *I need to work now,* Mary repeated to herself. She could always find another job if this one didn't work out. Once she made the decision, she stopped thrashing about in her bed, and slept.

***

Despite Mary's uneasy feeling, things had gone well at the office the first two weeks. Her employer was courteous to his patients and to her, although he was tardy about appearing for his appointments. Sometimes the office would be overflowing, and he would stroll in as if he had all the time in the world. This was a poorer section of the city than the one she had previously lived in. And the patients seemed to be happy just to have a doctor take care of them.

One day, Mary arrived early at the office. She remembered she needed to order some supplies. She stopped at her small outer office, hung up her coat, and picked up a writing pad. Last week she'd noticed some of the medications in the doctor's office needed replenishing. There were empty spaces in the medicine cabinet where not too long ago it had been full. Usually it was kept locked, but she knew where the doctor kept the key.

When she opened the doctor's door she was startled to see him. He stood in front of the medicine cabinet with his white shirt sleeve rolled up and was injecting something into his arm. Her eyes darted to a small vial on his desk, and she recognized Laudanum.

In his haste, the doctor jerked the syringe as he withdrew it from his arm, causing a small amount of blood to appear. "What are you doing here?" he screamed, his eyes wild.

Stunned, Mary took a step back. Even from a distance she could see the pupils in his light blue eyes were pinpricks. She hurried out of the office and went outside. For an hour she walked, her head buzzing with thoughts. *Good Lord, the doctor's taking drugs.*

There were many medical books in the office, and when the doctor was not in the office, Mary would read up on some of the medical conditions and the drugs some of the patients were taking. She knew Morphine was in Laudanum and that it was used mainly for pain, but it also had psychological effects. Euphoria was one.

She returned to the office and stood outside until Dr. Ludwick's patients began to arrive. At the end of the day, she rushed putting on her coat. When she looked down, the buttons were done up crooked. Hastily her fingers made the adjustment. Grabbing her purse from under the desk, she raced toward the door. Before she could open it, a loud voice called out her name. She grabbed the doorknob and looked over her shoulder. "Yes?"

Dr. Ludwick was standing in the doorway to his office. Peering over his glasses, he said, "Mary, I assume you won't mention to anyone what you *think* you saw this morning. It was only some vitamins."

"Of course, of course. Good day Dr. Ludwick," she said, as she scooted out the door. Her breathing slowed as she rode the streetcar home, thankful to be away from the doctor. Thoughts flashed through her mind like bolts of lightning. She couldn't go back. *He's menacing.* She didn't like the look in his eyes when he spoke to her as she left. *Threatening.* She knew what she saw, and it wasn't vitamins.

That evening, Mary devoted serious thought to her future. She berated herself for not following her intuition about the doctor. From now on she would listen to it. Another idea was troubling. She'd tried not to think about it, but it kept surfacing. She shuddered at the thought. A few mornings last week she'd been nauseated when she rose in the morning, and she vomited once or twice. She knew vomiting in the morning could be an indication of pregnancy. Pregnant or not, one thing remained clear in her mind: she wouldn't go back to Dr. Ludwick's office, and she would leave Toronto. It was becoming threatening. But she would call Andrew before she left and thank him for all his kindness.

Perhaps he is still at the old telephone number at his father's house.

CHAPTER 30

Burlington, Ontario

The Region of Halton had a newspaper index. Detective Selby went to his office first and checked to see if Mary Ryan's name appeared in any newspapers in 1939. As he sat at his desk tapping away, her name and a date appeared in the *Burlington Gazette*, October, 1939. The Burlington Central Library had all the editions of the *Gazette* on microfilm. He didn't find her name in any other newspapers in the area. He'd scoot over there now.

Snowflakes swirled around his head as he slipped out of the Ford and hurried into the building. He approached a young woman at the Information desk. "Could you tell me where you keep the microfilm of all the old *Burlington Gazette* newspapers?" he asked.

The blonde young woman took her eyes off her computer and looked at Selby. "Certainly, sir. They're on the second floor. You can take the elevator." She looked over his shoulder and pointed a finger.

Selby hoped the young woman at the Information desk didn't think he looked too decrepit to take the stairs, which stood to the other side of him. "Thanks, I'll take the stairs." He sprinted up them. When he got to the top, he looked back at the 25 or 30 steps and exhaled. He was not in bad shape, only a little out of breath.

A library worker replacing books on a shelf from a cart caught his eye. "Excuse me, Miss, where are the microfilms of the old *Burlington Gazette* located?" he asked.

The woman was in her mid-forties and wore thick eyeglasses. *Probably reads too much and wore out her eyes.* Wool plaid pleated skirt, a beige cardigan sweater set, and sensible

Oxford shoes completed her wardrobe. Selby smiled to himself. *The perfect stereotype librarian.* She wore a nametag. "Ms. Booker," it pronounced. *It figures.*

She looked at Selby, brushed a strand of dark brown hair away from her forehead, and smiled. It changed her whole face. She was lovely. When she spoke, her voice was low and intimate. "Wait one moment, and I'll take you there." She removed the last book from the cart, placed it on the shelf, and came around to stand in front of Selby.

"Follow me, and I'll set you up."

Selby followed, noting her bouncy step as the pleats in her skirt swayed. They stood in front of a bank of small drawers and boxes filled with film, much like the Toronto Reference Library, only smaller. "Which year and month would you like to see?" she asked in a low confidential voice.

He told her.

Ms. Booker sat down at the reader, threaded the machine, and scanned the dates to the appropriate place.

"OK, you're on your own now. If you need any help, I'll be here." She flashed that transforming smile again and left his side.

Selby started at the second week in October and worked forward. Then on the first week in November, he found it: an article about a Mary Ryan from North Shore Blvd. and a picture. All the details of the face were clear and sharp. He was struck by her beauty. Light wide set eyes, a thin nose, and full lips. *Too bad it's not in colour.* She reminded him of an old-time film star, Maureen O'Hara, who was Irish. He'd make a photocopy of the picture from the *Burlington Gazette*, enlarge the copies from *The Globe*, and drop them off to the forensic artist and Dr. Pallotta.

Selby turned up the collar on his jacket as he hurried to his car. A stiff wind swirled brown, crisp leaves around his feet. When he opened the door, he threw the large manila envelope containing the pictures across to the passenger seat. As he sat behind the wheel, he pulled out his cell phone and keyed in Dr. Pallotta's number at the morgue. She answered on the first ring.

"It's Roy Selby, Dr. Pal... Lisa."

"Good to hear from you, Roy. Got any new info?" she asked.

"I've obtained some photographs of a missing woman from way back in the day—1939, to be exact. I don't think I told you, but my dad, Detective Doug Selby, worked the case at the time. Tried to solve it, but any clues they worked dried up. He thinks there is a possibility there may be a connection to our skeleton."

"That's a long shot, Roy. But the remains *do* appear to have been buried for a long time."

"I'd like to come in now and show you the photos and talk about facial reconstruction."

"OK. I have a small office here. Ask the receptionist to show you where it is. See you soon."

Twenty-five minutes later, Selby sat in front of the anthropologist and opened the manila envelope. As he passed the photos across to her outstretched hand, he noted no wedding ring. "One of the photos is of the missing woman, Mary Ryan. At the time she went missing, it appeared in the *Burlington Gazette*. And the others are photographs of a *Titanic* survivor, Mary Flynn, taken shortly after the rescue ship, the *Carpathia*, landed in New York. And another photo was taken in Toronto."

"Where did you get the pictures of the *Titanic* survivor?" Lisa Pallotta asked.

"The Toronto Reference Library."

"Good work, Roy. When did you say the missing woman from Burlington disappeared? 1939?"

"Uh-huh. About the facial reconstruction—I have a forensic artist here in the Hamilton-Burlington area who does work for the Police Department sometimes. It may be faster to have the construction done here."

Lisa's forehead puckered. "I would rather have the Forensic Centre in Toronto do the job. They already have a lot of the evidence from the burial site."

"Yes, but they're always back-logged quite a bit, and it would take longer," Selby offered.

"OK, then. Call the artist in to take a mould of the skull, and ask how fast we can have the reconstruction. What's the artist's name?" Lisa asked picking up a pen and pad.

Selby took a few steps forward to stand beside Lisa as she wrote. A clean, light floral scent drifted by his nose.

"Caroline Sauvé," he answered. "Her telephone number's at the station. I'll call this afternoon."

"Great," she said as she put the name in her lab coat pocket and looked at Roy. "Excuse me now, Detective, but I have to get back to work."

Selby didn't move, but stood looking a bit awkward. "Ah...I know you're new in the area. I was just wondering if you would have dinner with me one evening?"

Lisa appeared to be taken off her guard and hesitated for a moment. Then a soft, slow smile replaced her moment of surprise. "Tempting, Roy. But I'm not up to dating just now. And I'm still settling into my new surroundings. Sorry, maybe another time."

Selby tried not to look disappointed and said, "OK, another time."

Lisa nodded and changed the subject. "After your artist makes the mould, I'll send the skull to Forensics in Toronto. They can do a computerized version, superimposing the photos on the skull."

"Right. I'll let you know when the forensic artist will go to your lab." Selby left the lab whistling a happy little tune. And thinking, *Well, she didn't say no, just maybe another time.*

CHAPTER 31

Toronto, 1922

After a restless night of tossing and turning, Mary rose early, dressed quickly, and walked to the Queen streetcar. She'd decided to sell her furniture back to the used furniture dealer. Afterwards, she'd visit St. Vincent de Paul Church, her former parish, and ask Father O'Neill for advice. It had been whispered among the girls at choir practice that when a girl gets into a certain kind of trouble, Father O'Neill knew of a place that would help her. Never in her wildest dreams did she think that one day it would be her.

Mary trembled as she raised the brass knocker in the shape of a Celtic Knot. She dropped it quickly after two raps and pulled her hat down closer to her eyes. A pleasant woman with a white apron moulded to her chubby body opened the door.

"Good morning, Miss, how can I help you?" she asked smiling.

Some of the tension in Mary's shoulders relaxed as she looked into a kind face.

"I need to speak to Father O'Neill on an urgent matter."

"Step inside, dear. I'll get the Father."

A few moments later, Father O'Neill strode into the foyer. His blue eyes sparkled through round horn-rimmed glasses, and his black hair looked blue-black against his fair skin, like the 'black Irish' back home. "Good to see you again, Mary. I remember you from the choir. We've missed your sweet soprano voice. I'd heard you moved away," he said, smiling and extending a soft hand with long tapered fingers. His voice had a musical timbre to it, which conveyed happiness. "Let's sit in the parlour."

She liked him.

After hearing her story, Father O'Neill sat back in his tufted armchair and rubbed his chin. There was nothing judgmental in his voice as he spoke. "You've had a hard time of it, lass, but you've kept your head. You made the right decision coming here."

A sigh escaped Mary's lips. "Thank you, Father."

"There's a convent near Hamilton, about 50 miles from here. The good sisters take in young women in your predicament, see them through their time, and help with the child after delivery. I'll call Mother Superior today and tell her I have recommended you."

He rose and went to his desk where a pad and pencil lay on the blotter. "I'll write down the directions to the convent."

Mary felt a weight lifted from her shoulders as she watched him rip off a page from the pad and hand it to her.

"Now, you said you wanted to go to confession before you left. We can go into the church and use the confessional there if that would be more comfortable." He led Mary out the side door of the rectory where there was a pathway to the church.

***

After Confession, Mary walked down Roncesvalles Avenue feeling more optimistic about her future. The horizon didn't look quite as dark and frightening. Without warning, she felt strong fingers dig into her arm. She jerked it away and turned to look into the face of her attacker.

"Going somewhere, Mary?" the man said, as he looked at the valise she clutched in her hand. His clenched jaw jutted out.

Her green eyes widened, and her throat tightened. She felt like screaming or running, but stood her ground and blurted out, "I'm going to see my doctor. I believe there may be two of us soon. And you best keep your distance sir, because I feel sick to my stomach right now. You'll be hearing from me when the time is right." And with that she did a lively trot down the street looking back over her shoulder once or twice.

He stood stock still in the middle of the sidewalk with an astonished expression.

Trembling from the encounter, Mary popped into a small tearoom. It was the one she and Detective Paul Kennedy had stopped in. The warm aroma of fresh baked bread smelled enticing, and for a few moments her mind drifted back to a more pleasant time.

"Miss, Miss, what would you like?"

Startled, Mary snapped back to reality. A middle-aged woman with brassy blonde hair stood in front of her, a pencil hovering over a pad.

"Tea, toast and jam please, and the ladies-room," Mary said.

The waitress pointed to the back of the tearoom before walking away. Her gait was slow, and she leaned back on her heels.

Poor thing, Mary thought. *It looks like her feet hurt. Probably standing up since early this morning.*

The trembling increased, and Mary had a hollow feeling in the pit of her stomach. She needed a drink right now. She dashed to the ladies-room, locked the door, and withdrew a small silver flask from her purse. She'd picked it up at a second-hand store, took it home, scoured it, and put it in boiling hot soapy water. The flask was thoroughly cleansed before she poured her "tonic" into it. Mary took a long, slow swallow before replacing the cap. In a few seconds, the wave of fear washed back out, and the warmth of the alcohol gave her strength. Back at her table, that strange feeling of nausea began to surface. She knew food would quell the sensation. Her snack sat in front of her. She ate in a hurry, swallowing the bread before it was fully chewed, and gulped down the fragrant tea.

Patting her mouth with a napkin, Mary dislodged a few buttery bread crumbs and pushed the small plate away. Her eyebrows arched when she looked up. She could hardly believe her eyes. Her lips parted and she raised a hand to cover her mouth. There was a slight tremor in her hand and she quickly placed it in her lap. The son of the rapist stood before her, frowning. She found him peculiar in a way hard to describe, furtive perhaps. When he walked into the room he didn't make a sound, quiet as a cat. Around the same height as Mary, he appeared to have had one dinner too many. His skin bore an unhealthy pallor, and his hair looked like a curled, brown leaf.

Mary's mind flashed back to the time when she had been doing some bookkeeping for his father. He had hovered around her until she looked up and stared at him. "Yes?"

"Nothing, nothing." He ambled over to the other side of the room and fiddled with some invoices.

Now, he sat down at Mary's table without waiting for an invitation. The man spoke in the same sarcastic way as he had in the past. She could hear it now in his voice as he feigned interest. "Mary, you look distressed. Is there anything I can do?" he asked.

"No, nothing, thank you. I'm perfectly fine." Shocked to have encountered both of them, father and son, on the same day, a knot began to form in the pit of her stomach. "I was just leaving." She gathered her gloves and purse and bent over to pick up her valise.

The man sprung from his chair and placed a vice-like grip on her arm. She froze for a moment. Her arm began to ache as he held fast and pressed her down on her chair. His smile turned to a grimace, and his grip tightened.

"Sit down Mary," he said as he pressed harder on her arm, forcing her down. "I've something I would like to discuss with you," he snarled from between clenched teeth. He let go of her arm.

As soon as her arm was free, she sprung out of her chair. "I'm in a hurry. I have to go." He grabbed her arm again and forced her back into her chair.

Panic rose in her mind, and her throat became dry. She looked around to see if the waitress was nearby and could see her signal, but she was busy with another customer. The only other customer was at the front of the tea room. All she could think of was getting away from this brutal man as fast as possible and boarding her train. But judging by the tight expression on his face, Mary guessed she was not going to like what he had to say. His steely gaze frightened her and kept her glued to her chair.

He cleared his throat and paused, seeming to gather up his words. "I was at home several weeks ago when Chief Inspector Braithwaite from the Toronto Police came to see Father. They had met previously when Father made a large donation to the Policemen's Benevolent Fund. The Inspector was adamant that his visit not be misconstrued. He seemed somewhat embarrassed that he'd come to our home."

I think I know what's coming, Mary guessed.

"In any event, he told Father that you had gone to the police station with some wild accusation about him. The Chief Inspector assured him that in no way did he believe your ridiculous story, but he thought Father should be made aware of the complaint and be on his guard in the event of any further trouble from you."

Mary's back stiffened and her hand clenched into a tiny fist as she listened. Her lips tightened. She could feel anger welling up. Her chair grated on the floor as she bolted out of it and stood several paces away from the table. Still focussed on the pale face with midnight blue eyes hard as flint, she said, "There will be consequences for your father's actions, but that will be in the future when the time is right. I'm dealing now with the result of that horrible day when your father attacked me." His face slowly registered recognition of what she was saying.

"And if I were you," Mary said, "I'd stop fiddling the books. You're going to be caught soon enough." His face flushed, and she could see a large vein bulging in his neck.

"If you pursue any avenue to harm me or my family in any way, you'll wish you hadn't," he blustered.

"And good riddance to you," she flung at him as she quick-stepped toward the entrance. She turned back just once to see him sitting motionless, his face flushed with anger. She guessed he got her drift.

Outside the tea shop, the air was cool and refreshing as it caressed Mary's face and gave a gentle lift to her hair. She walked at a brisk pace down to the train station thinking, *I'm not leaving a moment too soon, but I'll call Andrew Henry before I leave and thank him for all his kindness.*

***

Mary dialed the telephone number at the Henry home while waiting for her train. A woman answered.

"Henry residence."

"May I speak with Mr. Andrew Henry, please?" She wondered who the person answering the phone was. Perhaps a maid.

"Mr. Andrew no longer lives here," came the quick reply.

"Can you please give me his new number? My name is Mary Flynn, and I used to live there. Andrew is a friend of mine."

"Would you please repeat your name, and I will ask Mr. Henry senior if I have permission to give it to you?" she said in a brisk tone. Mary heard a soft bump as the woman put down the receiver.

Within a minute or two she picked it up. "Mr. Henry says I'm permitted to give you his son's telephone number."

Mary carefully wrote down Andrew's number and dialed it straight away. While she waited for someone to answer, she thought about what reason she would give him for leaving. Mary grimaced. *I may have to lie.* She hated the thought, especially since Andrew had been such a good friend.

"The Queens Hotel," the operator answered.

"I'd like to speak with Andrew Henry please."

Andrew picked up on the first ring. "Hello."

"It's Mary Flynn, Andrew. I'm leaving Toronto, and I just wanted to say goodbye before I leave and thank you for all your kindness and for being a good friend."

"Mary, I'm so glad you called. I've been wondering how you're making out. Mother told me you tried to reach her a while ago, but she was away from the house at the time."

"That's true. I haven't had time to get back to her."

"But why are you leaving? Are you well?" Andrew asked, concern in his voice.

"Yes, yes, I'm fine. Don't worry, Andrew. Something's come up, and I just have to leave for a while, and I don't know when I'll be back."

"Is there anything I can do to help?"

"Would you tell your mother goodbye for me? She's been very kind and helpful."

"Of course."

"Before I leave, tell me what you're doing, Andrew."

"I've taken rooms at the Queens Hotel. My friend Charles Simmons has also taken rooms there to help me when I need it. Having one leg can be difficult at times."

"Indeed. I remember Charles from the train station when you left for the war. He was there to say goodbye to you."

"He was. And I couldn't stay in Father's house after the shooting. I couldn't bear the sight of him after what he did to Mother."

Mary could hear the anguish in Andrew's voice. She knew he loved his father, but his emotions were torn between his mother and father. She felt compassion for him but knew there was nothing she could do. Only time could heal the rift. And even then, who could tell?

"I understand Andrew. I'm glad you have a good friend to be by your side at a time like this."

"Thank you, Mary. Good luck. I'll miss you. Perhaps we'll meet again someday. Goodbye."

As Mary rose from the bench the Station Manager called out, "Train for Hamilton arriving in two minutes."

CHAPTER 32

Oakville, Ontario, November 2000

Detective Selby drove to the evidence room. Officer Burbank was on duty at the counter. "How's it going, Burbank?" he said smiling. He'd met her several times at the courthouse over the years. Now nearing retirement, she'd been assigned to the evidence room. A pleasant woman, with a wide smile and short, curly blonde hair, she had been on duty when he signed in for the boxes of Mary's clothing.

"What can I do for you today, Detective Selby?"

"If it's possible, I'd like to retrieve some old notepads of my dad's. I don't know if you know it, but my dad was on the Force for 30 years—a lot of notebooks."

"Yeah, I'd heard something about him. Good cop. He'd just left as I began my career. I guess you inherited some of the bloodhound, eh? OK," she said, standing and fishing in the desk drawer for the key.

"How far back you want to go?"

"Latter part of 1939—October, I think." He had his doubts, but it was worth a try.

"Whew. I don't know if we keep them that far back. We have to destroy the old ones to make room for the new. Well, sign in and you can have a look-see." The officer unlocked the door to the room and pointed to a corner where banker boxes were stacked. Each was labeled with a date and officer's name. "Good Luck, Detective Selby."

Once inside, Selby went to the box where he had found Mary's clipping and slipped it back into the skirt pocket. A photocopy of the clipping was in Mary Ryan's file at the office.

As he scanned the notepad boxes, a look of disappointment creased his face when he noted the dates only went back as far as 1975. *Crap!* His shoulders slumped after reading the last date. *It's up to Dad now.* He hoped his father's forgetfulness and packrat behaviour would be an advantage and that there would be some old notepads at home in the basement.

CHAPTER 33

Toronto, 1922

The train felt warm and comfortable, with plush seats and a large window. Still some daylight left, it streamed through the glass. Mary looked out, not really seeing the countryside roll by, but engrossed in deep thought. She felt some satisfaction, having stood up to the rapist's son, but she was still apprehensive.

Mary hated the thought of lying to the nuns, but she must change her name. Father O'Neill said he would call Mother Superior right away and inform her of his referral and Mary's imminent arrival. She assumed he would give her name as Mary Flynn. Some of Mary's history would also be given he said, so the nun would know what to expect.

The idea gave her some relief. She wouldn't have to go into the ugly details again. Mary would tell the nuns to use her married name, Ryan. *Yes, Ryan seemed like a good alias*—her mother's maiden name. She liked the sound of it. If anyone came looking for her, the nuns would say they didn't know a Mary Flynn.

All the money Mary earned from her weekend typing at home had been saved, as well as some of her wages. Her living expenses were unusually low as she made all her own food from scratch and even baked bread on the weekends. She made her own clothes and purchased only boots or shoes and toiletries. The one thing she missed was her sewing machine. She sold it with everything else. Oh well, she would get another used one in time. For the present, she could sew by hand.

"Oakville next," the conductor announced, striding up the aisle. "Oakville next." His voice startled her, and she took the train schedule from her purse. It wouldn't be long now. *Burlington and then Hamilton.*

***

The train arrived in Hamilton on schedule at 7:00 p.m. There were black taxis waiting for fares. Mary stepped into one, reached into the bottom of her draw-string purse and drew out the scrap of paper with the address of the convent, and handed it to the driver. "Would you take me to this address, please? It's a convent."

"Yes Miss, I know. I'll have you there in two shakes of a lamb's tail."

Dusk began to descend as they approached the convent, which stood on the outskirts of Hamilton. Mary looked out the taxi window and could see dust rising from the road as they approached the ebony gates of the convent. The building stood on a small hill, silhouetted against a darkening sky. She craned her neck to look at the top of the three-storey building. Dark green ivy crept up the face of the building to the second floor.

Stillness hung on the air. No birds chirping, no wind whining though the trees. Just a hush all around. Black wrought iron fencing ran across the front of the property and up the sides of the building. Two tall gates opened to the grounds. The latch stood in an upright position. Goosebumps rose on her arms and she hugged her chest. *It probably looks better in the daylight*, she thought, trying to cheer herself up. *Right now, it looks like some medieval castle in Ireland.* She paid the driver and hesitantly approached the front door.

Humming a little tune, she placed her hand inside the circle of the black knocker, lifted and dropped it twice. She could hear it echo inside. An iron grill covered a small window near the top of the door. She could hear the soft singing of prayers in Latin as she stood on the threshold. A light came on overhead, and the oak door creaked open. A nun stood in the opening. She wore a white wimple with a cream habit. A long, brown rosary circled her waist and hung down in front. The beads looked the size of acorns. A large crucifix hung at the bottom. A faint smile slipped across her unlined face, but otherwise it bore little expression.

"Mary, is it? We've been expecting you, my dear. Please come in."

Mary stood in the foyer gazing around her. In the grey stone wall, a niche had been carved out. A statue of St. Theresa was sheltered in it. "Excuse me, Sister, if my eyes don't deceive me that's a statue of the Little Flower—St. Theresa. One much like it stood in the hallway of my school."

"Quite right, my dear. I see you know your saints."

Mary nodded. "When I was in school in Ireland we learned about many of the saints. St. Christopher, the patron saint of travellers, and St. Anthony, Finder of Lost Articles, with whom I am well acquainted," she gave a small laugh, and so did the nun.

"My name is Mother St. Agnes." She crossed her arms and her hands disappeared in the voluminous sleeves of her habit. "I'll take you to Mother Superior now. She has some forms to fill out for you and she needs to give you information about your duties and your stay here."

***

Mary sat in a large, sparsely furnished office. Just a few bookcases, a filing cabinet and a medium-sized highly polished dark desk, with an oak swivel chair behind it. Off to one side of the desk, another smaller desk with an Underwood typewriter on it.

The door had been left open, and Mary heard a swishing sound and the click of a heel on the stone tile.

Mother Superior glided into the room. A tall woman, she appeared to be around six feet. Her pencil thin body could be seen, even under the excessive amount of fabric of her garment. In a few sweeping steps, the nun crossed the room and sat behind the desk.

"Good evening, Mary. I am Mother Superior and in charge of the convent. Unlike the Catholic schools where you called the teachers 'Sister', in here we are all referred to as 'Mother'."

Mary nodded her head. She didn't like the idea. The only person she'd ever called "Mother" was her own mother, but she would comply.

"Have you completed your studies?" she asked.

Mary sat forward in her chair and proudly answered, "I have. And I've been working as a private secretary and a medical secretary where I transcribed medical reports dictated by the doctor. I've done some bookkeeping, too."

Mother Superior sat silent for a moment and stared at her. Mary found it hard to read the nun's expression. Her face appeared like an unpainted canvas, void of any brush marks of expression, but her tone seemed pleasant enough.

"Very well then, perhaps you could help with the studies of our younger girls. Would you like that?" she asked.

Mary wanted to please, as she was being given sanctuary and care as she prepared for the birth of her child. "Of course, uhh...Mother Superior. I welcome any task you choose to give me."

"Good."

A slight upward turn appeared at the corners of her mouth. Her eyes were a pale, watery blue or grey—Mary couldn't tell which—and there seemed to be weariness in them, or a great sorrow.

"It's close to the girls' bedtime now, but I'll take you to your dormitory. There are fifteen beds in each dormitory and we have three large rooms with washrooms attached. We rise at six a.m. and go to Mass. There will be a nightgown on the end of your bed," she said, rising.

"Oh, I've brought my own gown. I won't need one."

Mother Superior didn't speak for several seconds, and gave a cool stare as if she were assessing Mary. "All the girls wear the same nightgown, but in a few different colours. We make them here. There are no exceptions. Please wear the one provided."

Although she detected no anger in her tone, Mary wondered what Mother Superior thought of her. She had an inkling of numerous rules she would have to obey. It would be a challenge for her, after living on her own for several years. But if she could survive the *Titanic* and several other grave misfortunes, surviving the convent's rules for a while shouldn't be too hard to bear.

"I will," Mary answered.

The nun's cool eyes brighten as she rose and came around the desk to stand in front of Mary. She rose. The nun towered over her as they stood facing each other. "There's a lovely chapel on the second floor. It's large and airy with tall windows on one wall," she said, walking toward the door.

"Do we go to Mass every morning, Mother Superior?" Mary asked, walking quickly to keep up with the nun.

"Yes, we do. After we have said our morning prayers you can wash and dress, then follow the dormitory Mother downstairs to the chapel. After Mass is finished you can go directly to the dining room for breakfast. Just follow the rest of the girls and I'll send for you as soon as breakfast is over. We can plan your tasks then. Come with me now and I'll get you settled," Mother Superior said.

***

Mother Superior entered the dormitory in front of Mary and beckoned her to follow. Some of the girls were still getting ready for bed. Others appeared to be sleeping. The quiet whisper of women breathing could be heard from some. And an occasional short cough. The dormitory was large, with plenty of space between the beds. Mary could see a light coming from another room near the entrance. She suspected it was a washroom.

Mother Superior led Mary to her cot near the back of the room and close to a window. A sliver of a new moon shone a pale light on the neatly made bed with a white spread. There was a locker on the window wall near the bed with number 52 on it. The nun whispered, "Hang your clothes in there," pointing to the locker. "Goodnight," she said and slipped away as quietly as a falling star.

Mary picked up the nightgown and went into the washroom to change. Judging by the inside seams, the gown had once been a bright blue, but it'd been washed so many times it now appeared grey and drab. When she crawled between the cold sheets, she was glad the nightgown was flannel and warm against her cool skin.

Sleep eluded her. Her mind felt like a roiling sea, so much fear tumbled about. *Will he find me here? No, how could he? Still…And the baby, will it be all right? When the time comes will it be painful?* She jumped out of bed and prayed, *Lord, please take care of me.*

The cold, linoleum floor pressed hard against Mary's knees as she said a quick Hail Mary, and bounced back into bed. For a few seconds, she lay there tugging at the covers, when a slight movement at the front of the dormitory caught her eye. The moon beamed a weak light into the room, and she became aware of a dark figure sitting on a chair at the front of the room, off to one side. She could hear a clicking sound. Then the dark figure moved, and there was a louder clicking. *Beads—that's what it is. All the nuns must have the same rosaries around their waists like Mother Superior.* She wondered why she was sitting there.

Two hours later, the bed sheets twisted between her legs, Mary lay awake. The guilt she felt about lying to the nuns about her name came bubbling up. But, if anyone began looking for her, it would be Mary Flynn they would be searching for, not Mary Ryan. *Not to worry.*

After what seemed like hours, Mary twisted onto her right side. She heard one long click and saw a slice of light enter at the end of the room. The figure at the front of dormitory disappeared through a door near where she had sat. Mary relaxed and let sleep overtake her.

CHAPTER 34

Six a.m. A weak light fell through Mary's window and a loud school bell clanged as if it had a life of its own. She put her hands over her ears, sat up and looked around. Bedcovers were being thrown back, and everyone knelt beside their beds. The nun who had rung the bell began a quick morning prayer.

After the prayer, the women and girls began to chatter as they rushed to the washroom. The tepid water removed some of the drowsiness as she splashed her face. She had brought her toothbrush and gave her teeth a vigorous scrub and hurried to her bed.

Back in the dormitory, some of the girls were already dressed and making their beds. Some were combing their hair and sitting waiting for everyone to finish. Heads began to turn in Mary's direction. And it seemed to Mary, all fifteen pairs of eyes were asking, where did you come from? And who are you? Their cream-clad guardian clapped twice, and everyone filed out of the room. Some glanced back at Mary. *Odd—the nuns seem to communicate through clapping twice when they want your attention to do something.* The procession descended one floor to the chapel.

When Mary first approached the convent, she noted there were three storeys. She was curious to see the whole building. So far she had seen some of the first floor, now the second, and she had slept on the third floor. *Soon enough, soon enough.*

Caramel-coloured linoleum covered the chapel floor. It gleamed is if sunlight permeated it. Hard as concrete. Praise the Lord, it wasn't a High Mass—only a low one—so it didn't last very long. Her knees couldn't take much more. When she stood and looked down, a large red patch stained each knee.

Trying to take everything in as she left the chapel, Mary straggled at the back of the line of girls. A door partially open down the corridor caught her eye. She paused, cocked her head, and meandered over to it. She inserted a toe in the crack and peeked inside. Two loud, fast claps sounded. She froze and glanced over her shoulder. The dormitory nun was rushing down the hallway and looked as though she had the wind behind her, habit flying out like wings. Her brow furrowed, and a deep crease lay between her eyes. Mary hadn't heard a sound or a word before the clapping.

"What are you doing, young lady?" the nun gasped.

Mary could see annoyance on her face and wondered if there was a penalty for snooping.

"Just exploring a little, and trying to get my bearings, Mother."

The nun reached in front of Mary and pulled the door shut with a slam. "This is Father Walker's private parlour, which he uses when he comes to say Mass. Only one of the young women is allowed in there to clean and dust once a week. Otherwise, it is off limits to everyone else. Do you understand?"

Wide-eyed, Mary backed away from the door. "I…I'm sorry Mother. I didn't mean to break any rules."

The nun's face relaxed. "Well, come along now. I'll take you to breakfast," she said as she stepped in front of Mary and hastened to the dining room.

There appeared to be about 80 young girls and women in the dining room. Their ages ranged from approximately eight years old to around 18 or 19. They sat at round tables with white tablecloths, four girls to a table.

Mary sat on the chair which the nun had pointed out to her. "Hello, I'm Mary. What's your name?" she asked the placid looking woman to her left. The woman gave a surprised look and put a finger to pursed lips. *Oh dear! I forgot the rule—no talking at the table.* "Sorry, I forgot," she whispered. The other two girls turned a questioning eye on her.

The girl on her left had curly brown hair, which she piled on top of her head. Except for the back, where it hung down in something that looked like ringlets. Mary thought the girl's hair resembled a bird's nest, and she had to suppress a grin as she looked at it.

"Rose," the girl mouthed, smiling. Mary thought the young woman had the sweetest face she had ever seen. She handed Mary a bowl of porridge from the centre of the table.

"Where did you live?" Rose mouthed the words.

Mary mouthed, "Later."

After it appeared everyone had finished eating, the nun monitoring the dining room clapped her hands twice, and all the girls rose and began filing out. Rose sidled up to Mary, and asked again, "Where did you come from?"

Mary hated lying. But she had to keep her identity and where she came from secret in case someone came looking for her. She'd tried hard to lose her accent, but a trace still remained. It could be a clue to her identity.

Mary heard one of the girls in the Toronto choir speak of Barrie. She'd been there and said what a beautiful small community it was, situated on Lake Simcoe, several miles outside Toronto.

"I came from Barrie," Mary said, "but my parents came from Ireland, and I picked up their accent and manner of speaking." She tilted her head slightly down and to the side, in case her expression gave her away. She knew she was a rotten liar.

Rose nodded. "I'm from Toronto. Ever been there?"

"Ah...No I haven't. Ever been to Barrie?" Mary prayed to God Rose hadn't.

"Nope."

Mary breathed an inward sigh of relief and hoped there would be no more questions. If the girl asked anything more, she would refuse to answer.

Rose seemed satisfied for the moment and walked on.

***

Mother Superior appeared in the corridor a moment later and beckoned. "Come to my office, Mary."

Mary held her breath for a second, wondering if she had done something wrong as she followed the nun to her office.

When they were seated, Mother Superior asked, "Do you like music, Mary? If you do, one of our Mothers is a piano teacher."

A pleasant surprise. She exhaled with relief. It appeared Mother Superior wanted to find something recreational for her to do during her stay. "Sure and I do. I used to sing in a choir."

The nun seemed pleased, gave a shadow of a smile, and nodded her head.

"Very well, then. Next Tuesday someone will take you to the music room. And I understand you sew and make your own clothes. That skill will serve you well here. I'm assigning you to the sewing room where you can teach a few of the girls."

Mary leaned forward in her chair. "Thank you, Mother. I would like that." *What an unexpected and delightful surprise.* She looked away and peered into the distance. A sweet memory floated into her mind's eye. She could see herself sitting beside her mother sewing.

"What is it Mary? Do you have a question?"

The nun's voice stirred Mary out of her reflection. "No, no, just a thought about sewing with my mother."

Another thought occurred to her. "When will I be visiting the doctor to be sure everything is fine with the baby?"

Mother Superior treated Mary to a peculiar stare for several seconds before answering. At times like this, Mary wondered what was in the woman's mind. Sizing her up perhaps? After what seemed like a minute, the nun began to speak. Her facial expression did not change. It remained an unreadable slate.

"I'm happy to see you want to take care of your health and that of your child. There are two other young women here who also need to see the doctor. The three of you will be taken to a physician in Hamilton once a month." Mother Superior rose, crossed her arms and placed her hands inside the flowing sleeves of her habit. "I'll take you to the sewing room now where you can take up your duties."

Once Mary was inside the sewing room, the supervisor, Mickey, came over and introduced herself. Her hair was wiry, short, and black, with a few strands of silver, and her face was as plain as a plank. She wore thick, shiny eyeglasses. "Ah, a girl who can sew," she said.

She appeared happy and relaxed to meet Mary. "Sit down my dear and tell me where you learned to stitch and what you have made." Mickey took Mary's hand and clasped it with both of hers.

Mary liked her immediately. "My mother taught me, and I make most of my clothes," Mary said with pride.

"Very good, Mary. I'll enjoy having you here." She led Mary to a sewing machine and a chair. "Let's get started now."

***

Several months passed. Mary saw the doctor monthly. Delivery drew near and preparations were made to take her to the hospital. The doctor told her, "Don't wait too long. When your contractions are five minutes apart, leave for the hospital, unless your water breaks, then come right away." He added, "Any day now."

Mary began to feel afraid. She thought nothing could scare her anymore after the *Titanic*, but she began thinking, *If I don't get to the hospital soon enough, what then? Stop it, stop it!* she yelled under her breath. She'd survived being at sea in a lifeboat. She would survive this.

Mother Theresa monitored the dormitory where Mary slept. She had just placed her head on the pillow when she felt the first contraction. Rolling out of bed, she waddled to the front of the dorm. "I want to go to the hospital now. The baby's coming."

"How far apart are the contractions?" Mother Theresa asked.

"I've had only one," Mary answered.

With a slight grin, the nun said, "We must wait awhile. It's too soon. Five minutes apart, the doctor told us, after you've had a few."

Mary swallowed the panic inside her and tried to speak calmly. "The doctor said, 'don't wait too long.'" She gave a small tug at the nun's sleeve. "We must go now," she pleaded.

"Just a moment, and I'll get Mother Superior."

Mother Theresa hurried away and returned with Mother Superior, and the three of them left for the hospital.

The night was long and painful. The next day, March 21st, 1923, Mary delivered an eight pound baby girl. She called her Hope. The appearance of a small abnormality worried her. Hope's baby toe rested on top of the one beside it.

"Nothing serious," the doctor said, smiling. "It's a rare trait called Clinodactyly that quite often runs in families."

Mary thought for a moment. Did anyone on her side of the family have funny toes like her baby? No, none that she knew of, so...it must be coming from Hope's father's side.

***

Lying to the good sisters about her name was bad enough, but now more lies. The nurse presented her with birth registration papers. Mary registered the infant under the fictitious name of Ryan. Hope Ryan, the baby would be called. Mary supposed she was a criminal now, duping the government and all. The thought made her cringe. Mary left the space for the name of the father blank. She guessed that to be a lie of omission. She felt embarrassed when the nurse collected the form. Mary hoped she wouldn't read it and notice the empty space. *Ah well, nothing to be done about it. That's the way of it.*

CHAPTER 35

The Convent, 1925

Over the ensuing years, Hope grew strong and healthy. Mary cared for her in the convent for two years and taught sewing to the some of the women. One day she asked to see Mother Superior. An atmosphere of peaceful silence permeated her office. As Mary waited, she recalled her first time in this office—she had been scared and apprehensive. Would she fit in? What would the nuns think of her? Would her assailant find her and do her harm? All her fears had vanished over the last couple of years. Silently, she thanked the kind nuns for the care they'd given her during her pregnancy.

Mother Superior slipped into the room. Her habit made a swishing sound, and the wooden rosary beads made a familiar clacking as they swayed back and forth down the front of her cream habit. She glided past Mary and sat at her desk. "I understand you want to speak with me, Mary." She sat upright in her chair and folded her hands in front of her on the desk.

Mary sat close to the edge of her chair and began speaking in a hesitant voice. "Thank you, Mother, for all you've done for me these past two years. Now I feel I should be kicking out on my own, finding a job and a place to live."

A hint of a smile appeared on the nun's face, but otherwise it remained serene. She leaned back in her chair. "I appreciate your sense of responsibility and independence, Mary. Actually, I was going to speak to you about this very subject next week."

Mary let out a small breath of relief.

"Will you be taking the child with you when you find employment and a place of your own?"

Some of the young children remained living in the convent with their mothers after they'd been delivered, Mary had noticed.

One young mother told her she would be leaving her child in the convent for a few years to be educated. "If it's possible, I would like to leave Hope here for a while, so she can go to school. I would take her to my home every weekend once I settled some place and began earning a wage. Later, I would pay you for her keep."

Mother Superior nodded and gave a slight smile. Mary sensed the nun's approval of her decision. "The elementary years would be fine, but I would want to take Hope home permanently and have her attend a school outside the convent for her secondary education."

Mother Superior had been nodding her head as Mary spoke until now. "That sounds like an excellent idea, Mary, but Hope could stay on a bit longer and receive some of her secondary education here."

Mary wiggled in her chair. "It's a kind offer Mother, but you've already done so much for me. I don't want to impose on your goodness. For a while it will be fine, but I don't want to promise past Grade Eight." She gulped when she had finished.

Some of Mother Superior's satisfaction faded. "Well, of course you don't have to decide everything right now, but it all might be a bit too much for you. We'll speak again after you've found employment."

***

The *Hamilton Spectator* lay spread out on a desk in one of the empty classrooms. Mary circled a few advertisements that interested her. One ad for a dressmaker—*Sure and I could do that*—another for a medical secretary—*better stay away from doctors for a while.* A smattering of ads for teachers. *Hmm… maybe.* And one for a secretary to an architect, which offered accommodation. *That one sounds promising. No need to search for a room.* She'd call the telephone number tomorrow.

The next morning Mary woke early, knelt beside her bed and said a quick prayer, adding, *Please Lord, help me find a good job.* She rose and went downstairs.

She approached Mother Superior's office and rapped on the door.

"Enter," a voice said from within.

Mary stepped inside and stood near the door with her hands behind her back. "May I use your telephone, Mother? I need to call about a position."

The nun looked up from her writing. "Oh, it's you Mary," she said rising "Certainly. And what kind of position would it be?" she asked.

"A secretarial one." She handed the newspaper with the job circled and the telephone number underlined.

"I see, the employer is offering accommodation also." The nun frowned and cleared her throat. "Do you think that is wise? A young woman can't be too careful, you know."

Mary hesitated for a moment. "We'll have to see about it first, I think." If Mother Superior only knew what she had been through with men, she'd realize that there was no need to warn her to be careful. The nun left the room, and Mary sat at her desk with pencil and paper. She dialed the number in the ad.

"Ted Martin speaking," the man answered.

"I'm calling about the ad in the newspaper for a secretary. My name is Mary Ryan, and I wondered if I might see you for an interview."

"You may, Miss. Ryan."

She received instructions to his home on North Shore Boulevard, thanked him, and hung up. She felt a surge of excitement and hopefulness, and began to sing.

***

Aldershot, (Burlington area) Ontario

"Tell me, Mary, do you have experience being a secretary?" Mr. Martin asked. They sat in his elegant library, which doubled as an office. The walls were panelled with a rich mahogany. His desk looked as if eight could be seated for dinner. Books lined the bookcases, and long rolls of architectural paper lay on his desk. The ad in the newspaper mentioned he was an architect. Mary assumed the rolls were blueprints.

"I have, Mr. Martin, several years of it working for various employers."

"And where did you go to school?" He lifted a glass which was standing on his desk and took a sip of water. He leaned forward, picked up a pencil and held it poised over a piece of paper. He stared directly at Mary and waited for an answer.

"Shaw's Business School in Toronto," Mary answered. *Oh dear.* She hoped he didn't ask too many questions. She must keep the past dark for her own protection. It would mean more deceit, but it had to be.

"Indeed, I've heard of it. Seems to be a good school. Some of my colleagues have secretaries from Shaw. What did you study there?"

Mary spoke with confidence, although she didn't feel much of it. She hadn't worked for some time, and although she had kept up her typing and shorthand, she still felt apprehensive. "Typing, shorthand, and bookkeeping. Also, composition of business letters," she replied.

"And your employers, what kind of businesses were they in?"

Perspiration began to trickle down her sides. *Dear me, here it comes.* She hoped he didn't want names, but she guessed there were a couple she could give him. Mary leaned forward in her chair, hands clenched in her lap. "Mr. Howard was an engineer, and an executive of the Superior Railway, and then Dr. Tricklebank, a family doctor." She held her breath for a few seconds hoping that would be enough. She was relieved she didn't have to lie about them.

Mr. Martin wrote as she spoke. He stopped and looked at Mary. "Do you have any letters of recommendation?"

She thought about the letter Mr. Henry gave her to take to Mr. Howard. She wished she had a copy of it now. "I did have one. I gave it to Mr. Howard, but he was taken by the Spanish Flu some time ago. I didn't think to ask for one from Dr. Tricklebank."

"I see..." Mr. Martin averted his eyes and looked out the window for a moment. A magnificent white and pink magnolia tree stood a few feet from the library window. It was in full bloom. He seemed to study it for a moment. Then he turned to her. "Just a few more questions, Mrs. Ryan. How is it you're applying for a position in Burlington, when you were working in Toronto?"

Mary crossed her fingers and ankles, preparing to tell a whopper. "A friend of mine lives in the Burlington area. She invited me to come and stay with her when my husband was run over by an automobile and went to hospital."

"Oh, I'm sorry to hear that, Mrs. Ryan."

"Thank you, sir. Well, when he left hospital, he went out to celebrate. I think he may have had one too many and wasn't looking where he was going. He was hit by a tram and died."

"Good Lord, what a tragedy!" Mr. Martin said with a stunned expression.

"Oh, it was a terrible time, sir, and I was left alone with a small child to rear," she said with a silent 'whew' under her breath. She watched for his reaction. Was the lie going to pass muster?

Mr. Martin leaned forward in his chair. His brow crimpled. "You really have had a rough time of it, young lady. How long ago did this happen?"

Mary lowered her head and nodded. "My misfortune began three years ago," she said, raising her head. At least now she could tell the truth about this last question.

Mr. Martin smiled as he pushed away from his desk and rose. "How soon could you start?"

Mary picked up the signal and rose also. "In one week's time, if that suits you, sir."

He nodded. "Now, about the accommodation. Please follow me," he said strolling toward the door.

"There's a small house down the hill, not too far from the entrance to the property. It used to be the groundskeeper's, but now I have a company come to tend the landscaping. You could use it if you like. I'll take you to see it now."

They walked across the manicured lawn, which was lush and green with a trace of dampness. The green blades brushed across Mary's ankles and tickled. As they neared the house, Mr. Martin produced a long, silver key from his pocket. A few seconds later they stepped into a small, wallpapered foyer. The paper was heavily patterned with colours of rich brown, cream and burgundy.

"We've cleared it out, and cleaned it. Did a bit of decoration, and added some furniture. I hope you find it suitable."

"Oh, Mr. Martin, this will do very nicely," she said as her eyes swept over a large room. It had a few pieces of white wicker furniture and an old green velour chesterfield. Mary followed Mr. Martin through the living room and into a small kitchen at the far end of the main room. Then a few steps back to the living room, and down a short hallway off to the left. One bedroom and a bathroom completed the house.

"Well, Mary, that's it. You'll need a few things of your own, but then it should be comfortable enough for you," he said looking at her with an expectant expression. "You have the job, if you want it."

Mary's face lit up. She visualized chintz curtains on the kitchen window and a small carpet in front of the chesterfield.

"I do. Thank you so much, Mr. Martin. It's more than I could ask for."

On her way back to the convent, Mary pedaled her bicycle at twice the speed. She could barely wait to begin packing and tell Mother Superior about Mr. Martin and that there was nothing to fear. Mary just had a sixth sense about him.

CHAPTER 36

Spring, 1939

The years passed by like the scenery on a fast-moving train. Mary's job with Mr. Martin could not have worked out better. She found him pleasant and not hard to please.

As she had no rent to pay, she saved a large part of her salary and bought herself a second-hand automobile: a black, 1931 Ford Auburn for $510. Of course, she still sent money to the convent for her daughter's support. But that would be ending soon. Hope would be coming to live with her full-time.

Mary had just entered the Martin residence to begin her day's work when Mr. Martin asked her to step into his office. "Mary would you please deliver these blueprints for me? Here's the name and address I want them to go to," he said, as he handed over the plans and a separate piece of paper with the address.

"Certainly, Mr. Martin," Mary replied.

"Do you know where the street is?" he asked.

"I believe so. It's across from First Street, not too far from the lake."

"That's right."

The bright sun made her squint as she left the house. A cool breeze blew in from the north and she enjoyed the freshness of it as it swept across her face. The client's house was a mile or two from the Martin home.

Mary parked in front of the house on Balmoral Avenue. She stood on the sidewalk for a few seconds and admired the large house. Clad in pale yellow and brown bricks, it rose two storeys and appeared higher because it was on an elevated piece of land. Green sprouts poked up from the charcoal soil and a large, orange-breasted robin hopped along the neat lawn as Mary walked to the entrance. A large Silver Maple tree shaded the front of the house.

She pressed a white ceramic buzzer. The door opened, and a lean man in his mid-forties stood in the doorway. "I have some plans for Mr. Tipley. Is he home?"

He nodded. "I'm David Tipley."

Mary wondered why he just kept staring, seemingly amused. She extended her arm with the tubes. "Mr. Martin asked me to give these to you."

He didn't look at the tubes in Mary's hand. His eyes were riveted on her. They were sparkling blue, like the sea with the sun shining on it. They were made all the more attractive by his fair skin and black wavy hair—like she'd seen in Ireland many times.

Finally, Mr. Tipley took the plans. "Thank you very much. And what might your name be?"

His stare made her nervous, and she stuttered as she said her name. "Mary..., it's Mary. I'm Mr. Martin's secretary." She felt a flash of heat on her face. "I have to be on my way now. Well, good day, Mr. Tipley."

Mary turned and held the black railing surrounding the porch and descended as fast as she could. She didn't like what she felt. She remembered another time when she first cast eyes on Paul Kennedy, and she knew how that turned out.

Mary hit the bottom step and was about to hurry down the front walk, when she heard, "Wait—wait a moment please."

She turned on her heel and looked back.

"It's quite chilly today," David Tipley said. "Won't you come in and have a hot drink before you start back?" He beckoned and stood sideways in the entrance.

As much as she felt attracted to him, she couldn't go inside. They might be alone in the house and she would be vulnerable. No, she couldn't—too dangerous. Although her assault was in the distant past, it had left searing scars. "I have a vehicle, and I don't have far to go. Thank you for your concern." In spite of her fear, she couldn't help adding, "Perhaps another time," as she walked away.

***

A few weeks later, David Tipley arrived at Mr. Martin's home. Mary sat working inside when the doorbell rang. Mr. Martin had left the house a short while earlier to go to the pharmacy to pick up some medication for his wife, Elaine. She was asleep upstairs, so Mary answered the door.

"Hello, Mary," he said, his face breaking into a grin. "What a pleasant surprise. I have some building specifications for Ted. May I come in?" he said, putting one foot on the threshold.

Mary's heart gave a little flip-flop. "Certainly, come in." She'd be all right. Mrs. Martin slept upstairs, and Mr. Martin would be home soon. She stepped aside and opened the door wide. Cold air whooshed in, and she closed the door quickly.

"Mr. Martin will be home in a little while. Would you like to wait in the library? Or you can leave them with me, and I'll give them to him." She held out her hand.

David pressed the large manila envelope close to his chest. "I would like to wait, if you don't mind. Some of the specs need a short explanation."

Mary's hand dropped to her side. "The library's this way," she said, turning.

David picked a green wingback chair near the window. "May I get you a cup of tea, or coffee—perhaps water, while you wait?" Mary felt pleased he had decided to

213

come in. In spite of her apprehension, she enjoyed his company.

They chatted a bit about the weather, and then David said, "Do you enjoy the pictures, Mary?"

She nodded.

"I'm planning on going next week. There's a great musical starring Ginger Rogers and Fred Astair playing at the Hume theatre. It's called *Top Hat*. Would you like to go with me and see it one evening?"

She fell silent for a few moments, thinking, *I guess a movie would be all right.* "When would you like to take me?"

"How does next Friday night sound?"

Mary couldn't help but notice how delighted he seemed. She felt flattered. She'd kept her guard up ever since that awful day. Now she believed she could let it down a little. Her shoulders relaxed. *He seems like a decent sort, and we're going to a public place. I'll be safe.*

***

After a few more dates, Mary began to trust David. They still went to the movies, but now there were church dances and some picnics in LaSalle Park during the warm months. Sometimes they would meet at the library. They both loved Agatha Christie novels and would take out several. *Murder on the Orient Express* was one of their favourites.

The July sun shone on them as they picnicked in the park. Mary guessed she would not be rejected if she told David about her daughter Hope.

David stretched out on Mary's blanket. He lay on his side with his hand supporting the side of his head. Mary sat sideways with her legs bent under her. A soft breeze blew a few strands of auburn hair across her face.

"David, I have something important to tell you." Her voice quivered—not so much because she was going to tell

David about her daughter, but because she would have to lie again about how the pregnancy occurred. She could not bring herself to reveal the truth.

"I have a child, a daughter." She pressed her hand down firmly on the blanket and waited for his reaction.

David sat upright, a look of astonishment on his face. "A child—" Slowly, a smile slipped across his face as he waited for Mary to continue.

"After the baby arrived, and with my husband dead from an accident, I came to Burlington to live with a friend." Careful, she must tell the same story as the one she'd told Mr. Martin. Who knows? One day the topic might come up in a casual conversation between the two men.

David leaned toward her and took her hand, "You've had a rough time of it these last few years, darling."

Mary took a deep breath, and said, "There's more. My daughter lives at the school she attends. I bring her home most weekends. You've probably noticed on weekends when you've asked me out, I've always given the excuse that I had work to do. But that's not true."

David listened intently and took her face in his hands. "It's all right, Mary. It doesn't make any difference to how I feel about you. I'd very much like to meet your daughter. The three of us could do things together. It would be fun."

"Really, you don't mind?" she asked, delighted. Smiling, he shook his head. She flung her arms around him and kissed the side of his face.

***

Mary shared the Catholic faith with David, and some Sundays the three of them would attend church. It was a satisfying time for Mary, and she began to believe that the effects of her sexual trauma were behind her. Until one night.

David had always been respectful, had never tried to take liberties with her. Oh, a sweet kiss goodnight and that was all, until one evening after the movies. He had just parked his Ford in front of her cottage. They heard King, Mr. Martin's German shepherd barking, as David's tires scrunched the pebbles on the driveway.

"Well, King knows a strange vehicle and person are nearby," Mary said smiling. "Funny how he doesn't bark when it's my car, but I've noticed he does when we're in your car. Smart dog, eh?"

"They are quite intelligent, that's why the police use them a lot," David said. "I've read that they have the intelligence of a seven-year-old child. Fancy that."

"And his sense of smell is at least fifteen times greater than ours. So, I guess he knows the scent of my car and that of yours," Mary said, proudly. "I love that dog."

David got out of the car and walked around to the other side to open the door for Mary. He took her hand as they approached the bungalow. Mary stood on the threshold and turned to David. "Thank you very much. It was a wonderful picture. Cary Grant and Irene Dunne were hilarious. It certainly was *The Awful Truth.*" She hesitated for a moment, wondering whether she should invite him in. David stood very close to her. She could smell the woody scent of his aftershave lotion.

"May I come in for a moment, Mary? I have something important I want to discuss." His voice became slightly hoarse, and he seemed to speak with a nervous hesitation.

"Alright, but just for a few minutes. I'd like to get to bed soon. I've had a long day and I have to rise early."

They entered Mary's bungalow, and she hung her coat in the foyer closet. She did not ask for his coat.

"Come, let's sit in the living room," she said, leading the way to the couch.

When they were both seated, David looked directly at her and said, "We've been seeing each other for several months now, Mary, and I've been in love with you for almost that long. I haven't pressured you because I sensed reluctance on your part about getting too involved. But now marriage is on my mind." With that he pulled her close and kissed her with such intensity that she drew back and gasped. This was not a sweet kiss, but one full of passion. He began kissing her neck.

Mary placed her hands on his shoulders and pushed him back. She had a flashback of another time when a man was kissing her with such abandon, and a sick feeling began in the pit of her stomach. Breathless, she gulped out, "I can't do this, David. I'm sorry."

He sat back with a stunned look. "Why, Mary? What's wrong?"

"I...I just can't do this. I can't." Her eyes welled up. "I had a terrifying experience with a man a long time ago. I thought I was over it, but apparently not." She looked at David's wounded face, and she teared up. She did care for him, but this was more than she could bear. Over the years, Mary had a few romantic encounters, but they all ended the same way. As soon as the relationships progressed and became more intense, she backed away and ended them. But she thought this one was different.

Although she trusted David, she just couldn't go any further, not just now. She wanted to—desperately—but the fear overcame her desire. Fear that she couldn't enjoy a sexual relationship once they were married. And fear that David would leave her someday if she couldn't get over her fear of sex. "I'm sorry David, but you'll have to leave," she said rising from the chesterfield.

David stood up and took Mary's hand. "I'll help you get over this, Mary. We can see someone who's an expert in these matters and we'll work it out."

Mary looked at David with doubt in her eyes. She knew he could see it too. "Perhaps later, dear. I'm not ready for it just now. I think we shouldn't see each other for a while. I need time to think about this. Just for now—don't try to get in touch with me. I need to be alone. I'm sorry. I know this hurts you dear, but it has to be this way."

Sadness and disappointment creased his face as he said, "All right, darling, if that's what you want." He squeezed her hand and left.

Mary felt heavy-hearted as she closed the door behind David, and she had a sinking feeling she might not see him again.

CHAPTER 37

Burlington, Ontario, 2000

Roy Selby parked his Ford in the driveway on Locust Street. His dad had hired the next door neighbour's son, Brian, to shovel the driveway and walkway whenever it snowed. With irregular working hours, Selby had no time for household chores. Now the snow lay in neat rows on either side of the walk. He hurried to the front door. The cold weather nipped his nose and cheeks. Inside, he stamped his boots on an all-weather rug. "Dad, I'm home." *Odd, no odour of food cooking.* "Dad...Dad?" Silence. His father's balance had not been good lately, and he hoped he hadn't fallen. A small knot began to form between his shoulder blades.

Walking into the kitchen, his eyes swept the room. The basement door was ajar. He swallowed hard and strode toward the stairs. "Dad...Dad are you down there?"

A muffled response emerged from the basement. The light was on, and Roy could see his father bent over into a large cardboard barrel. Doug's head and the upper part of his body was buried inside the container. Selby hit the first step running. "Dad!"

His father emerged from the barrel with a wide grin. "Got 'em."

"Whew. You scared the crap out of me when you didn't answer, and you weren't in the kitchen. I thought you had fallen or something."

Doug took a few wobbly steps toward his son clutching several black notebooks. "I guess I wasn't a very good cop. I forgot to hand in all my notebooks." He chuckled as he took his son's arm.

CHAPTER 38

Aldershot (Burlington area), October 1939

A few weeks had passed since Mary had last seen David. She sat at her desk in Mr. Martin's home, typing, trying to concentrate, but her final conversation with David kept running through her head. She could picture his face—puzzled, sad, and hurt like she'd stuck a knife into his heart when she rejected his advances and offer of marriage.

"You're very quiet today, Mary," Ted Martin said. He stood beside her desk and looked at her while she typed. "Anything wrong?" The keys just kept clicking. "Mary?"

Suddenly she stopped and looked up. "I'm sorry, Mr. Martin, what did you say?"

"I was just asking if you were all right. You've been unusually quiet today."

Mary's eyes turned toward the window and saw the fallen oak leaves. They were brown and crispy, like they had been fried by the sun. Her eyes shifted back to her employer. "No, No, I'm quite well. Just a bit sad to see summer go," she lied.

"Some fresh air would probably do you good, Mary. I have an errand for you to do in downtown Hamilton. A client wants some drawings in a rush. Would you deliver them for me?"

Mary rose and nodded. "And you're probably right about the fresh air. I'll get my coat."

***

As Mary strolled along James Street in Hamilton, she stopped every now and then to look into the store windows. They displayed red and green Christmas decorations. A large and fully decorated tree with blue and white bulbs and gold ribbon had been placed in a large window. The blue lights on the tree shone onto happy and expectant faces.

She sighed. *So soon. I'll have to start thinking about a Christmas present for Hope.* She pivoted and started in the direction of the parking lot, when she saw a frightening, familiar face striding toward her. She could see sparks of recognition in his steel-grey eyes. They widened with surprise. He did a double-take. She stopped abruptly and the woman behind her bumped past. Mary froze for an instant in front of Robinson's Department Store.

Holy Mary, Mother of God, it's him! With the speed of a rabbit, she ducked into Robinson's. She pushed by and dodged shoppers with an "Excuse me, excuse me." A woman turned toward her and frowned.

She'd been in the store before and used a ladies' room on the second floor. She found the escalator and flew onto it like a startled bird. Her heart hammered. She thought bystanders could hear it. Her breathing slowed to almost normal when she saw the washroom just in front of her.

Dear Lord, how did he find me? Was it just a chance meeting? No matter, he knew now she lived in the area, and that could be dangerous. She would have to move. Her sweaty palm left an imprint on the brass plate of the washroom door as she dashed inside.

A pleasant, plump woman worked inside the washroom, mopping up around the sinks. Her skin shone like polished ebony. She glanced over her shoulder when she heard footsteps. The woman wadded the paper towel and trudged toward the wastebasket.

Mary stood near it, her face pale like fresh fallen snow.

"Could I help you, Miss? You don't look well. Maybe an aspirin, or something else?" the woman asked.

"Just some water, thank you." Her breathing hadn't found a resting place yet. Mary collapsed into an upholstered chair in the corner. The attendant returned carrying a cone-shaped paper cup of water. Mary took it from her and drained it. "Thank you, I'll be alright now. You're very kind. I'll just rest here for a while," she said and pressed a coin into the woman's hand.

"Thank you," the hard-working woman said, and smiled as she dropped the coin into her grey uniform pocket.

Fifteen minutes later Mary left the washroom, found another escalator, and exited the store. She'd left her automobile on the lot next to the store, so she didn't have a long walk. She kept looking behind, but she didn't see him again. Relieved, she spotted her car and dashed to it. She shoved the key into the ignition so forcefully that her fingernails hit the steering column and some of them broke. She drove slowly until she was off the parking lot and then tramped on the gas. It took Mary a lot less time to get back to her home on North Shore Boulevard than it had taken her to get to Hamilton earlier.

Once inside her house Mary took a deep breath and sank down on the sofa. *Well, that's it. I'll have to move.* She'd give notice to Mr. Martin tomorrow and say her sister in the United States was terminally ill and needed her help. She'd pick up Hope in a couple of days and they would leave together. Perhaps Oakville. No… too close. She'd think of someplace else. With a plan in mind, some of the tension and fear left her body and she began packing.

***

The stunned man stood on the street for a moment overcoming his surprise. He craned his neck and saw Mary duck into Robinson's Department Store. He hurried into the store. Once inside he could feel the adrenaline pumping through his arteries as he looked to the left and to the right. No sign of her. Shoppers crowded the store, and there was a din of voices between customers and salespeople. Pushing his way through the crowd, he scanned the main floor. Damn! He'd lost her. And he didn't think he'd ever find her in this crowd. It'd be like looking for a four-leaf clover in a field of three-leaf clovers. The frustration gradually left him as he experienced a tinge of satisfaction knowing Mary lived in the Hamilton area. A shadow of a smile crossed his face. He'd find her.

A *No Parking* sign had been placed outside Robinson's. So he couldn't bring his Buick to the front of the store and watch the doors leading in and out. Besides, the store had more than one exit. He strolled back to his Buick in the parking lot next to the store. Instead of starting the car right away, he lit a Players cigarette. His fingers shook. It had given him quite a start when he saw her. Excitement pulsated through him now as he wondered what to do next.

Finally, he finished his cigarette and jammed the key into the ignition. Might as well call it a day. He'd begin to investigate tomorrow. A woman hurrying across the parking lot caught his eye. Incredible! He couldn't believe his good luck. It was Mary. Scrunching down in his seat he raised his collar and watched. Unknowingly, he'd parked just a few cars away from her. Shaking fingers tugged his fedora down.

A pencil and pad lay on the dashboard. He scribbled down her licence plate number as her vehicle passed by. He could get her name and address from the licence number from the Motor Vehicle Registration, or he could follow her now.

Easing his car out from the parking space he followed, keeping several yards behind. *Don't get too close,* he cautioned himself.

Mary sped along the Queen Elizabeth Way, going east. If she didn't slow down, the police might stop her for speeding, and he could lose her. He let a black Chevrolet get between them, in case she looked in her rear view mirror. He stayed a short distance behind the Chev, though, with his eyes glued to her vehicle as she moved over to an exit lane. Now two cars behind, he followed onto the cut-off. Eventually they ended up on North Shore Boulevard in Aldershot. She slowed down. There weren't too many vehicles on the street. Her view in the rear vision mirror would be unobstructed, so he dropped further behind, even pulling over a few times so he wouldn't catch up.

After driving a short distance along the road, she braked and turned into a driveway. He waited a minute or two before creeping up to the entrance where she had exited. Surreptitiously, he peered up the driveway and saw Mary's vehicle parked beside a small bungalow. The bungalow was off to the side of the main road, which led up to a much larger home. The Tudor estate sat on elevated land with brown wooden slats over white stucco. He sat there for a few minutes, his mind churning.

Should he approach her now or wait for another time? No...Not now. *Night-time would be the best time.* Also, he wanted to observe her comings and goings for a few days to ascertain if anyone else lived in the bungalow. And it would give her time to feel secure again. *Yes, next week would be soon enough.* After all, he'd given up hope of ever finding her, so what was another few days?

CHAPTER 39

Three times last week, he parked his vehicle close to a wooded area about 50 yards to the side of Mary's house. At dusk, the man would creep close to the edge of the woods, lay down and spy on her. If anyone else lived there, he saw none.

Now here he was, one week later. A gentle mist covered his windshield. He opened the window a fraction. Dampness crept in. Nine p.m. *Dark now.*

Gravel crunched under his wheels as he took the fork in the road to her bungalow. A cedar hedge ran along the near side of her house, its pungent scent floated into the automobile. He parked behind the hedge where the car wouldn't be seen from the Tudor mansion behind her house. The stalker gave a gentle rap on the door, and Mary opened it a crack.

Quickly he jammed his foot into the opening and said, "It's all right, Mary. I just want to speak with you for a little while."

She tried to shove the door closed. When it wouldn't close the fear in her eyes gave him pleasure.

"What are you doing here? I don't want to see you. Go away."

He could hear the tremor in her voice. It delighted him. With a smile, his voice lowered to a soft whisper. "I told you I just want to talk to you for a little while."

"No, leave!"

She surprised him with the amount of strength she exerted trying to close the door. He could feel a painful pressure on his foot.

"I will, and I won't return, if you'll just give me five minutes."

She hesitated, as if weighing his words. "Five minutes, just five minutes then," she said as she relaxed her hand on the door.

In an instant he leaned his shoulder against the door and pushed his way in. His eyes swept around the living room. Across the room a Duncan-Fyfe coffee table stood in front of a cream sofa. He strode across the room and plunked down on the sofa.

On the coffee table in front of him lay a few books— *Gone with the Wind, The Great Gatsby,* and a recent copy of *Reader's Digest.* Sitting there, he got a faint whiff of alcohol. A glass tumbler, half full with an amber liquid, rested on a coaster at one end of the table. An empty crystal candy bowl sparkled beside the glass. The small brown radio on a side table played the soft strains of "They Can't Take that Away from Me."

Mary remained standing, hands on her hips, her eyes narrowed. "Wait just a minute. I didn't say you could sit down!"

He didn't answer, but averted his eyes and jerked his head sideways toward a brown leather suitcase half full, resting on a chair beside a hallway. Brown shoes jutted out from it. And beside them were what looked like fluffy sweaters, and some soft pink items that looked like lingerie. When his focus shifted back to Mary, her eyes were riveted on him.

"Going somewhere, Mary?"

"I...I just returned from a weekend trip and haven't had time to finish unpacking," she said nodding in the direction of the suitcase. She spoke quickly with her eyes averted.

He guessed she was lying. *Probably going to leave town before I could find her.*

"Tell me why you are here?" Mary asked. She did not smile and remained standing several feet away from him. "Well?"

He patted the cushion beside him. "Come sit beside me and tell me, did you have the child?"

Mary did not move, just nodded.

"Where is the child now?" he asked. Just then, something that sounded like a kettle singing caught his attention.

Mary swung around and disappeared for a few moments into a small kitchen at the end of the large living room. He could see half of it from where he sat. A small pop could be heard and a whiff of gas entered the living room. In a few seconds she came back and sat at the far end of the sofa near her glass. She reached across the table and took a large gulp from it and smoothed her skirt. He could see white knuckles as she clasped the glass.

"I put the child up for adoption soon after it was born."

He sat sideways on the couch, his eyes roving over her face and body. "Was it a boy or girl?"

"It was one or the other," she said tight-lipped.

"Do you know who adopted the baby?" he asked.

"The authorities don't tell you such things," she said in a sharp tone. "Well, that's it then, if that's what you came to find out."

He looked at her set jaw as she pushed her shoulders back. Clearly he was not going to get any more information from her. *Liar*, he thought. Maybe she did have the child adopted out, but he doubted it. In any case it won't matter after tonight. Probably the child doesn't know anything about their past association anyway, he surmised.

The ice cube in Mary's glass had melted, as she took another gulp of her drink and said, "Now, it's time for you to go."

Standing, the intruder unbuttoned his jacket. "May I use your washroom before I leave?"

"Just down the hall, second door on your right, and then I'll be saying goodbye."

Once inside the washroom, he contemplated his image in the bathroom mirror. His full lips curved at the corners in a sadistic grin. The dark brush above his upper lip, clipped with precision, pleased him.

He snatched a piece of tissue and pressed it down over the toilet handle. The sound of gushing water completed the impression he wanted to make. Next he held the tissue over the tap handle and ran some water for a few seconds. He withdrew a black snake-skin belt from around his waist, and wrapped it around one hand and put it in his pocket. Small and out of sight, just right, he almost laughed out loud at his pun. A few seconds later he returned to the living room.

Mary perched on the edge of the sofa like a bird ready to take flight. He pointed to a picture on the wall behind her. "That's a lovely picture. It's a Renoir print, isn't it? May I have a closer look?"

Without waiting for an answer, he sidled behind the couch. Mary did not turn around or look up—just nodded, and took another long swallow from her glass and replaced it on the table. Her fingerprints smudged on the cold glass.

The man glanced at the picture for a second, then whirled around and withdrew his hand from his pocket with the belt wrapped around it. In a split second he twisted the loose end around the other hand, and pulled it taut. Sweat made the belt slippery as he clutched it, like a seagull holding a fish in its closed talons.

Mary tilted her head to the side and said, "It's time for you to be off and…"

Lunging forward, he swung the belt over her head, straightened and squeezed back. It was done in one smooth action. She sputtered and struggled, trying to get her fingers under the belt as it dug into her flesh.

He thought he heard her say a word which sounded like 'ope', then nothing. His grasp held firm for a few minutes until he felt her body go slack, like a balloon with the air let out. Perspiration beaded on his brow. A few droplets caught in the hair on the sides of his face. He replaced the belt around his waist. His breath came fast and hard. Surprised at her strength, she'd fought for longer than expected. Now, it was over.

***

The killer lounged at one end of the sofa, a cigarette dangling from his fingers. Leaning back, he took a puff, tilted his head, and blew a few smoke rings into the air. As he watched the rings dissipate, he felt peaceful. Killing was easier than he'd imagined.

There was a window at the side of Mary's house. He sauntered over to it, pulled back the lace curtain and observed the mansion across the lawn. Most of the lights in the house had been snuffed out. *Getting ready for bed. It won't be long now.* A thrill ran through him. Only a pinprick of light burned through the mist from a fixture that hung over the front door.

The killer decided to wait a little while longer just to be sure no one remained up and about, and then he would bundle her up and toss her into the Buick trunk. He strolled back to the sofa and picked up the *Reader's Digest* from the coffee table and began browsing through it.

After a while, he tossed the magazine aside and looked at Mary. She lay sprawled at the other end of the sofa, her green eyes open, with a frantic expression in them as she stared unseeing into space. Miniscule red dots were visible now in the white of her eyes. He wondered what they were and if they had been there before. If so, he hadn't noticed them. He stretched over her slim frame and with a manicured thumb, pressed her lids shut. Her reddish eyelashes fell like a fringe on her milk-white skin. One limp arm hung down the side of the couch. She was even more beautiful than he remembered. He cocked his head as he peered down at her. His lips curled. *Pity, but she had to go. As long as she remained alive, she would be a threat.*

Too soon to leave, he flicked his Ronson and lit another Players. His thoughts drifted back in time to fifteen years earlier. Mary was a bright young woman then, and she must have known it would be dangerous for her to remain in Toronto. And just like the wave of a magician's wand, she'd vanished. He'd tried everything in his power to find her.

He went to her rooming house. A woman with curlers in her salt and pepper hair cautiously opened the door. "State your business Mister—and if you're sellin' anythin', I'm not buyin,'" she said.

He pressed splayed fingers on the door jam and held it open. "I'm looking for Mary Flynn. I have some typing for her. Do you know where she is?"

The woman eyes narrowed. "She ain't in any trouble is she?"

"No, no, nothing like that. I just need to find her. I have some work for her."

"Mary was a nice girl, she was. Always prompt with the rent and never made no trouble, always polite. And oh, that lovely red hair." She touched her head. "One day she just paid her rent, up and left. Only God knows where she is." And with that, she shoved the door shut.

He'd hired a private detective, who traced her to the Parkdale train station at the foot of Roncesvalles Avenue. The C.N.R. ticket clerk remembered her from his description. "Nervous Nelly she was," the clerk said, "with a suitcase almost bigger than her." But he couldn't remember which train she took.

***

Then last week, after fifteen years had passed, to his amazement, he'd come face to face with her on James Street in Hamilton. He slapped his knee, lifted his arms over his head, stretched backward, and pushed himself up from the sofa. A sigh escaped his lips. *Time to stop reminiscing and get to work.*

A shaft of light from the washroom illuminated the hallway. It lit the bedroom across from it. He strolled in and for a few seconds stood there, his eyes roving around the room. They fell on a dark blanket folded at the end of her bed with another dark knitted garment lying on top. He snatched them up, took them to the living room and placed the dark blanket on the floor, then the black knitted triangle on top.

He rose and studied Mary on the sofa. Her head drooped forward onto her chest, and her feet were slanted sideways on the maple syrup coloured floor. A graceful left arm hung down the front of the sofa. He could see some of her nails were broken. Flecks of blood were under some of them. It looked like she had just fallen asleep. He bent down and slid one arm under her shoulders and the other under her knees. Her head flopped back when he picked her up, and he could see an angry red circle around her neck. A silver chain with a crucifix on it partially rested on the crimson semi-circle. He stood there for a moment contemplating whether to take the chain or not. Should he remove it? *What difference would it make anyway? No one is ever going to see it.* So he left it.

The lightness of her body surprised him. He heard a muffled *bump* as he dropped her onto the coverings, crossed her arms over her breasts and straightened her legs. First, he folded the black knitted garment over her, and then the dark plaid blanket. Last would be the rope in the trunk of his car. He opened the front door with caution and listened. The only sound was an occasional whooshing from a few cars on North Shore Blvd. Stepping outside, the murderer opened the trunk of his vehicle. A loud click sounded. He paused and looked up to the mansion and then down to the road. Nothing. Silence. Everything was going according to plan. He was getting away with it, and no one…no one…would know. He chuckled.

The straw-coloured rope lay coiled like a cobra off to one side of the trunk. A shovel nestled in the corner. He picked up the rope, left the trunk open, and slunk back into the house. It took only a minute or two to wrap the rope around Mary as she lay bundled on the floor. He'd parked only a few feet away from Mary's front door. With Mary flung over his shoulder, he bent and flipped her into the open trunk. The heady scent of the cedars hit his nostrils as he got behind the wheel. Just as he turned onto the fork in the road, a dog barked. He looked sideways. Through the fog and the dim light on the front porch of the main house, the killer could just make out the outline of a man and a dog. The dog seemed to be straining at his leash, barking and looking in his direction. He tramped on the gas pedal.

CHAPTER 40

Burlington, 2000

Roy and his dad sat at the kitchen table. "Before we look at the notebooks, I want to run a couple of things by you," Roy said.

"Alrighty."

"I'd like to speak to Daphne Essex again."

"What about?"

"I want to ask her if Mary would ever let anyone she didn't know into her home."

"What's got that bee in your bonnet?" Doug asked.

"Well, from what you've told me about your investigation of Mary Ryan's disappearance, it didn't appear that anyone local would have a motive. So, I think Mary may have known the killer from the time she lived in Toronto," Roy said.

"Yeah, but where? Toronto's a big city even back in the early 1900s."

"I'm wondering if Mary gave any indication which part of the city she worked and lived in. I'm going to give Mrs. Essex a call and ask if we can see her again," Roy said.

***

A few days later Selby and his dad arrived at the Essex home. Mrs. Essex greeted them warmly. "Nice to see you again, gentlemen. Please come in." Mrs. Essex had prepared tea, coffee, bottled water, and cookies. She led them to the kitchen. Once everyone was settled, Selby began.

"I'm trying to pin down approximately where Mary lived in Toronto. Did she ever mention anything about where she lived?"

Mrs. Essex put her finger to the right side of her head. "Hmm, let me think."

The men watched her and waited patiently.

"I seem to remember Mary mentioned an orphanage nearby, and the lake was not too far from where she lived. And oh, yes, a park where she would walk sometimes. That's about all I can remember just now."

Roy stood and said, "Thanks, Mrs. Essex. I'll work on finding the location."

Mrs. Essex looked at the detective, resignation written on her face, "Oh well, I don't see how it all matters now. Mary's long gone, and whoever killed her, that is, if someone did kill her, she or he is probably dead by now."

Roy Selby smiled at the sweet, wrinkled face, and said, "Well, I guess it's just the detective in me wanting to tie up loose ends."

Doug nodded vigorously. "Me too, Mrs. Essex."

"Before we leave, do you have any idea how Hope and her husband met?" the detective asked.

"I do. When I attended the wedding, I asked her."

"That's right. I remember now, you mentioned it to me at the time. I'd forgotten," Doug said.

"Well," Mrs. Essex continued, "Hope said her mother-in-law, Mrs. Stone senior, was a Patron of the Arts, and she and Wesley attended a performance at Massey Hall. After the performance there was a reception for the audience to meet the cast. Hope was among the cast, and she was introduced to Wesley. Hope told me sparks began to fly between them at the first meeting."

"Did they begin dating right away?" Roy asked.

"I think it was quite soon after. Wesley Stone called the theatre company, and asked if he could leave his telephone number and have Hope call him. She did, and a few days later they started dating."

Doug turned to Roy. "Sounds like love at first sight."

"Thank you, Mrs. Essex," Roy said as he turned and walked toward the front door with his dad following.

***

Once in the car, Doug asked, "Earlier, back at the house, you said there were a couple of things you wanted to discuss. What was the other one?"

"I was thinking about us moving into a condo, Dad. I'm afraid the basement stairs are getting too much for you, and I'm afraid of you falling."

"OK. If that's a worry for you son, I won't go downstairs unless you're home," his dad said.

"Good. I really don't want to move, because if Laura ever comes home, I want us to be here for her. I was just fearful of you falling when you went down to the basement. We'll stay here."

Roy coughed. "And one more thing—I've been thinking of marrying again."

"What?"

CHAPTER 41

Aldershot (Burlington area), 1939

The killer had chosen a burial ground for Mary when he'd spied on her the previous week—some kind of park down the road that had fallen into disuse. A gentle rain patted on his windshield as he drove. There was no other car on the road at that time of night as the area was sparsely populated. Then he saw it: a black and white sign that was tilted sideways. The faded paint said *LaSalle Park*.

The entrance was mostly obscured by trees, some leaning precariously, and tangled bushes mixed in with long grass commented on its disuse. He'd driven about a mile down the road from Mary's house. The rain stopped as he entered the park. The moon came out and shone on the darkened remains of a burnt-out structure.

The beam from the headlights of the 1938 Buick shone on the area. Late fall, and the pungent scent of burning leaves hung on the cool night air. The park stood on a bank overlooking Lake Ontario. The gentle lapping of waves against the shore could be heard. Stillness hung in the air. Because the area was so deserted, he felt no fear of being discovered. Only peace, now that Mary would no longer be a threat.

He parked behind the brambles near the entrance, got out of his car, and walked behind it. The killer opened the trunk, picked up Mary, and slung her over his shoulder. He walked toward the shrubbery and dropped her on the ground near it. Returning to the car he retrieved the shovel. Hurrying now, he dug a grave, close to encroaching bramble bushes and a short distance away from an oak tree. It took him 20 minutes to dig down a few feet, the dark earth softened by the fall rain. He cast the shovel aside. Stooping over, he picked up Mary—slung her over his shoulder and dumped her into the grave. She landed with a thud.

Although the air was cool, he perspired as he strained, lifting the soft soil and covering Mary's crumpled body. A blanket of crisp red, yellow, and brown oak leaves covered the spot. Now he was done. A feeling of satisfaction made him smile. No one would ever know the events of this night, and his secret would be safe.

CHAPTER 42

Burlington, Ontario, 2000

Roy Selby stood behind his dad as they climbed the basement stairs. His father's knuckles shone white as he clutched the railing on the wall. Breathing hard, he walked into the kitchen and dropped the small black pads on the table.

"There's more down there," Doug said, pulling out a chair and plopping down. It took a few moments for him to catch his breath.

"How many, Dad?" Roy asked.

"About three or four. Some might be from different cases though, but we'll have a look-see later," he said.

"I think we'd better get the rest of them now and fit them in. I'll get them. You wait here and start reading."

When Roy returned, two piles of books lay on the table. "I've sorted this pile chronologically. Some are from other cases," he said, pointing to the second pile. "I found six more."

"How could you miss turning in this many books?"

"Well, after 30 years I made a few mistakes. If you average it all out, it really isn't that many."

Roy looked at his dad with eyes wide and eyebrow raised, and then a smile appeared. "Yeah, I guess I made a few too."

His dad picked up the first small, spiral notebook and started flipping the pages. "The first notepad I wrote in on the Ryan case isn't here. I looked already. These notes begin further along in the investigation, but it's all coming back to me now," he said with a sigh.

"Tell me what you remember from the beginning, Dad." He leaned forward in his chair and placed his forearms on the table.

Doug collected his thoughts. He turned his head sideways and gazed out the kitchen window.

Roy followed his father's gaze. It rested on a tall, barren oak tree which grew close to the house.

His father had told him that he planted it years ago when he first began working on the Ryan case.

When his dad looked back to him, Roy could see a faraway look in his eyes as if he were reliving the time.

"I remember like it was yesterday when the call came in," Doug said. "I was writing a report on an investigation. My partner, Senior Detective Sergeant Stan Burkowski, sat across from me in the squad room and answered the call."

***

Burlington, October 1939

"Detective Burkowski speaking," he said picking the call up on the first ring.

"Hello, Detective. This is Ted Martin calling from North Shore Blvd. Would you please send an officer out here? I think we have a missing woman."

As Doug Selby watched, Burkowski pointed at him and to the telephone on Doug's desk. One of the buttons on the phone was lit up. Doug pressed it and lifted the receiver so he could hear the conversation.

"What makes you think she's missing, Mr. Martin?" Burkowski asked.

Ted Martin described the morning to the detective, and added, "This is very unlike her.

"What's your address, Mr. Martin?" Burkowski asked as he fished a small, black notebook and a pen out of a drawer.

"My partner Detective Selby and I will be out this afternoon around one o'clock," he said hanging up the phone. "Got that Doug?"

Douglas Selby, a new detective in his late 20s, hovered around five feet ten and looked as sleek as a greyhound. His brown hair measured a little longer than most officers, but was still within regulation. He'd been assigned to partner with the experienced Burkowski.

Stan Burkowski leaned back in his swivel chair and clasped his hands behind his head. A large man, well over six feet tall, with bulging muscles and hands like ham hocks, he'd been with the department for 25 years plus. Square jaw and wide set blue eyes with a hint of fatigue and scepticism in them.

Douglas Selby admired him. Rough around the edges, but he'd solved a car-load of cases. Burkowski lumbered over to his new partner's desk and slapped the address down.

Doug studied the writing. It looked like chicken scratches. "Would you translate this, Stan?"

Burkowski smirked and snatched the address away. "We'll go over around one o'clock this afternoon," he said. "Probably out with a boyfriend, but who knows."

***

The sun gave off tepid warmth, and dew still clung to the grass in low-lying patches. The detectives located the property on North Shore Blvd. The address stood out in large brass numbers on one of the pillars, at the entrance. A wide, white gravel road ran up to a large Tudor-style house. It perched on a slight elevation. Before the road reached the main house there was a fork in it which led to a small red brick bungalow.

Doug Selby noted the secluded area of the small house and the cedars sheltering the entrance. A person could park beside the house, enter, and not be seen by anyone in the Tudor house. The bungalow nestled in a slight hollow. The entrance faced North Shore Blvd., but blue spruces close to the main road blocked the view of the house. A small forest ran down the east side of both properties. A few white birch trees stood out, intensifying the various shades of the evergreens. Other trees appeared almost black.

As the men approached the entrance, the rhythmic sound of water lapping the shore of Lake Ontario could be heard. Doug made a mental note of the distance between the two houses. If something happened in the bungalow, he didn't think it would be heard in the main house.

Burkowski thumbed the doorbell. Soft melodic chimes sounded and a dog's deep bark followed. The door opened, and a blonde-haired man stood in the doorway with a German shepherd by his side. "Good afternoon," he said.

Burkowski flashed his badge and said, "Detective Sergeant Burkowski, Sir. And this is Detective Selby," he said, tilting his head in Doug's direction.

The dog sniffed the detectives and calmly sat down beside his master. A thin woman hurried out from somewhere in the back of the house and stood beside Mr. Martin. He held the door wide, "This is my wife, Linda, and my dog, King, detectives," Mr. Martin said.

Mrs. Martin lips quivered as she said, "Good day," smiled, and clamped onto her husband's arm. Doug noticed the small white handkerchief bunched up in her hand. He guessed Mrs. Martin depended on her husband for most things. He wondered whether she was just upset about the missing secretary, or if something else was troubling her.

"Come in, come in, gentlemen," Mr. Martin said, stepping aside.

Once they were in the foyer, Mr. Martin and his wife seemed glued to the spot. "May we sit down some place, Mr. Martin?" Burkowski asked.

"Certainly. I'm sorry. I seem to have forgotten my manners. Mary's disappearance has me rattled. Please, come into the study. I'll have our cook bring in some refreshments." The aroma of fresh baked ginger cookies wafted into the foyer.

Doug smiled and opened his mouth to say something, but Burkowski answered quickly, "Thank you, but nothing just now, sir."

When they were all seated in the study, Doug glanced around, taking in the décor. Burgundy leather-bound books stood in the cases lining one wall. Mr. Martin sat at a massive mahogany desk with a green banker's light on it. Original oil and water-colour paintings hung on the far wall. Doug's hobby was oil painting, and he had an appreciation for fine art.

Earlier, the two policemen had arranged between themselves that Burkowski, being the senior detective, would ask the questions, and Doug would take notes.

"When you called the station, Mr. Martin, you said you wanted to report a missing person. Who would that be? And why do you think they are missing?" Burkowski asked.

"It's my secretary and assistant, Mary Ryan. She lives in the red brick bungalow you saw coming in. I'm an architect, and I work from home," Mr. Martin said. "Mary comes in every morning at 9:00 a.m. This morning she never arrived. My wife and I thought perhaps she was ill or had slept in, so we went over to the bungalow. I have an extra key, so when no one answered, I attempted to use it, but the door wasn't locked."

Burkowski took a quick breath before he asked, "Did you touch anything?"

Just then a middle-aged, portly woman entered the room carrying a large silver tray with coffee, tea, and cookies. She wore a starched, white apron.

"Just leave it over there, Jane," Mr. Martin said, as he waved his hand toward a credenza on the other side of the room.

"No, we didn't. We found the cottage deserted and everything neat and tidy, except the coffee table," Ted replied. "Linda and I were puzzled though, because Mary's car remained beside her house."

Linda Martin rose from her chair. "Excuse me gentlemen I'm going to pour myself a cup of tea."

Doug turned and watched her take small dainty steps across the room. Attractive in a delicate sort of way, but he sensed she was not well, very pale and thin.

"Mary is a fastidious person, Detective Burkowski. Always kept herself and her surroundings in immaculate order, as she did with her work," Mr. Martin added. "She didn't require much supervision. Made decisions on her own as to what had to be done."

Doug continued to take notes and looked up at the Martins whenever Burkowski asked a question.

"So, it was out of character for her not to show up for work or telephone in sick? That's why you called and reported her missing?"

The Martins nodded in agreement.

"I'd like a physical description of your secretary, Mr. Martin."

"She has short, wavy auburn hair and green eyes. Stands around five feet and a few inches, approximately 120 pounds, in her late 30s, or early 40s. And she has a slight Irish accent." Turning to his wife, he asked, "Does that sound about right, Linda?"

She fiddled with a cameo brooch pinned on the lapel of her stylish suit and nodded in agreement. "It is, I believe."

"Just one more question before we look in the bungalow and around the property, if you don't mind. Did either of you hear or see anything out of the ordinary last night?" Burkowski asked.

"Well...yes. I did see something just as I was about to walk King." The dog, which had been lying on the floor at his master's feet, looked up at Ted, with an expectant look on his face. Doug leaned over and petted him.

"It was around 10:00 p.m., when I saw a dark coloured auto—judging from the outline, I think it may have been a Buick, but I'm not sure. It approached the fork and headed down to the main road. Mary doesn't have many visitors that I know of, and it wasn't her car."

Doug shifted in his chair and turned a page in his notebook.

"Could you see who was in the car?" Burkowski asked.

"Unfortunately, no. It was dark and drizzling. And the only light came from the porch, and the fog didn't help any," Ted Martin answered.

"OK," Burkowski stood up, "that's about it for now. If you'll take us over to the bungalow, we'd like to have a look around and then we'll take a stroll around the grounds."

The three men walked the short distance across the lawn. Once inside the bungalow, Doug noticed a grey ash on the carpet and a few Players cigarette butts squashed in the candy dish on the table. "Was Mrs. Ryan a smoker?" he asked.

Burkowski jerked his head sideways to see what Doug was looking at and shot him a penetrating look. Doug shrugged and mouthed, "What?"

"Not that I know of," Mr. Martin replied.

"Get an envelope, Detective, and pick that up," Burkowski said, nodding toward the ash on the carpet. "And empty the butts in the candy dish too."

Selby retrieved a small brown envelope from the breast pocket of his suit, put his lips close to the envelope and gave a small puff. He scooped up the ash and cigarette butts with the flap of the envelope.

They strolled down the hallway and checked out the bedroom. Doug could see nothing out of order. Bed made, and the rest of the room neat. No clothes lying about. *Too neat.* He didn't think anyone had slept in the bed last night. They returned to the living room.

"Looks like our secretary was going somewhere, or had just arrived back," Burkowski said eying an open suitcase on a chair near the hallway.

"I don't think she'd been away on the weekend. I saw Mary and her daughter getting out of Mary's auto Saturday afternoon when I took King out to do his business."

"Daughter? Tell me about her daughter, Mr. Martin," Burkowski asked.

"I don't know much. Mary is a very private person. All I know is what she told me when I hired her," Ted Martin said.

"What was that?"

"She was a widow, and had a child who stayed with a friend during the week. When Mary first started working for me, which was about twelve or thirteen years ago, I would see a toddler with her on the weekends. Then over the years I saw the child bloom into a lovely teenager," Ted Martin said, smiling.

Linda Martin had sat silently beside her husband listening. Now she broke into the conversation. "Mary called the child Hope," she offered. "We met her one Sunday when all of us were leaving for church at the same time. Mary introduced us to her. At the time she would have been about five years old. Beautiful child! Mirror image of her mother with auburn hair and green eyes." Mrs. Martin had a pleased look on her face. She seemed happy that she could contribute.

"We didn't attend the same church. We're Anglicans and belong to St. Matthews, on Plains Road, and Mary is Catholic, so we didn't see her again that day," Mr. Martin volunteered.

Detective Selby stopped taking notes and glanced at Burkowski, who was rubbing his chin.

Selby jumped into the lull. "Do either of you have an address where Hope stays during the week?"

Burkowski swung his head sideways and frowned at Doug.

The Martins both shook their heads.

"But I know where the daughter goes to school," Linda answered. "When we met Mary and her daughter that Sunday I did ask the child where she went to school. And she said in a convent. The sisters taught her."

"Do you know where the convent is?" Burkowski took the reins again while Doug jotted down the new information.

"Sorry, I don't," Mr. Martin apologized.

"It's OK, we'll find it. Just one more thing. Do you know the name of the church Mary attended?" Burkowski asked.

"It's either Holy Rosary Catholic Church, on Plains Road, or St. John The Baptist, at Pine and Elizabeth Street," Mr. Martin answered.

***

As the detectives drove down to the main road, the wind came up from the lake and gently rocked their car, and there was a low whining in the air. "Well, what do you think Stan?"

Burkowski's brow creased. "It could be just a night out with a boyfriend. Someone was at her house last night, according to Mr. Martin, and she probably left with him seeing as her car is still parked at her home."

Doug had his thumb under his jaw. "I don't think so. I think she was forced to leave by some kind of coercion and taken somewhere. Or, maybe killed in the house, and then brought out and dumped. Maybe the lake. From what we've heard so far, she doesn't sound like the type who would just pick up and leave with someone in the late evening. Then there's the kid."

Burkowski turned onto the main road. "I've seen cases like this before Selby, and the missing person usually turns up in a day or two. Maybe she drinks and is hung over someplace. We'll wait awhile and then check back with the Martins."

***

A couple of days later the telephone rang in the Burlington police station on Elizabeth Street. The desk sergeant picked it up. "Constable Maloney here."

"Hello, this is Mother Superior speaking from St. Theresa's Convent. I would like to speak with a police officer regarding the mother of one of our resident students," she said.

"Hold the line, Sister," the sergeant answered.

After a few clicks, a deep voice said, "Detective Burkowski."

"Detective, this is the Mother Superior at St. Theresa's Convent. The sisters and I are very worried about the mother of one of our students, Mrs. Ryan. The student's name is Hope Ryan, and she's crying all the time and won't eat. Her mother comes every Saturday without fail and takes her daughter out for the weekend."

Burkowski's eyebrows arched. "I just looked up the address of the convent and was about to visit you Mother Superior."

"Oh… why is that?"

"We'll talk about it when we see you."

"I see. It's just that Mrs. Ryan is a very devoted mother and never fails to pick up her daughter. So when she didn't arrive or telephone this weekend, we began to suspect something was amiss. We've tried calling her home, but there's no answer. Everyone is worried something has happened to her. Could you help us?"

"We'll be there in 30 minutes."

Burkowski strode over to Doug's desk where he was bent over examining fingerprints with a large magnifying glass.

The detective clapped him on the shoulder. "Another phone call reporting Mary Ryan missing. Her teenage daughter, who's been stashed away in a convent school, is all keyed up wondering where her mother is. Looks like you might be on to something, Doug. Grab your coat. I said we'd be there soon."

***

As the two detectives left the station, Doug observed the thermometer hanging on the outer wall of the station. 28 degrees. *Winter's almost here.* Both men wore grey fedoras and black winter overcoats.

They found the convent easily. Burkowski gave a slight smile and said, "Looks medieval doesn't it?" Grey stone with dying ivy covered most of the walls, and only weak light escaped the small windows.

Doug shivered and tugged his overcoat tighter around his throat.

Burkowski lifted a large brass knocker, dulled by wind, and pitted by rain and snow. A nun's face appeared behind the small grilled window. Detective Burkowski held up his badge. The heavy oak door creaked opened.

"Detective Burkowski and Detective Selby to see Mother Superior. She's expecting us."

A tiny nun with dark brown owl eyes ushered them in. "Wait here gentlemen. I'll fetch Mother Superior."

A tall, thin nun appeared and said, "Good day, Detectives. Please follow me," as she guided them into a library. The ceiling appeared several feet above average height, and a diffused beam of sun filtered down on them from stained glass windows high up on the south wall.

After introductions, Burkowski spoke. "Tell us how and when you met Mrs. Ryan, Mother Superior."

"Mrs. Ryan's parish priest called us from Toronto and referred her to us. She arrived at our convent approximately fifteen years ago. She had gotten into trouble and needed help, so Father O'Neill told me." Mother Superior said. "Many of our girls are expecting when they arrive. They need shelter and assistance."

Again, Doug took notes, occasionally looking up at Mother Superior. There was something about her that reminded him of a principal he'd once had. Middle-aged, tissue-paper white skin and the palest blue-grey eyes— almost no colour. He perceived an inner toughness. Outwardly, she seemed calm and direct. He sensed no prejudice from the nun regarding Mary's condition when she arrived.

"And the father of the child—what did she say about him?" Burkowski asked.

"When I asked if we should contact the father of the child for any reason, a look of fear came into her eyes, and her hands trembled."

"Did she give you the name of the father?"

"No. She acted very afraid of him to the point of fearing for her life, or so it seemed. She said he mustn't know her whereabouts. Well, we took her at her word, and she stayed here until the baby was due. Mother Ignatius and I took her to the hospital when her time to deliver arrived."

Burkowski nodded. "When was that Mother Superior?"

She paused for a moment.

Doug peered at her with pen balanced above the paper.

"Approximately sixteen years ago. Mother Ignatius and I brought Mary and the baby girl back here when her time to leave the hospital came."

"What did Mrs. Ryan do next, Mother Superior?" Burkowski asked.

"She asked if she and the baby could stay here for about 12 months until she stopped nursing, then she would start looking for employment."

"And you agreed to that?"

"I did. The plan we worked out was that she would work in a private home as a secretary, or take a room in a boarding house. We would keep the child in our foundling nursery. Mary would pick up Hope on the weekends."

"And did she do that? Did she ever miss a weekend?"

The nun responded immediately. "Never a one. We also planned that when the child became of school age, her schooling would take place here. When Hope completed her elementary education, Mary planned to take her home to live with her. Hope would receive her secondary education in the community. I agreed with the plan, and our relationship progressed along that line."

"So, Mrs. Ryan's daughter would be around fifteen now. Is that correct?" Burkowski asked.

"Correct," Mother Superior answered.

"If the girl is fifteen now, she must have completed her elementary education, but she's still here. Why did the plan change?" Burkowski asked.

"Hope wanted to take the bookkeeping course that we had available. So she stayed on a bit longer to complete the course. We were happy to oblige," the nun smiled and leaned back in her chair.

Burkowski looked over at Doug. "Did you get all of that, Detective?"

Doug nodded, and blurted out, "Could we speak with the child now, Mother Superior?"

Burkowski coughed, drummed his fingers on the desk, and gave Selby a withering look.

"Is there anything more you can tell us, Mother Superior, before we speak to the child?"

"Well...Mrs. Ryan...we called her Mrs., although there was a doubt in my mind as to whether she was married," Mother Superior said.

"Why the doubt?" The detective leaned forward.

Mother Superior's face took on a thoughtful expression. "It was her aversion to any talk about the father, and the fear I saw in her eyes when I first broached the subject. Of course, I could be wrong. It was just an intuitive thought, but the fear I saw was real," she said.

"Did she ever speak of a girlfriend or a boyfriend, Mother Superior?"

"Excuse me," she said, as she lifted a pitcher of water standing on a side table and poured herself a glass. The nun shook her head. "Only once. She mentioned a friend from the choir at her church. A young woman—I believe Mary called her Daphne."

"Do you know the name of the church, Sister?" Burkowski asked.

"Yes. I have it in her file."

"Could we speak to Mrs. Ryan's daughter now?" Burkowski asked.

Mother Superior rang a small brass bell on her desk and another nun appeared in the doorway almost before Mother Superior could replace the bell.

"Mother Ignatius, would you please fetch Hope and bring her here?"

"Thank you, Mother Superior, for the information. It's helpful. We'll check out Daphne at the Church," Burkowski said.

"I think you should know, Detective Burkowski, Mary Ryan was a doting mother. I can't imagine her abandoning her child."

Hurried footsteps approached the library. Mother Ignatius burst into the room. She gasped for air as she spoke, and her face was tinged pink. "Mother Superior, Hope's gone and so is her bicycle!"

CHAPTER 43

Doug Selby got behind the wheel of an unmarked Ford. "Sounds like there really is something to this, Stan. What do you think?"

"I think you should stick to your note-taking and leave the questioning to me." He rolled down his window and spat. With a cigarette clenched between his teeth, Burkowski struck a wooden match and cupped his hands. The pungent odour of sulphur clobbered Doug's nostrils, and he held his breath for a few moments. He didn't smoke. The smoke meandered upwards.

The detective took a drag on the cigarette before he spoke. "We need to get back to the missing lady's house pronto and speak to the Martins. I hope they haven't been in there mucking around. We need to make sure the door is locked and put some rope up to cordon off the place."

***

An hour later the detectives were back at the Martin home.

"Hello, Detectives. Please come in. I was just going to call you," Mr. Martin said.

"Do you have some new information sir?" Burkowski asked, as he and Doug stepped across the threshold.

"I do. Mary's daughter showed up here a while ago, looking for her mother. She was panicky and crying, so when she asked to go into the house to see if her mother had left a note or something, I said 'Alright'."

Doug heard Burkowski groan and curse under his breath. "Shit."

"Did you go in with her?" he asked

"I did." And added, "I'm sorry Detective. I didn't touch anything and I don't think Hope did. She just dashed around from room to room, and I followed her. She said her mother didn't show up on the weekend, and told me she was going to check with a friend of her mother's and dashed off."

"We're investigating further now, Mr. Martin. Keep the cottage door locked and don't let anyone else in. I'm sorry, Mr. Martin, but that includes you."

"Certainly, certainly, I understand."

"We'll be putting some rope around the property also," Burkowski said.

Ted Martin nodded vigorously.

"May we have the key, sir?" Burkowski asked. "Detective Selby and I want to look around again."

Once inside the cottage, they stood near the entrance and peered into the living room. "Looks the same as before, Stan", Selby said. "The suitcase is still there on the chair. Doesn't look like it's been disturbed." He looked into the tumbler sitting on the coffee table. It had been there before, but he hadn't looked at it closely. It was one third full and a familiar odour emanated from it. Doug leaned over and sniffed the glass. "Rye—Canadian Club by the smell of sweetness."

"How the hell can you tell it's Canadian Club rye? Are you a connoisseur of whiskey or something?" Stan snarled.

"I'm not. It's just that once I tasted C.C. Rye, and found it too sweet. I never forgot the smell. More to the liking of a lady, I thought."

Doug walked around the coffee table. "I think she left, or was taken away in a hurry by the looks of the coffee table. She hadn't bothered to clean it up, Stan. The *Reader's*

Digest is open and turned face-down. I think she was reading when someone knocked at her door."

"Check the kitchen, and see if there's anything out of order," Burkowski said.

Doug strolled around the living room first—his eyes slowly roving over everything in the room, and then he stepped into the kitchen. A kettle rested on a back burner. He touched the side of it cautiously—stone cold. And an opened bottle of Canadian Club whiskey had been placed at the back of the kitchen counter. He walked to the other side of the living room. Doug assumed the bedroom, or bedrooms and washroom would be there. He walked down the hallway and found Burkowski standing in the doorway of the bedroom.

"Just the same as before. Nothing out of place. Not a speck of dust anywhere. I'd pay a pretty penny to have a housekeeper like this. There is one thing, though. It's getting pretty cold at night now, and there's no blanket on the bed, just a thin bedspread. Hmm," Burkowski said.

With a small grin, Doug said, "I found a bottle of Canadian Club sitting on the kitchen counter. I told you it was C.C., Stan."

Burkowski smirked and asked, "Is there a fingerprint kit in the car?"

"Yeah, I think so."

"Go out and bring it in. And the ash and cigarette butts you picked up when we were here before, did you send them off for testing?" the detective asked.

"Ah...not yet."

Burkowski gave Doug an icy stare.

***

Rain drizzled down the windshield of the Ford. It was warm inside and condensation formed on the window. The detectives wore overcoats, and the smell of wet wool permeated the air. They pulled into the parking lot of Holy Rosary Church. "Did you phone ahead and tell the pastor we were coming?" Burkowski asked.

"Yeah, he got all jumpy and asked if there was a problem with one of his parishioners. I guess the police don't visit the church that often, not on official business that is. His name is Father Breen."

The two men stood on the porch of the rectory waiting for someone to answer the bell. "Do you attend church, Stan?"

"Uh-huh, but not here." He opened his overcoat and gave it a shake.

A tall, elegant-looking man with silver hair answered the door. "Hello gentlemen. I'm Father Breen. You must be the detectives who just called."

"We are. I'm Detective Sergeant Burkowski and this is my partner, Detective Selby. May we come in? We're here to ask what you know about one of your parishioners, Mary Ryan. She sings in the choir, and we'd like to know where we could find her friend, Daphne."

Father Breen stepped aside. "We'll be more comfortable in the office. Follow me. Yes, yes, I know both young women. Mary and Daphne...Daphne Essex. Lovely sopranos, both of them."

"When did you last see Mrs. Ryan?"

Doug took out his notebook.

The priest put a cupped hand on his chin, "I believe it was not last Sunday, but the Sunday before. I remember last week our choir mistress, Miss Pitch, came to me and said Mary had missed choir practice. She was quite concerned. Said it wasn't like Mary to miss practice, and not call." Doug could see the concern clearly written on the priest's face. The priest leaned forward in his burgundy chair. "I hope nothing has happened to her. She's a lovely person."

"Would you have Daphne Essex's address, Father?" Doug chimed in, and turned the page of his notebook.

Burkowski turned slowly in his chair and gave Doug a long penetrating look, with his head slightly cocked.

Father Breen rose, "I can get it for you in a moment. Let me look in the church's list of parishioners."

He returned with a piece of paper in his hand. "This is Mrs. Essex's address."

Burkowski took it.

CHAPTER 44

"I'll drive," Burkowski said in a gruff voice, and lifted the lever to push the car seat back to its last position. "You're doing it again, Doug! I told you before, just shut your trap and leave the interview to me."

Selby sunk a little lower in his seat and said, "Well, the address had to be written down, and I had the pen."

"OK, OK, but this is the last time I'm going to tell you—leave the interview to me. If it happens again, protect yourself."

Burkowski pulled up in front of the address Father Breen had given them. The dark green paint on the front door looked cracked and flaking. A child's wagon with its wheels rusting lay on its side in the grass on the front lawn. Only a few red patches of paint remained on it.

When the front door opened, a woman who appeared to be in her early 30s, greeted them. She had a worn-out look about her, thin as a sapling, and was wearing a shabby housedress.

"Yes?" A crease materialized on her forehead as she waited for the men to speak. She glanced behind her and put her index finger to her lips. "Shh, my son's sleeping. What is it?"

"Detective Burkowski and Detective Selby, ma'am. We'd like to speak with Daphne Essex." He flipped open his wallet containing his badge.

"I'm Daphne. Is it about Oskar? Oh…well, Oskar's not here, if that's why you've come. Went out for cigarettes a week ago and I haven't seen him since."

Doug could hear the disgust in her voice.

The next second her eyes widened and she leaned forward. "He's not dead, is he?"

Another missing person? What's going on? Doug asked himself.

"We're here to speak to you about a friend of yours, Mary Ryan. May we come in?" Burkowski took a step forward.

Mrs. Essex's eyes darted from one policeman to the other. A question mark and a tinge of fear crept into them. She opened the door wide and stepped aside. "We can sit in the kitchen, straight ahead at the back. I was just making tea, and I have some oatmeal cookies, just baked. Would you like some?"

Doug scanned the room. Faded linoleum on the floor, the pattern nearly worn off. A yellow and white flowered cloth covered the table. He could see a small, frayed hole in the corner, but the cloth was clean and ironed. A cast iron wood-burning stove, with an elevated warming oven attached to the back, like the oven in his grandmother's Aga stove, stood against the wall near a window. It shone.

"Thank you, but just some water," Burkowski said.

"I'll have some water too, if you don't mind," Doug added.

Daphne brought some cookies on a plate, and set it down on top of the hole in the tablecloth. She ran the tap for a few seconds and then returned with two tumblers of water.

"Mary's a good friend of mine," she said as she poured herself some tea. "Has something happened to her?" she asked in a voice with a slight quiver.

"We don't know, ma'am. That's why we're here. When's the last time you saw her and where was it?"

"She was at choir practice two Fridays ago, and at Mass the following Sunday. We came here afterwards for a cup of tea, and something to eat. We'd been fasting for Communion, and we were in need of a snack."

"Did she say she was worried about anything, or that she might be going away for a while?"

"No, not going away or anything like that. But she was confused and sad about her boyfriend."

"What's the boyfriend's name?" Burkowski asked.

"Now, look, I don't wanna get him in trouble or anything. I've met him and he's a decent sort. Pretty well off too, so Mary told me."

"You won't get him in any trouble, Mrs. Essex. We just want to speak to him."

She took a sip of her tea. "OK, if that's all…his name is David. Last name is something like Tipple… Tiplady, or Tipley. That's it, Tipley. He lives in a posh neighbourhood, Mary told me."

"What did she say troubled her?"

Doug stopped writing for a moment. "May I?" he said, as he reached for a cookie.

Mrs. Essex nodded.

Turning to Burkowski, Daphne continued. "They'd been going steady, Mary and David, but now for the last few weeks, it appeared they weren't seeing each other."

"Is there anything else you can tell us?" Burkowski asked.

"Ummm." She leaned forward, her hands tightly clasped in her lap, and there was a slight tremor in her voice. "I've been worried about her myself. She usually calls me a couple of times a week, and I haven't heard from her for days. I telephoned a couple of times, but the phone just kept ringing. Miss Pitch, the organist at the church, is worried too. Mary didn't show up for choir practice last time and didn't call."

Burkowski took a sip of water. "Do you know if Mary saw any other men, or did she have any other girlfriends or any family?"

"No men friends since I've known her, other than David. And maybe another girl or two, but we were the closest. No family, other than her daughter, Hope."

"Yeah, we know about the daughter. Can you tell us anything else?" he asked, staring at the woman, who stared back with a worried look in her eyes.

Daphne averted her eyes and focussed on the corner of the room. "See that Singer sewing machine?" Daphne pointed to it. "It was my mother's, but I didn't know how to work it. Mary taught me. There's not much money to buy clothes, so she helped me make some for my kid and myself. Oskar doesn't always work. And with the Depression not far behind us—not many jobs out there."

Just then a child's cry came from somewhere in the house. "Excuse me, detectives, it's time for little Jimmy's lunch."

"Thank you, Mrs. Essex. Give us a call if you hear from her or think of anything else," Burkowski said, pushing up from his chair. Doug tucked his notebook in his breast pocket and followed the senior detective out.

The two men drove in silence for several minutes, each man lost in his own thoughts. Burkowski broke the silence. "You may be right, Doug. Perhaps there's foul play here."

CHAPTER 45

The Selby kitchen, December 2000

"I need a break, son. Let's have a snack. There's some peanut butter in the cupboard, and some bagels in the fridge. You can put them in the microwave for a few seconds—warm them up. And get me a beer. All this talking has me dry as a bone."

"OK. Can you remember the rest of the investigation, Dad?" Selby asked.

"Yeah, the notebooks helped a lot. And seeing Mary Ryan's photo too. But let's eat first, and you can tell me about Dr. Pallotta."

"Well, she's pretty attractive and, of course, smart. The next time I see her I'm going to ask her out to dinner. She looks a bit like Demi Moore—long black hair, green eyes and dove white skin. You know Dad, the star from *Ghost*? Only difference is Demi Moore's hair was short in that picture."

"Oh, yeah. I loved that picture. She looks that good, eh?"

Roy nodded and bit into his sandwich. The men were silent as they enjoyed their snack.

Saying it out loud, that he was going to ask Lisa out, made it real. He wondered if he still knew how to interact in a romantic situation. He had been married for 25 years before his wife died. Roy could still see her face when he began to think about the past. And her voice—it had a musical lilt to it. Suddenly he felt tightness in his chest and a lump in his throat. Maybe it was too soon to start dating. And then there was his age, 55—too old? Dr. Pallotta looked to be around 40.

"OK, I'm ready," his dad said, swiping a few crumbs off his face. "Let's see…we left off at Daphne Essex's house. She told us Mary's boyfriend was a David Tipley. Burkowski and I went back to the station."

CHAPTER 46

Burlington Police Station, October 1939

Doug Selby sat in the Burlington police station looking in the telephone book. "Here it is Stan," he yelled across the room.

Stan was speaking on the telephone. Without looking up he stuck a hand in the air, palm out, facing Doug. A couple of minutes later he hung up. He hovered over Doug, "What is it that can't wait, eager beaver?" Burkowski asked.

"I have David Tipley's address."

A short while later the two detectives stood on the porch of a yellow and brown brick house. It was on Balmoral Avenue in Burlington and stood on a small hill several feet above the sidewalk. Tall, silver maples lined the avenue. Burkowski leaned to his right and thumbed the white, ceramic doorbell. The muffled melodious tone of chimes greeted their ears. The door opened promptly, and a well-groomed man stood in the doorway. "Yes? Can I help you?"

"Detective Burkowski and Detective Selby, Sir," Burkowski answered, showing his badge. "We would like to speak with David Tipley."

"I'm David Tipley. Is there a problem, detectives?" He looked from one face to the other. A stiff breeze came up from the north and whipped his blonde hair into his face.

"May we come in, sir? We're conducting an investigation and have just a few questions," Burkowski said.

Tipley ran his fingers through his hair as he stepped aside. "Yes, yes, please come in." He led them to his library. A large black and grey tabby cat lounged on his desk. It got up and stretched when the men entered. "Away you go, Kenny," Tipley said, as he brushed the cat on its hinny. The feline meowed as it leaped down, and leisurely sauntered across the room and hopped up on an empty bookcase shelf where he could watch the interview.

Tipley slid behind a cluttered mahogany desk, and gestured to two wingback chairs which were placed in front of it. "Have a seat, gentleman, and tell me what this is all about."

"I understand you were acquainted with a woman by the name of Mary Ryan?" Burkowski said.

"I am, yes—I am," his brow puckered. "Has something happened to her?" Tipley asked. A bump appeared in his throat and he swallowed hard. Small beads of perspiration appeared on his forehead.

"She's been reported missing by several people. When was the last time you saw her?"

"Several weeks ago. We'd been out to the movies. I haven't seen her since."

"Is there any particular reason for that? I mean was it normal you would go that long, without seeing each other?"

Tipley hesitated. "Well…no, but that night we had decided to break it off for a while."

"And why was that?" Burkowski leaned forward in his chair.

Doug could see Tipley getting agitated, shifting in his chair, picking up a pen from his desk and twirling it between his fingers. He's holding something back, Doug thought.

"It's personal!" Tipley snapped. "Mary Ryan is a fine woman, and I care about her a great deal. I'll not discuss our private conversations."

Burkowski leaned back in his chair. "Hold on there, Mr. Tipley. Settle down. We're just trying to learn something that might help us find her."

Tipley took a couple of deep breaths. "Have you spoken to Ted Martin, her employer?" he asked.

"We have. From all accounts her disappearance is unusual. We're told he considered Mrs. Ryan a reliable employee, but Mr. Martin hasn't seen her since last week.

"Mary has a daughter, Hope. Have you spoken to her?" Tipley asked.

Burkowski glanced at Doug, who had stopped taking notes.

Doug, stared at Tipley—trying to size him up

Burkowski's lips were pressed together in a fine line. "We're working on it. Now tell me, where were you last Thursday evening, Mr. Tipley?"

A look of horror darkened David Tipley's face. "Surely to God you don't think I had anything to do with Mary's disappearance? I'm in love with her and want to marry her, for God's sake!" He looked down and shook his head side to side.

Doug heard a harshness creep into Burkowski's voice. "Just tell us where you were last Thursday night, sir."

David Tipley slumped in his chair and sighed. He reached over and flipped a few pages on his desk calendar. "I had dinner with friends, Mr. and Mrs. Vincent Terrizini. He's one of my suppliers. I'm a builder."

"Can Mr. Terrizini verify that?" Burkowski prodded.

Tipley snatched a piece of paper from a pad on his desk and jotted down Terrizini's phone number and proffered it to the detective. "Call him. Here's his number."

Burkowski stretched out from his chair and grasped the paper. "Where did you eat?"

"A Chinese food restaurant, Tien Kue," David replied.

"Just one final question, sir," Burkowski said, pushing himself out of his chair. "Is there anyone you know of who might have had a disagreement with Mrs. Ryan?"

Tipley stood. "Absolutely not. Everyone that I know of spoke well of her. She is a kind, understanding woman and an excellent mother from what I could see."

The detectives buttoned their coats and turned toward the door. "Thank you for your co-operation, Mr. Tipley. If you think of anything that might help us, call this number." Burkowski held out his white police information card. "Good day, sir."

***

"I believe him. His story has a ring of truth. He seems genuinely concerned," Doug said once they were back in the cruiser.

The engine roared to life when Burkowski twisted the ignition key. "And maybe he's just a good actor. I've seen men and women cry like babies, while denying they had murdered their spouses or kids. And when compelling evidence comes in, they still deny any involvement with the deaths of their supposedly loved ones. Only when the evidence has their backs against the wall do they admit to some—I say *some*—involvement."

"Uh-huh," Doug muttered, and lowered his head to the headrest.

***

The next day, at eight o'clock in the morning, Burkowski burst through the door of the Detectives' room, shouting, "Doug!" The welcoming aroma of fresh coffee greeted him.

Doug dropped his pen and looked up expectantly at his partner striding toward him.

"What?"

"In the excitement at the convent last week, I forgot to find out more about the priest who referred Mrs. Ryan to the convent. I remember Mother Superior said he was in Toronto. You got his address?"

Selby fingered a few neat piles of paper on his desk, and then withdrew his small black notebook from the second pile. "Yeah, that's right. I have his name and address. Father O'Neill, St. Vincent de Paul Church, on Roncesvalles Avenue."

The two men left the station, slid into their vehicle, and headed out toward the Queen Elizabeth Highway on their way to Toronto.

A few snowflakes whispered down, settling on the shoulders of the detectives' overcoats as they hurried up the stairs of the rectory of St. Vincent's. Doug reached up and pulled the brim of his hat closer to his face. Burkowski clutched the brass knocker and let it drop twice. Doug could hear it echo inside the house.

An elderly woman with sensible black Oxfords opened the door. "Yes, may I help you?" She peered out over glasses so thick they reminded Doug of Coca-Cola bottles, as the saying went. Snow-white hair surrounded her head like a puffy cloud.

"We'd like to see Father O'Neill, please," Burkowski said. He held out his badge.

"Oh dear, oh dear," she said, placing bent arthritic fingers over the lower half of her face. Her eyes widened with alarm. "I'm afraid I can't help you. Father O'Neill died a few years ago."

Doug watched as Burkowski's face dropped, and he gave an audible sigh. "Could we speak to his replacement, then?" he asked.

Damn, it looks like this lead may fizzle out, Doug thought.

The woman's small pink face brightened. "That would be Father McGuigan. He's here. Just a minute." The woman left the door ajar as she tip-toed away, and a few flakes of snow crept into the foyer, leaving small puddles on the hardwood floor.

A young priest appeared almost as quickly as the snow melted on the threshold. "Step inside please. We can go into the library. It's more comfortable there. I'm Father McGuigan," he said as he led the way. "Mrs. Malloy tells me you're police officers, and you were asking for Father O'Neill. Sorry, but he died quite suddenly a few years ago. How can I help you?" he said as they entered the library.

Doug dropped into a hard backed oak chair and took out his notebook. He began writing in it at once. "How do you spell your name, Father?" he asked politely.

The priest had the kind of vivid blue eyes that sparkled, and his mouth curved slightly when he answered. "No 'a' after M, just a small 'c'." And then he spelled the rest of it.

Father McGuigan took a seat in a chair behind his desk. A curious expression replaced the smile, as he leaned forward.

Burkowski glanced at Doug and dropped his eyes to Doug's notebook and then back to Doug's face. Doug caught the look and remembered Burkowski's threat. *No asking questions. Just take notes,* the silent message said.

Burkowski wiggled around, trying to get comfortable, his backside overhanging the chair. "Father McGuigan, we're conducting an investigation into a missing person. Her name is Mary Ryan. Possibly sung in the choir here, and we've been told she was referred by Father O'Neill to a convent near Hamilton. And I don't know if it's helpful, but she had a slight Irish accent."

"I don't know if I can be of much help, Detectives. Father O'Neill didn't keep many notes on the parishioners. But if she was a member of this parish, there may be something."

A small filing cabinet stood off to one side of Father McGuigan's desk. He opened a drawer and began fingering the folders. After a minute or two he straightened and said, "I'm afraid there is no record of a Mary Ryan. But, as I said, Father O'Neill didn't keep many records. Sorry."

Another dead end. Doug's heart sagged.

"Thanks anyway for your trouble, Father," Burkowski said. The detectives rose, disappointed, and left.

CHAPTER 47

Burlington, 1941

Hope and Daphne lingered at the kitchen table one morning. "I'll have to find a job soon, Daphne," Hope said. "I must pay my way. I know you don't have much to go 'round, and I'm grateful you've given me a place to stay."

"You're welcome to stay as long as you like, dear. It's the least I can do for your dear mother." Daphne put her arms around Hope and hugged her.

"Anything new from the detectives?" Daphne asked.

Hope's face clouded, as she looked down and shook her head. "No…but I telephoned them every few weeks before I left the convent. Nothing. It's been almost a year since I last heard anything."

Daphne patted Hope's hand. "Something will come up one day dear, mark my words."

Hope's sadness faded as she looked up and said, "I think I'd like to try my hand at something in show business. At the convent we put on small plays, and I did some singing and dancing. Mother Superior hired a ballet teacher for us. She thought it might be a fitting recreation for us, and give us poise. The teacher came once a week. I loved it."

Daphne frowned. "I don't like the idea of you going to a strange place by yourself, dear. Your idea about performing is fine. But I worry because you'll have no one to discuss things with."

Hope smiled. "I'll be OK. I'm going to stay at the YWCA in Toronto. Only women are allowed. Also, I read in *The Toronto Daily Star* that some radio announcers in Toronto were banding together to form a group. It'll be for announcers and performers. Something like a union, I guess."

"That sounds useful."

"Perhaps I could join them after I've had some training as an actress. I could always sing, and the dancing lessons I took at the convent may be helpful. As far as the singing goes, I guess I inherited my mother's voice."

Daphne clapped her hands together and gave a huge smile. "Well then, I feel better about your going. If you can sing like your mother, you're on your way. And you've been blessed with more than her voice—her good looks, as well."

Hope smiled and blushed. "Give me your telephone directory, Daphne. I'll start looking for a coach right now. I'll take a part-time job to pay my way, and hopefully have enough left over for the acting lessons."

The black box telephone hung on the wall beside the kitchen table. It beckoned to Hope.

CHAPTER 48

Burlington, 2000

Doug Selby leaned back in his chair and said, "All this talking has left me dry as a bone. I need to wet my whistle. Any beer left in the fridge?"

Roy pushed away from the table. "Nope. Just some diet Canada Dry. Anyway, you're only supposed to drink a small amount of alcohol. Remember your diabetes, Dad."

Doug smiled, "Ah, well. A bottle now and then can't hurt."

Roy sauntered over to the fridge and pulled out a can of the ginger ale. The soda fizzed up as he poured it into the glass. Back at the table he passed it to his dad.

"Thanks." Doug took a long sip.

After a few swallows, he said, "There, that's better. So, where was I? Oh yeah, we got nothing from the priest. We interviewed everyone who knew Mary Ryan to no avail. The meagre clues dried up. It appeared that Mary Ryan had no known past, except for a long-ago conversation with Father O'Neill and her time spent at the convent. One day Burkowski approached me.

"'I guess we'll have to put Mary Ryan's case away in the unsolved crimes for now,' he said. 'There's been nothing new for more than a year, although her daughter, Hope, still keeps calling. Poor kid.'" Doug shook his head, still smarting from that early failure.

The Mary Ryan case really got to Doug for some reason. He didn't want to give up on it, but he had to agree with Burkowski.

"I'd like to do one last interview with Daphne Essex. She may have thought of something," Doug told

Burkowski. "And if Mary's daughter is still there, maybe she has remembered some small detail. She may think it's not important, but you never know."

It was just past one o'clock Monday afternoon. A ray of sun began to slant into the detectives' office. The phone rang. Doug Selby answered it.

"It's Hope Ryan. I haven't heard from you in a while, so I guess there isn't any news of my mother, is there?"

"Sorry, Hope. Are you still staying with Mrs. Essex?"

"For a while, anyway."

"I was just about to call you. Detective Burkowski and I would like to drop by this afternoon and run a few things by you and Mrs. Essex."

Burkowski sat at his desk opposite Doug, eating a ham sandwich. He looked up when Doug coughed and raised his voice. "I'll see you later today, Hope."

The detective put his sandwich down on the wax paper and looked at the row of buttons on the telephone to see which one was lit. He gently pressed it down and removed the receiver.

"I just want to let you know I'm moving to Toronto. I'll call and give you my address and telephone number when I get settled," Hope said.

"How soon will you be leaving?" Doug asked.

"Well, this week, on Friday, I think. Mr. Essex has returned home and it's getting a bit crowded."

Selby could hear something odd in Hope's voice. He couldn't quite put his finger on it.

Burkowski leaned backwards in his swivel chair. It gave a loud squeak. He picked up his sandwich with a large piece of ham with mustard hanging out of the bread. He swiped it with his tongue as he listened.

Doug's eyebrows drew together. "Do you know anyone in Toronto, Hope?"

274

Hope was silent for a few seconds. "As you know, Detective, all my relatives have passed. My mother told me they all drowned. She didn't say how. I got the impression she didn't want to talk about it, so I just left it."

"Sorry, Hope," his voice softened.

"Don't worry about me, Detective Selby. I'm going to stay at the YWCA."

Doug made a note, lowered his shoulders, and smiled.

"I thought I might try my hand at acting and singing. Maybe do something on the radio. I've been listening to some radio shows. There's one Sunday night where they do performances of famous movies."

"What's it called?" Doug asked.

"Lux Theatre. Anyway, there are a lot of different ones. And then there are commercials."

"Well, good luck, Hope. Here's Detective Burkowski. He wants to speak with you."

"Hello, Hope. I'll be watching out for you. Don't forget to give us your number once you get one. Break a leg!" Burkowski said, and laid the receiver back in its cradle.

A thoughtful expression appeared on Doug's face. "Stan, I want to ask Mrs. Essex if Mary told her anything more about her family. We know none of them are alive, but how and where did they drown? Maybe she told her, or another friend."

"Wait, I'll go with you."

"I want to go alone this time, Stan," he stood and put on his Macintosh.

Burkowski frowned and then relaxed. "OK, see you later."

***

When Doug Selby knocked on the door at the Essex home, a man with several days' growth on his face answered the door in his undershirt. Black hair protruded from the circular neckline. His left arm bore a tattoo of a heart with 'Mother' scratched across it. "Whadda you want?"

The sour smell of beer made Doug want to hold his nose. He flipped open his wallet. "Police."

The man scowled. "So?"

"I'd like to speak to Mrs. Essex, if you don't mind, Sir," he said, taking a step back.

"I do mind. I'm her husband. What's this about, copper?"

"If you'll get Mrs. Essex, you'll find out."

Just then Daphne Essex appeared behind the man, holding a toddler. She leaned over her husband's shoulder. "Let him come in, Oskar. I know him," she said smiling at Doug.

"You know him? How?" A suspicious look appeared on his mug.

"It's OK, Oskar. It's about my missing friend, Mary Ryan. The detective was here when you were away. This is my husband, Oskar, Detective Selby."

Oskar nodded, but didn't extend his hand. Grudgingly, he stepped aside. Daphne led Selby to the kitchen.

"Glad to see you home with the family, Mr. Essex." Selby seated himself at the kitchen table after Daphne sat down. "Would you like some tea, Detective? I just brewed some Lipton's," she said passing the child over to her husband. Mr. Essex took a seat in the far corner of the kitchen holding the child on his lap.

"The last time we were here, Mrs. Essex, we didn't discuss your friend, Mary's, family very much. Do you recall anything more about them? Her daughter tells us all she knows is that they are all dead. What, if anything, did Mary tell you about them?" Out of the corner of his eye, Selby saw Mr. Essex lean forward.

Daphne's eyes flitted in her husband's direction, and then back to Selby. "Sorry, Detective, but I can't be of much help there. Mary never spoke much about her background. From what I remember, she told me that her twin brother and mother and father had all drowned when a boat they were on ran into trouble and sank."

Selby pulled his chair closer to the table. "Did she say when this happened?"

"Afraid not."

"We know she came to this area from Toronto. Did she ever mention any old friends?"

"The only thing I can think of is…she told me that she had a score to settle with someone there. And one day she would, when Hope was older."

"Did she ever mention a name of anyone from her past?" *If only I had a name, maybe that could lead somewhere.* A spark of hope ignited in him at the thought. Selby put his hand on his notebook and picked up his pen.

Daphne lowered her head and shook it side to side. Doug leaned back in his chair, deflated. He'd thought for a second he was on to something.

"Guess I'm not much help. I wish I could tell you more. The only other thing is that when she told me about the score to be settled, she seemed edgy."

"That's alright, Mrs. Essex. Thanks for what you did give me today. Who knows, we may be able to use it in the future."

"Oh, I just remembered something. Hope and I went to Mary's home a while back and packed up some things. She gave me a box with some clothing in it and a few odds and ends. Mary and I were the same size, but I wasn't interested in everything. Just a minute I'll get it for you." She disappeared for a moment.

Doug Selby shifted in his chair and looked at Mr. Essex, who glared back at him.

Daphne returned with a large box. "Here it is. I took out some dresses and a few knick-knacks. I'd like to keep something to remind me of her. The shoes don't fit me. Take them with the rest. Some of it may be useful to you down the road."

Doug took the box and left. He sat in his car for a few minutes, and then fished his notebook from his breast pocket. When he was finished recording the conversation with Daphne he put the notebook away and sighed. *Not much to go on without a name.* But he'd tell Burkowski what he'd learned when he got back to the office. *We can go through the box together. Who knows what'll turn up in the future?* Just now, Detective Douglas Selby had happier things to think about. He had married a year and a half earlier, and a baby was on the way.

CHAPTER 49

Burlington, 2000

"Your mother liked the name Roy Robert, so on September 17, 1942 you were born." The kitchen chair scraped across the ceramic floor as Doug rose and stretched. He'd been talking for a very long time. "OK, Roy. Let's get Hope's wedding invitation out and try to track her down. That is, if she's still living."

The two men approached the cellar door on the other side of the kitchen. Roy stepped down first and stood on the second step. "OK, Dad, you follow, so if you become unsteady, I'll stop your fall."

Doug could easily reach the railing on the side of the stairs. He grabbed it and held tight.

"Right, lead the way. See the tall bin with papers on top? It's in that one. I saw it a few days ago when I was rooting about," he said, smiling and looking pleased with himself.

He stood in front of the barrel and pushed a few papers aside. "Bugger! Where did it go? It was here a few days ago. Did it grow legs and walk away? You put something down for a minute and it disappears." He scanned the room and his eyes landed on another container a few feet away. One paper lay on the lid. He sauntered over to it and looked at the card. "Bingo!"

The invitation was yellow around the edges, but the rest of it had received protection from the numerous papers piled on top. He carefully picked it up, and his hand trembled as he held it. "Let's see what we have here. It's still easy enough to read, even after all this time." The two men stared at the white and gold invitation. The ornate gold print was elevated above the white background in a graceful, swirling script.

Mrs. Pricilla Stone
Requests the pleasure of your company at the marriage of
Her son, Wesley, and
Hope Marie Ryan
Saturday the Ninth of August
Nineteen Hundred and Forty-Five
At One o'clock in the Afternoon
Our Lady of Sorrows Church 3055 Bloor St. West, Toronto
Reception to follow at The Old Mill
21 Old Mill Road

Roy Selby took his father's arm and led him to the foot of the staircase. "Let's get upstairs and see if we still have a Toronto telephone book in the house. If not, we can try 411. See if they're still listed."

"There's a chance, son. I'm still here, and I was several years older than Hope when I first met her. People are living longer today, you know. Seems every month someone has a 100th birthday. Look at Kirk Douglas."

"Who?" Roy asked smiling.

"The actor. You know, *Spartacus*? He's nearing 100. And I believe George Burns, the comedian made it to 100 in 1996, when he died, so the newspapers reported. They also mentioned that he felt too sick to attend his birthday party. The family ate the cake though, in his honour. Couldn't let a good cake go to waste."

The two men climbed, making a slow, careful ascent. Doug's knuckles appeared white and shiny as he clutched the banister. When they reached the kitchen, he took two deep breaths and said, "I think I saw a Toronto telephone book in the front closet last week, all dog-eared. Let's look there first."

Roy strode ahead. He knew his father probably couldn't reach the top shelf. He'd shrunk in height over the last few years. The upper shelf of the closet held scarves, caps, toques and gloves.

Doug held out his grabber, a long plastic stick with a handle at one end and something like a claw on the other. He used it sometimes to reach things. "Here, Roy, use this," he said holding out the grabber.

"I'm OK, I think I can reach it."

The telephone book appeared larger than two *Encyclopaedia Brittanica*s. Roy tugged at it, until it dropped into his hands and made his knees buckle. He pivoted toward his father, and saw anticipation in his eyes.

The mahogany dining room table and chairs stood just a few feet away from the front closet. Roy cleared away some of the clutter which had accumulated there. "Really Dad, you've got to get rid of some of these newspapers," his forehead wrinkled.

"Yeah, but I haven't read them all yet," Doug replied in a defensive voice.

"Yeah, and you probably never will," Roy said, heaving the telephone book onto the table.

The book smelled like the mothballs his mother had put in a small canvas bag a long time ago, and his dad was not one to throw things away. With the wedding invitation open on the table beside him, Roy flipped the pages of the telephone book till he came to 'S'.

His finger moved slowly down the S column. *Stitch, Stock, Stokes, Stone, WT*. "Look, here's a W.T. Stone in the Kingsway area."

Doug got excited, and dropped his glasses on the floor. He almost stepped on them when he leaned over to retrieve them. "OK, let's try the number."

Roy brushed some of the papers aside and found the telephone half buried, dialed the number and put the call on speaker. A man answered.

"Is this the home of Wesley Stone?" Roy asked.

"No, it's Walter Timothy Stone's home."

Their faces sagged and darkened with disappointment.

"Sorry to disturb you, sir," Roy said, and hung up.

"I thought sure it'd be Hope's home," Doug said and slumped back on his chair.

A sour expression lingered on both men's faces as they looked back at the telephone book. After several seconds of silence, Roy's countenance took on a hopeful look. "Let's try the Internet, 411." They went to the far end of the dining room table where the I.B.M. computer lay dormant. A few taps and they were in the directory. As they scrolled down again, Doug put his hand on his son's shoulder and watched. Again, Roy went to the *S*s. Pretty much the same as the telephone book. Nothing.

"Roy, go back up to the top of the list. I saw something there that might be helpful."

He began scrolling down again.

"Go slow, son," Doug said, watching intently. "OK, stop!" he cried out when Roy arrived at *H.M. Stone.* It's possible this could be Hope Marie. That's what it says on the invitation, isn't it?"

Roy glanced at the wedding invitation. "Uh-huh," he said with renewed hope and a grateful smile at his dad. Good old Dad. Still on his toes.

Roy's finger quivered slightly as he poked in the numbers. Three rings. A pause.

"Hello," a soft, female voice answered.

He felt his father's body stiffen as they both listened. "This is Detective Roy Selby speaking. Is this Hope Marie Stone, formerly Hope Ryan speaking?" he asked holding his breath as he waited for an answer. A sudden intake of breath could be heard by both men. Silence and a pause.

"Why, yes. And the name Selby is familiar. It's a name I haven't heard for a long, long time." Her tone sounded excited. "Would you be related to another Detective Selby?"

"I am. He's my father, and he's right here with me now."

"Oh, is he well?" she asked. "I always liked him, better than the other detective, I might add. Seemed smarter too," Hope Stone said with a chuckle.

The men looked at each other and smiled. "And is your husband, Mr. Stone, well?"

"He is," she replied.

"Good," a bit of excitement bubbled up in Roy Selby's voice. "Mrs. Stone, I'm calling now because I'm working on a case that may be related to your mother's disappearance."

Another gasp. "It's been such a long time. I'd despaired of ever finding out what happened to my mother. I know she never would have left me of her own accord. Something terrible must have happened to take her away from me."

Hope's voice broke a little, as she spoke. Selby could hear longing and sadness in it. And he knew the feeling. At first, anguish, and fear of what have must have happened to his daughter, when she disappeared without a trace. The painful wondering, *Why?* It felt like a piece of him had been ripped away, leaving a wound which had never completely healed. But someday...someday we still might find out, he thought. "I'd like to visit with you and your husband tomorrow afternoon, Mrs. Stone. Could I come around 3:00 p.m.? I want to run some information by you."

"Just a moment."

Roy and Doug could hear her asking someone if they would be available the next afternoon.

"Alright, that's fine. My husband and I will both be here. And why don't you bring your father along? It'd be nice to see him again," she said.

"Seems like you made quite an impression on Hope back in the day, Dad," Roy said, replacing the receiver.

Doug just smiled.

"I want Hope to know what we have, and maybe she'll have something to add."

CHAPTER 50

December, 2001

The crusted snow sparkled on either side of Bloor Street as the bright winter sun kissed it. Roy thought it looked like a handful of diamonds had been sprinkled over the city. He and his father were pensive as they drove past Park Lawn Cemetery. Roy spotted the Kingsway on the left and turned. The street was exceptionally wide, with the houses set well back from the sidewalk. They drove about one kilometre up to Kingsway Crescent where the Stones lived.

The residence appeared large and sprawling and was situated even further back from the road than the others. The red brick provided a sharp contrast to the snow piled high on either side of the black asphalt driveway.

Roy picked up the brass lion's head knocker and let it drop twice. His shoulders felt tense, and his breathing had shortened. After all this time, were they closing in on the mystery of Mary Ryan's disappearance? Perhaps. It was still a long shot.

A butler in a faultless white shirt and black suit opened the door.

"Detectives Selby to see Mr. and Mrs. Stone. They're expecting us," Roy said, flipping his wallet open to display his badge.

The butler nodded. "Follow me please," he said in a discreet and friendly tone.

The detectives were led through a massive foyer. Fresh white and yellow chrysanthemums with green fern had been placed in a crystal vase on a side table. The butler led them to the back of the house.

Roy could feel moist warmth on his face, and his clothes began to cling to him. The butler stopped, opened an oversized door, and announced the visitors. Roy and his father gazed around them. Roy had never seen such elegance. Chaise lounges with red, yellow, and blue cushions were scattered around an indoor swimming pool. Two of the walls were glass and the third had hanging plants attached to it. Steam covered the two glass walls half way up. An elderly couple wearing white bathrobes lounged at a patio table off to one side of the room.

"Oh, sorry, Detectives, we were swimming and lost track of time. Please excuse our appearance," the gentleman said, rising. "Come in and sit down."

Roy approached with outstretched hand. His father looked at Hope, smiled, and held out his hand. Before sitting, Roy peered out the floor-to-ceiling window. They were steamed up, but he could see a small patch of the Humber River at the bottom of the hill behind the house. Mostly frozen over, but in some spots the water bubbled to the surface. Roy lowered himself into a padded deck chair. "Thanks for seeing us, Mr. and Mrs. Stone. As I mentioned to you on the phone, I'm currently working on a case that may be relevant to your mother's disappearance."

Hope pulled forward to the edge of her chair. An expectant glint shone in her eyes.

"What is it, Detective?" she said.

She put her hands on the table and crossed them. Roy noticed a small tremor.

"The remains of a woman have recently been unearthed. We're working with a forensic anthropologist, and she informs us that the remains are that of a woman approximately 40 to 45 years old, around five feet, three or four inches, and she once had red hair. The anthropologist believes the woman's been buried for approximately 60 years, judging by the clothing and some other details."

Hope's eyebrows arched, and she uncrossed her hands. Her husband took one of them, squeezed and patted it. Love and concern hovered in his eyes.

"Anything else, Detective?" she asked in a trembling voice.

"Did your mother ever say anything to you about the *Titanic*?"

Mr. Stone's eyes averted to his wife.

"Why no, she didn't. Why do you ask?"

"We had everything analyzed that we found at the burial site, including a fragment of what appeared to be a wool blanket. A label was attached to it. It said, *Titanic*."

Hope's mouth opened and she put a hand over it. Mr. Stone leaned forward, his eyes wide. "The *Titanic*?"

Roy let that sink in for a few seconds. "Mrs. Stone, do you know of any relatives of your mother's?"

"I don't. The only thing she ever told me was that they'd all drowned, and she didn't want to talk about it. And that she lived in Toronto for a time, and there were some very good people and some very bad ones. She said one day she would tell me more when I was older. But then she disappeared."

Wesley Stone chimed in. "So many catastrophes happened back in the day. First, Hope's mother went missing, my grandfather died a horrible death—tortured and murdered by kidnappers when the family refused to pay the ransom. Then my mother developed diabetes. And lastly, when I introduced Hope to my father for the first time, he became agitated. And a few moments later he had a stroke and lost his ability to speak. He died when we were planning our wedding."

The detectives looked at one another and were silent. Mr. Stone's head was bowed.

Roy's eyes drifted downward, and he noticed a peculiarity in Hope's shoeless feet. Hope's baby toe sat on top of the next toe. It was the same on the other foot. Something stirred in Roy's memory. He raised his eyes to look at Hope. "I have some jewellery and some other items I'd like you to look at. And I'd like to take a swab from your mouth for DNA comparison with the remains we found. Could you and your husband come out to the police station in Burlington?"

"Yes, yes, when?" She looked at her husband and he nodded.

"Soon as possible. Tomorrow, all right? Around 1:00 p.m?"

"Of course," Mr. Stone said.

Everyone rose. Wesley Stone rang for the butler, and the Selbys were shown out.

***

Back in the Ford, Doug looked at his son. "Well, what do you think?"

Roy didn't answer right away. He was thinking about the funny baby toes. He'd either seen them somewhere before, read about them, or someone in the past had talked about the abnormal condition and said it was rare.

"Sorry Dad, what did you say?"

"I asked what you thought about the meeting."

Roy grinned. "First time I ever saw a private indoor pool." He wondered what that might have cost. "They were both pretty surprised when I mentioned the label with *Titanic* printed on it."

"Who wouldn't be?" his dad replied.

"Now that old memories have been awakened, Hope may think of something else about her mother that might be useful," Roy said.

"Well, I think we got pretty much everything she could give us at the time of her mother's disappearance."

"She was under a lot of stress at the time, Dad. And it's been proven stress can affect a person's memory. So now, something long submerged might float to the surface. Perhaps a long-forgotten conversation which seemed insignificant to her at the time might bubble up. Did you happen to notice Hope's feet?"

"What the heck are you talking about?" Doug asked, frowning.

"The abnormality in Hope's baby toes. Each baby toe lay on top of the next toe."

"Oh, that. I didn't notice Hope's feet, but I did see Mr. Stone's. And he had the same kind of toes. Odd, eh?"

Roy blinked, and his voice rose slightly. "He did?"

"Uh-huh. But I was wondering why you didn't tell Hope the manner of death your skeleton revealed?" Doug asked.

"She didn't ask, and I saw no reason to tell her now. That will come later when we know we're on the right track. We still don't know for certain if the skeleton is Mary Ryan's. I want to be 100 per cent sure."

"Oh, talking about remembering long-forgotten details of the case, I just remembered something. I put some ashes and two cigarette butts into a small brown envelope that I found in the missing woman's house. And then I put the small envelope into a large heavy envelope. There's a slight chance it's in the evidence room, or else in the basement somewhere."

"If the evidence box you put that envelope in hasn't been destroyed, we may be able to get DNA from the butts." A hunch began to germinate in Roy's brain.

When Roy awoke the next morning, the only light in his room came from his clock radio. He lay in bed, rubbed his eyes and looked at the clock. *Seven a.m.* The pleasant, heavy scent of coffee brewing lured him out of bed.

His father rose early, and the first thing he did was start the coffee. Roy threw on his plaid bathrobe and stuck his feet into plaid slippers. Not even a minute passed before he stood in the kitchen with a plaid-patterned cup of coffee in his hand. His father gave him the bathrobe and slippers at Christmas-time, as well as the matching coffee cup. Doug Selby liked things that matched.

He lounged at the kitchen table with cinnamon toast and black coffee. "'Morning. Come sit down and tell me what you've got incubating in that brain of yours, Roy. I know you. You've got some kind of plan for the Stones today."

"Uh-huh. First, I'd like Hope to look at the cross and chain that was found with our skeleton. And she's already agreed to let me swab her DNA. Then I want to get some DNA from Mr. Stone."

"I can understand why you would want Hope's DNA—see if it matches up with the DNA from the skeleton, but why Mr. Stone's?" Doug asked.

"I'll tell you later, after I speak to Dr. Pallotta."

Roy finished his coffee and raced upstairs to take a shower. When he returned to the kitchen his dad was washing up the dishes.

"I'd love to be a mouse under the table in the interview room when you show Hope the cross and chain. Too bad regulations won't allow me to be there. Think I'll kill some time and wander over to the station while I'm waiting to hear from you."

"Sounds like a plan, Dad."

"There are still a few guys working who came in shortly before I retired. I want to find out what happens to the old evidence boxes, the ones I used. I know you found the one Mary's friend gave me. But what about the older boxes that weren't there when you looked?"

"If there's any possibility we can find those butts and get DNA from them, we might be able to find out who killed Mary. Still, we'll need some other DNA to compare it with."

Roy picked up the land line, punched in Dr. Pallotta's number, and left a message on her voice mail. "See you at nine o'clock this morning."

***

At 8:50 a.m., Detective Roy Selby knocked on Dr. Pallotta's door at the morgue. He felt a twinge of excitement at seeing her again, and not just for scientific reasons. She really did appeal to him. He liked her long, black hair and green eyes. And, of course, her brain. Oh, yes, her brain.

He heard her melodious voice. Yeah, he especially liked that too.

"Come in," she called out.

Lisa sat at her desk, writing. She turned and smiled. "Nice to see you again, Roy. I picked up your message on my voice mail. Anything special?"

"Yeah, there is," Roy said. "A couple of days ago, my dad and I found Hope Ryan, the missing woman's daughter. Thankfully she and her husband are still alive."

"That must have taken some effort," Lisa said.

"Just some old solid police work. And my dad being a packrat helped a lot. He kept some items from the case of the missing woman. And over the course of the investigation, Dad and his partner became friendly with the daughter, Hope. He'd kept a wedding invitation Hope sent him. Using that, we were able to track her down."

Lisa Pallotta smiled and said, "Sometimes it's good to be a packrat."

Roy nodded and returned Lisa's smile. "Anyway, we went to visit Hope and her husband. We were ushered into a room with an indoor swimming pool, where Mr. and Mrs. Stone were sitting in their bathrobes, poolside. At one point I looked down and saw Hope's feet and noticed an abnormal characteristic. Her baby toe sat on top of her next toe. I've seen or read about this abnormality at some time in the past. But for the life of me I can't remember what it's called or its nature."

"Roy, you've stumbled on a rare abnormality. Only a small percentage of the population has this condition. And it's hereditary. It's called Clinodactyly."

"So that's what it's called. I didn't think too many people had it and you've just confirmed it. So the next bit of news will be a shocker for you. My dad noticed Hope's husband has the same anomaly." The detective studied Lisa's face and waited for her reaction.

"What?" Lisa's eyes widened and her lips parted as she straightened in her chair. "It's an unusual coincidence that a person with this rare characteristic would end up marrying someone with the same condition. But I suppose it could happen. They each could have inherited the condition from different relatives, of course, who have no connection to each other. Or..."

"They could be related," Roy said. "I'm meeting with Hope Stone and her husband in a few hours. I have some jewellery from the burial site, and of course the shoes we found with the skeleton and those in the box from Daphne

Essex. Then I'll get specimens for DNA analysis from both of them."

"How do you plan to do that?" Lisa asked.

"Hope has already agreed to donate a specimen. I'll get her DNA from a mouth swab. I plan to put a bottle of water and a glass in front of each of them. Hopefully, Mr. Stone will take a drink."

"It's a long shot, but good luck with that one."

Roy continued. "After I get the specimens, should we send them to the Centre of Forensic Science in Toronto, or should we get someone out this way to do the lab test?"

"Let's wait until you get the specimens before we decide on that, Roy."

"Right, and when are we going to have that dinner?" he asked as he strode out of the morgue.

CHAPTER 51

Detective Selby looked at his watch. *11:00. Still plenty of time.* He'd just picked up the cross and chain and the Oxford-type shoes from the evidence room. The jewellery lay nestled in a small brown envelope in a zippered pocket in his briefcase. He'd placed the shoes in a plastic bag, dropped them into the briefcase and drove to the station house.

As he sat at his desk, he pulled a sheet of paper from his drawer and constructed a chart of his father's missing woman, Mary Ryan, and the events surrounding her disappearance. Selby looked at his watch again—12:05. Time to grab a quick bite and a coffee at Tim Horton's. As he entered, he saw his father sitting in a corner with another senior.

"Hey, Roy," Doug said as he beckoned him over.

Roy gave his order to go to the cashier—a bagel with cream cheese, a black coffee, and two bottles of water, and sauntered over to Doug's table.

"This is one of my pals from the Department, Sid Cudmore. I asked him about the boxes in the evidence room. He says the old boxes are destroyed to make room for the new ones, but sometimes an old box get pushed behind and left, like the one you found."

"Thanks Sid, but I'm onto something else just now. I just want to grab a quick bite to go. See you later." Roy picked up his order and hurried back to the station and entered the interview room. He ate his lunch and placed two water bottles on the table, with paper cups.

He looked at his watch again—12:45. Hope Stone and her husband would be arriving in 15 minutes. He opened his briefcase and withdrew the envelope with the cross and chain and placed it on the table. As he looked at it, he thought, *What a story the cross could tell, if it could talk.*

At the sound of a gentle rap on the door, he sprang out of his chair. Mr. and Mrs. Stone stood in the doorway. His pulse quickened.

Once the three of them were seated, Selby said, "Feel free to help yourself to the water. Is there anything else you need?"

They both shook their heads, and Mrs. Stone said, "You're very kind, Detective, but I'm all right. Just excited to see what you have."

"If you don't mind, Mrs. Stone, I'd like to collect some cells from inside your cheek with a buccal swab." Selby reached into his briefcase and withdrew a container with a swab inside.

"Will this hurt?" Mrs. Stone asked.

"Not at all. Just open your mouth for a few seconds. I'll swab and then we're done."

After Selby replaced the swab in its container and a plastic bag, which he taped, he picked up the slender manila envelope. He observed Mr. and Mrs. Stone watching him intently.

"Mrs. Stone, when we unearthed the remains of the woman I told you about, we found a small, silver cross and chain under the remains. I'd like to show them to you, and ask you if you recognize them."

Mrs. Stone nodded and said, "Yes, yes, I'd like to see them."

Selby observed a slight tightness in her face. She reached for the bottle of water and the paper cup. A small tremor appeared in her hand as she poured the water. Mr. Stone put his arm around her.

Everyone's eyes fell on the envelope in Selby's hand. He nodded to Mrs. Stone, and she put out her hand. The contents slid into them.

Mr. Stone reached for his bottle of water and took a swig.

Hope gasped as she looked at the jewellery in her palm. She began to gently stroke the cross and turn it over. Tears started to well in her eyes and trickle down her pink cheeks. Her chest began to heave.

Selby felt a lump in his throat and had to choke back his own tears. He thought of his missing daughter and wondered if someday he would be in Mrs. Stone's shoes. The sound of silence enveloped the room, and the air seemed sucked up and filled with tension.

After several seconds, a small voice choked with anguish murmured, "Yes, yes, it's hers, it's my mother's." She turned the cross over. "Look at the engraving on the back, Detective."

He leaned in closer and read the engraving, *Confirmation 1907.*

"My mother told me she received this at the time of her Confirmation into the Catholic Church. That was back in Ireland." She closed her fist tight over the cross. "May I keep this?" she asked dabbing her tears away.

Roy felt mean having to say, "I'm sorry. Not just now, but if the remains turn out to be your mother's, I will return it to you later."

Mrs. Stone placed another hand on top of the one that held the cross. "It's my mother's. I recognize it. I'm positive the cross and chain are my mother's."

"There, there, my dear," Mr. Stone said. "The detective has to finish the investigation first."

"Mrs. Stone, we have to be completely sure the remains are those of your mother. Your DNA has to be analyzed. And the forensic artist is going to put a photograph of the skull on the computer, then superimpose an enlarged photograph of your mother."

Mrs. Stone fell silent. She looked away from the detective and appeared to be thinking back to something. "I remember I gave a photograph of my mother to your father so he could make posters. And it also appeared in the local newspaper. Is that the photo you have?"

"It is. Now about the cross, Mrs. Stone. Although we found it in the grave with the skeleton, it could have been stolen, or your mother could have loaned—"

"No! My mother never would have loaned it. She never took that cross off. Stolen, maybe, but not loaned," she said in a firm voice.

Selby felt in his heart and mind that the skeleton belonged to Mary Ryan, but it would be premature to say so without further tests. "As soon as we compare your DNA with the DNA from our lady's remains and we receive the forensic artist's report, I'll call you immediately."

Mrs. Stone rose from her chair and slowly offered the cross and chain to Selby. Her husband took her hand and stood by her side. "You promise to give it back to me, Detective?" she said, an anxious tone in her voice.

"Of course, just as soon as we know." Thank God, she didn't ask how the woman in the grave had died. That would be another delicate conversation.

As soon as the door closed behind the couple, Selby snapped open his briefcase and withdrew a plastic bag. He put on gloves and picked up Mr. Stone's water bottle, replaced the cap, and put it in the plastic bag. The detective taped, dated, and identified the bag. He felt pleased and excited. It'd been iffy whether Mr. Stone would take a drink. Once provided with Mr. Stone's DNA, perhaps his theory could be proven. Perhaps.

***

Two weeks later Selby received a call from Dr. Pallotta. "The results from the forensic artist are in, Roy," she said.

"Great. I'll be right over."

"That was Dr. Pallotta, Dad. She's received the results from the forensic artist," he said, as he pulled on his overcoat and threw a scarf around his neck.

Doug was on his feet before his son had finished speaking. He grabbed his parka and a toque from the closet. "I'm coming too. I'll wait in Tim Horton's. After all this time, I can't know soon enough whether it's Mary Ryan," he said, his eyes sparkling with excitement.

The crisp winter air felt refreshing on Roy's cheek, and the sun hung high and bright in a clear blue sky. He stepped into his Ford and his dad plunked down beside him.

After dropping Doug off at Tim Horton's, he hurried to the anthropologist's office. The detective could feel the pulse in his wrist pumping faster as he pulled into the parking lot at the morgue.

Dr. Pallotta sat at her desk with papers stacked neatly into two piles. "Hello Roy," she said smiling. "You didn't lose any time getting here. It seems like I just called you a minute ago."

"I've been waiting for this, Lisa. I must confess I feel excited. It seems ironic that this may be the closing of the case my father worked on way back in the day. He's wound up as tight as a violin string waiting for answers."

Lisa leaned over her desk, picked up a file, and flipped it open. "First, here are the results from the forensic artist." She slid the file across the desk to him.

Selby slowly opened the file and looked at the image result. The photograph from the *Burlington Gazette* had been enlarged, manipulated to the correct angle, and superimposed on the photo of the skull from the grave. A perfect match! The skeleton belonged to Mary Ryan.

Another photograph lay under the first one. This image portrayed some of the survivors from the *Titanic*, and had appeared in *The New York Times* in 1912. The people were on a train. One of the women in the photograph underwent the same treatment as the *Gazette* photo. *Bing*o. Mary Ryan became Mary Flynn.

Detective Selby leaned back in his chair, the folder still in his hand, and whistled. "So, Mary Ryan and Mary Flynn are one and the same. And she survived the *Titanic* disaster."

"She was lucky, Roy. Only a little over seven hundred passengers and a few crew survived," Lisa said.

"That must be what she was talking about when she told Daphne all her family had drowned," Roy said. "It appears Mary Ryan didn't want anyone to know her real identity or her *Titanic* experience once she moved to Burlington. According to my dad, even the nuns at the convent didn't know."

Roy told Lisa about his father's encounter at the convent and his investigation of the missing woman, Mary Ryan. "Mary Flynn (Ryan) appears to have left Toronto abruptly and appeared at the convent in Burlington. She was pregnant at the time and didn't tell the nuns her real name."

"Sounds like she was hiding out, Roy," Lisa said.

"Hmmm, yeah, but from whom?" Roy looked pensive. "When do you think you might have the results from the DNA?"

"In two or three weeks. I'll let you know as soon as I have them."

CHAPTER 52

Selby left Dr. Pallotta's office thinking about his father. There was something he wanted to ask him about the case. He stopped at Tim Horton's to pick him up.

Doug sat in a corner, sipping coffee and talking with another senior.

"Dad, let's go," Roy said approaching the table.

Doug looked up, an expectant glint in his eye. "Sure, son. I can hardly wait to hear all about it." He rose and said a quick goodbye to his friend.

Once inside the car Doug squirmed with impatience. "OK, let's have it—all of it."

"We got a hit on the photographs. And the DNA results will be available in two or three weeks."

"I knew it!" He clapped his hands.

"No, Dad, you didn't know it. You suspected the skeleton was Mary Ryan's, but you didn't know it. You even changed your mind once."

"Well, it *is* her isn't it?" Doug said in a triumphant voice.

Roy nodded and smiled. "Yes, Dad, you got it right. I wonder if you might still have some more evidence, packed away in those barrels and boxes in the basement?"

"Maybe. Whaddaya have in mind?"

"Those cigarette ashes and butts you found at the scene of Mary's disappearance. Any chance they're in one of the barrels?"

Doug cocked his head and a thoughtful expression appeared on his face. "Don't think so, but I did find a few more notebooks from that time. So maybe there's something else I've forgotten about. When we get home, I'll empty all the barrels and look."

On the ride home neither of them spoke, each lost in his thoughts.

Roy thought about the confirmation of the identity of the skeleton. It was Mary Ryan-Flynn, all right. He knew her real name now and that she had survived the sinking of the *Titanic*. Also, he knew something about the time she spent in Toronto. He believed someone in Toronto was responsible for her pregnancy.

He recalled his father telling him about the visit to the convent, and how Mother Superior said Mary became fearful when asked about the father of the child. And now, judging from the old newspapers with the photographs, she had changed her name. It would appear Mary left Toronto because of the pregnancy and fear of the father of the child. So who was the father?

He'd read in some police journals that the main cause of death in pregnant women was murder by the father of the unborn child. For various reasons, the murderer wanted to be free of the pregnant woman and his child. *Did the father of Hope or someone else kill Mary years later, long after the child had been born? And why?* Selby had a hunch.

***

When they arrived at their home on Locust Street, Roy dropped off his dad, and said, "I'm going for a drive. See you in about an hour."

"Okey-doke. I'll get busy emptying the barrels in the basement," Doug said as he waved goodbye.

The drive to North Shore Boulevard took only a few minutes. Selby wanted to see where Mary had lived. His father had given him the address a while back.

A fine rain fell on Selby's windshield, and the sky was a murky grey as he parked in front of the address. A small gatehouse stood off to the side of a road leading to a large Tudor-style house. The dwelling was around 200 feet away from where Selby had stopped. Both structures looked dark and weathered. English ivy partially covered both residences. It was curled and dry. A gloomy air pervaded his senses as he scrutinized the houses, looking for what, he didn't know. The murder took place in the gatehouse, so his dad believed. He concluded the reason the killer buried Mary so close by was that he was in a hurry and he wanted to escape detection. And besides, the park would have been deserted at that time of night. Selby lingered for a few moments, taking in the scene. Once or twice he reached into his breast pocket where he usually kept his cigarettes—damn! Nothing there.

***

When Selby returned home and walked into the kitchen, the rich aroma of spaghetti sauce simmering greeted his nostrils. Delicious. The basement door stood open and a light shone up the stairs.

"Hey Dad, I'm home," he shouted down the stairs.

Doug's head peeked around the railing at the bottom of the stairs. "Come on down, son. I may have found something," he said.

Roy hurried down the stairs, almost tripping.

Two work benches were covered with papers and odds and ends. Doug held up a small brown envelope. "I'd put the cigarette butts in an envelope like this. And I'm sure I turned it in."

"So, what do you have now?" Selby asked.

"There were a lot of ashes, and I vaguely remember putting them in another envelope so as not to dirty up the butts in the first bag. I didn't notice at the time, but a squashed-down stub was buried in the ashes of the second bag." He pressed the bag. "I can feel it." He held the envelope up between two fingers.

Doug cleared a space on one of the workbenches, put a piece of white paper down, and emptied the contents of the envelope. Most of the tobacco lay among the ashes. The cigarette paper showed ragged edges, but still a part of it had not opened.

Roy ran upstairs for a pair of tweezers and a plastic baggie. When he returned, he carefully lifted the small piece of yellowish cigarette paper and placed it in the new baggie.

"What are you going to do with that?" Doug asked.

"You told me you found the butts the day after Mary disappeared, and you told me her employer said she didn't smoke. My hunch is that these are the ashes from the cigarette the killer smoked before or after he killed her. I want to get DNA from the paper and stub if that's possible. I'm going to drop them off this afternoon."

"But who would you compare the DNA with?"

"I'll let you know later," Roy said. "First, we need to see the results of the DNA from the skeleton's bone, and the Stones' DNA."

***

Three weeks later, Selby received a call from Dr. Pallotta and dashed over to her office. Results of the DNA from the Stones and the skeleton lay on Dr. Pallotta's desk. His excitement flashed in his eyes as he took a seat across from the doctor.

"I expect you've already read the report, Lisa?"

She nodded. "I have, and it's fascinating."

"OK, let's have it."

"Remember what I told you about the Stones' toes?" Lisa asked.

"Uh-huh," Selby moved forward on his chair. His body tensed as he waited.

"I told you about a congenital condition called Clinodactyly involving over-lapping and under-lapping of the toes. Fingers as well are often involved. The condition is fairly rare."

"I remember, so…"

"The DNA from the various donors, Mary Ryan's bone, Hope Ryan, and Wesley Stone was compared. The results revealed a close familial relationship."

Roy took a deep breath. "And what is the relationship?"

Lisa picked up the file and slid it toward him. "It appears Hope Ryan's father, and Wesley Stone's grandfather was one and the same. Without a sample of Wesley's grandfather's DNA, they can't be positive, but some characteristics seem to point to this conclusion. If correct, it means that Hope Stone is Wesley Stone's aunt."

"You'll have to explain how the scientists worked that one out."

"Well, when the scientist examined Hope's DNA, he compared it with the sample of DNA taken from the skeleton. It proved a close match. So, the remains are definitely those of Mary Ryan. When the examiner looked at Wesley Stone's DNA, it appeared to have some similar characteristics with Hope's DNA, suggesting a familial relationship."

"OK, I'm following so far. Then what?"

"The evidence further suggests Hope's father was Wesley's grandfather, and Wesley's father, Gerrard, was Hope's half-brother. Therefore, Hope is actually Wesley's aunt," Lisa said.

"This is falling in with my hunch," Roy said. "I did some research on the Stone family and found out Wesley's grandfather's name was Angus. From what my dad learned during his investigation back in the day, Mary became pregnant as a result of having sex with someone in Toronto. And it was not consensual, according to what Daphne Essex told us."

"Unfortunately," Lisa said, "we don't have a specimen of Angus Stone's DNA. But, from some similar characteristics in Hope's DNA and Wesley's, it does suggest a hereditary connection. Your hunch appears to be adding up, Roy, with this new information."

"My theory is that when Angus Stone impregnated Mary Ryan, he already had a wife and a son, Gerrard."

"You've put names to the DNA results, so that's a lot to consider. Good work, Roy." Just then someone gave a light tap on Dr. Pallotta's door.

"Come in," the doctor said.

A neatly dressed FedEx courier stood in the doorway. "I have a delivery for Dr. Lisa Pallotta. Would you please sign for it?" he asked, proffering a large FedEx envelope.

She signed and opened the envelope. "It's from the Centre for Forensic Sciences."

"Good. This should be interesting." Roy leaned forward in his chair.

"It's the report on the hair and cigarette paper you dropped off at the Centre."

After scanning the report for a minute or two, Lisa passed it to Roy.

He gave a small nod as he read. "This confirms my hunch," he said, pushing the document back to Lisa.

"Tell me about it," Lisa said.

"I did some research on the Stone family. They were quite a prominent family back in the day. I back-dated my research to 1912. The patriarch of the family, Angus Stone acquired a fortune in the stock market.

"Around 1930, Angus was kidnapped and held for ransom. It became a sensational case. Gerrard, his son, refused to pay the kidnappers. And two days later, the police found his father's body floating in Lake Ontario. He'd been tortured—cigarette burns on the body and knife wounds in multiple places—before the kidnappers shot him in the face."

Lisa frowned. "That's a tragic end to a story. Did you learn why his son wouldn't pay the ransom?"

"In an interview a few days after the police found his father's body, he was asked why he didn't pay. He said the police advised him not to fork over a dime because the kidnappers would only come back for more."

"I suppose follow-up stories appeared in various papers for a while?" Lisa asked.

"They did. I read quite a few of them. Some acquaintances of the family told newspaper reporters that the Stone family were tight-fisted when it came to money, except when it came to themselves. Then they spent lavishly. And some believed Gerrard went along with the police's advice without much protest."

"Sounds pretty callous to me, if it's true," Lisa said, leaning back in her swivel chair. "So tell me, what's your hunch?"

"I think Mary Flynn fled Toronto to escape the man who impregnated her. He probably threatened her, and she feared for her life. I think that's why she changed her name to Ryan and hid out in the convent near Hamilton, a place where she could safely deliver her baby."

"That sounds plausible," Lisa said.

"Thankfully, at the time my dad was handling the case, he learned a fair amount from the nuns at the convent. I believe many years after Angus Stone stopped looking for Mary, his son Gerrard and Mary's paths crossed. I think he surreptitiously followed her, probably spied on her for a while, made sure she lived alone, and one evening he went to her home and murdered her."

"That's a lot of speculation, Roy, and I don't see how you can prove it," Lisa said.

"I can't. Almost all of the people Mary knew back in the day are dead. Although, the nuns at the convent confirmed for my dad that Mary appeared petrified of the father of the child when the subject was brought up. And of course, the coroner determined asphyxia by strangulation caused Mary's death."

"Roy, Forensics is saying that the cigarette paper you sent them showed similarities to the DNA on the water glass from Wesley Stone. What do you think?"

Roy paused for a couple of seconds, "I think it's Gerrard Stone's DNA."

Lisa sat forward in her chair again, and said, "But why him?"

Roy looked down and shook his head side to side. "Money, Lisa, money. I believe money was the motive. My hunch is Gerrard knew, or at least suspected his father's crime. And believed that someday Mary would confront the Stone family with Angus Stone's offspring. Gerrard knew Hope would be his half-sibling and he believed he may have had to share the riches from his father's estate with her. So he decided to stop Mary in her tracks."

A tap on the door. "Yes," Lisa called out.

One of the secretaries poked her head in the doorway, "Coffee, anyone?"

They both gave a vigorous nod.

Roy continued. "After the murder of his father, Angus, Gerrard would be next in line to inherit his father's fortune. But Angus Stone turned the tables on his son and left most of his wealth to his grandson, Wesley. Again, this was a dramatic turn of events and the newspapers covered it."

"And Mary's daughter, Hope, married Wesley, thereby sharing in her father's fortune. Isn't it ironic how things turn out sometimes?" Lisa said.

"Uh-huh. Too bad the hair from Mary's remains was too degraded to tell us much. I think it was probably Gerrard's," Roy said.

He shrugged and stood. "I have to call the Stones now to make an appointment to give Hope the news about her mother."

Lisa reached across the table, picked up the file and rose. "Are you going to tell her your suspicion about Wesley's father? And Hope's father?"

"I don't think so. I expect Hope's husband will be present when I speak to her. Why stir things up now? Gerrard Stone is long gone, as is Angus his father. So what's to be gained? It can only hurt and upset both of them, for no good reason."

"Don't you think they would still want to know?"

Roy rubbed his forehead and didn't answer for a few seconds. "Perhaps, but I believe this is the best way to handle it."

Lisa had admiration in her eyes when she spoke. "You really are a compassionate man, Roy."

"Well, Hope and her husband are both older now, and her days of conceiving a child are over. She doesn't have to worry about delivering a baby with birth defects because of the familial relationship. So, what's the point? I think it'll be enough for her to handle when I tell her how her mother died."

Roy held out his hand to Lisa. "About that dinner, Lisa..."

"Monday, next week at five o'clock. See you then," she said, with a broad smile and continuing to hold his hand.

CHAPTER 53

Detective Selby sat across the table from the Stones in the interview room. Hope's shoulders were hunched as she leaned forward. Her clenched hands rested on the table.

He could see mixed emotions: curiosity one second, and fear the next. The couple stared at Selby's briefcase as he began to open it. He withdrew a small plastic bag. "You may have your mother's cross and chain now, Mrs. Stone."

Hope gasped as she unclenched a hand and extended it toward the plastic bag. The necklace slid into her quivering hand. She smiled and drew it close to her lips and kissed it. "Ma-a-a."

A lone tear trickled down her pink cheek. Wesley pulled his wife close and patted the tear away with a Kleenex. "Thank you," they said in unison.

The detective coughed, cleared his throat, and straightened in his chair. "You were right, Mrs. Stone— your mother never gave the cross away. We positively identified the remains as that of your mother. And she was wearing it when she died."

"So now, after all these years, I finally know what happened to my mother. I knew all along that she never would have left me, but it's still a relief to know you found her."

Selby braced himself for what he expected would be her next question.

Hope took a tissue from her husband, wiped her nose, and settled back in her chair. "How did she die, Detective Selby?"

Selby paused. He hated this part of his job. "She met with foul play, Mrs. Stone, and died from asphyxia." He hoped that would do.

"You're saying she was strangled?" Hope asked with horror.

Selby looked at Hope and nodded. "I'm sorry, Mrs. Stone."

Tears welled up in Hope's eyes again. "But why?" she asked and put her face in her hands.

Her husband put his arm around his wife's shoulder. "There, there my dear. I know it's painful for you, but you finally know what happened, and there's some peace in that."

Hope turned to her husband and dried her tears. "I suppose you're right, Wes, but I would like to know why someone would murder my mother," she said with anger in her voice. "Do you know why, Detective?"

Roy Selby had hoped she wouldn't ask this question, but of course it was only reasonable that she would want to know. He couldn't tell her his hunch. After all, it was conjecture—at least part of it. "We don't know why, Mrs. Stone. But, we think it may have been connected to someone she knew when she lived in Toronto. Of course, they're all dead now, so we can't pursue anything there."

"Who, who, would do such a thing?" The lines on Hope's forehead deepened.

Selby shrugged, looked down, moved his head side to side and remained silent.

Holding her husband's hand, Hope sighed and rose. She looked tired and older since entering the room. "Thank you, Detective Selby, for all you have done. You have given me some closure."

Wesley Stone shook Selby's hand. "Thank you, Detective. My wife can relax a bit now. She's been tense for the last few weeks, waiting to hear from you."

Arm in arm, the Stones left the interview room.

CHAPTER 54

On his drive home, Selby glanced at a weak winter sun that was beginning to set. He wondered if he'd made the right decision not to tell Hope and her husband the whole truth—or what he believed to be the truth. After all, it was partly conjectured. And the genetic relationship shown in their DNA wasn't conclusive except for the mother-daughter relationship. Also, the cigarette paper DNA was too degraded to be used as evidence. So why mention it? It would devastate Wesley Stone and Hope.

Selby pulled into his driveway and sat there for a few seconds. His father opened the front door and peered out. When Roy saw him, he straightened his shoulders, and said under his breath, *Yes, I believe I did the right thing.* He turned off the engine and opened the door.

Roy plunked down on the sofa next to his father and told him the whole story, mentioning the evidence and his hunch. "Money, money, that's what makes the murder go 'round."

"Well, there are a few other motives, son. Like jealousy, revenge, and a couple more, further down the list," his dad offered.

"Funny, the way things turn out. I believe Gerrard Stone killed Mary so there would be no question of her child inherited anything from Mr. Stone, senior."

"But in the end, Mary's daughter got her inheritance anyway by marrying Stone senior's grandson," Doug said.

"Gerrard Stone must have keeled over when his son presented Hope. Daphne Essex said Hope was 'the spitting image' of her mother, wavy red hair and all. And Wesley told us how his father had become agitated on meeting Hope, had a stroke and died shortly after."

"From what I can see," Roy said, "it appears neither Hope nor Wesley is aware of any hereditary relationship."

Doug Selby sat with hands crossed over his stomach, not speaking for a few seconds. He eased himself off the couch and crossed the room. He lowered himself slowly into his brown La-Z-Boy. The drapes on the bay window were open. It was dusk, and the winter sun was descending on the horizon. "You did good son," he said gazing out the window.

"Ditto, Dad," Roy said smiling.

Margaret Iles is a retired medical secretary, living in Burlington, Ontario, Canada. She is of Metis heritage, born in Toronto. Her love of history led to studies at the University of Toronto.

Margaret is the mother of five grown children. Swimming and walking are her favourite sports.

She joined the local library when she was five years old.